# THE TRUTH
## BEYOND THE SKY

### THE EPIC OF ARAVINDA: BOOK 1

#### ANDREW M. CRUSOE

*There is a truth beyond
the sky... energy goes
where attention flows...*

— Andrew

2019.05.08

ISBN: 0-615-70391-7
ISBN-13: 978-0-615-70391-6

Version P7–20170207
Released by Aravinda Publishing
Cover design by Shookooboo

# DEDICATION

For all who have dared dream of the vastness of the cosmos.

# A NOTE TO THE READER

WELCOME to the Epic of Aravinda.

Unbounded goodwill and gratitude goes out to my earthbound family and friends. Without them, this adventure would have never been brought into book form, a process spanning over four years.

Since then, this series has grown considerably, and I can now afford to give away books. To be the first to hear about upcoming books and get your free Sci-Fi Starter Pack, sign up for the Aravinda Mailinglist: http://myth.li/newsletter/

I hope that this first book serves as a voice of optimism in a time when too many of the narratives we encounter are based in fear and a lack of faith, instead of acknowledging the true power of the heart, mind, and spirit. With that power, we can create a reality in which lack of faith crumbles in the face of compassion and fear melts away in the light of truth. The best days for Humanity are still ahead as long as we continue to purposefully create that brighter future.

And I know we will.

— AMC

# CONTENTS

# AD OMNIUM UNITATEM

"BEGIN with the first. How did they find the first one?"

*"The first stone? Well, before Zahn we knew only of a single Chintamani stone. Finding it set off a chain reaction that brought my dear friend face to face with the greatest horror of the galaxy. In the end, he confronted them with only a single stone, a humble starship, and a plan many would deem insane."*

"What did you think when you first met him? Did you know?"

*"When I met Zahn? Well, he wasn't a 'chosen one.' In many ways, he chose himself, never falling under the illusion that he was more important than the others. But I did not know what he was truly capable of. No one could have."*

"So will you tell us?"

*"Of course! I am the Chronicler. It is my purpose."*

"We start at the stolen moon, correct?"

*"If I started there, I would deprive you of the magic of the story. We begin in the twilight, just before Zahn's world was split open, with a young boy walking upon silvery sand. . . ."*

# CHAPTER 1

## GOOD MORNING, ASHRAYA

ZAHN OPENED HIS EYES.

He was a young boy, walking barefoot on pristine, silvery sand. Although this time, something was different. While the beach around him was familiar, it seemed unusual at the same time, and he couldn't discern why.

Zahn didn't realize that his entire world was about to come crashing down.

To his left, he could see the majestic Ashraya Bay opening up into the ocean, and beyond that, there were faint outlines of islands in the haze along the horizon. To his right, he could see a forest path leading around the edge of a canopy of blue leaves.

He drew himself back to the therapeutic feeling of the sand beneath his feet and the soft sound of the waves. The crisp scent of the ocean made him smile, yet the thought came to him once more: something wasn't quite right.

Zahn examined his surroundings again and realized that the sand looked strangely luminous, like no sand he had ever seen. But before he could investigate, he heard a familiar voice calling to him in the distance. He looked ahead and saw his mother farther up the beach, kneeling on the sand and waving him over as she called out to him. The way the sun glinted off of her light brown hair was almost surreal.

"Zahn! Come over here! You've got to see what I've found!"

"What is it, Mom? Is it the first rockturtle?"

"Nope, even better!"

Zahn ran over to his mother, who was looking into a shallow pit in the sand, and knelt down beside her. Inside the pit were hundreds of small, pearl-colored, rockturtle eggs gently sparkling in the afternoon sun.

"Wow! I thought none of them had laid their eggs yet."

Darshana smiled so big that even her eyes seemed to smile.

"Well, I guess today is our lucky day, Zahn. I'm going to take some measurements so we can estimate when they'll hatch. Why don't you take some photos so Dad can see later?"

"Good idea!"

From one of his pockets Zahn pulled out a palm-sized transparent disc that appeared to be solid glass except for a rim of bluish metal around the edge. He held it in front of the eggs and squeezed the edge of the disc. After doing this a few times from different angles, he put the device back into his pocket.

"Guess what?" Darshana said. "It looks like these eggs are going to hatch in about five days."

"Wow! So can we come back then? Please! Extremely please!"

"Of course you can come back! In fact, I'm assigning this mission to you, Zahn. Make sure these eggs stay safe."

"Oh, they will."

A look of worry crept over Zahn's face.

"Wait. You said I had to make sure, but you didn't say you would come. You can't come, can you?"

"I'm so sorry, Zahn. I don't think I'll be able to. Five days from now we have an important meeting at the observatory, and I can't miss it."

"More important than rockturtle eggs?"

"More important than rockturtle eggs, but I want you and your father to take lots of photos and tell me all about it when I get back, okay?"

"Okay…"

Still kneeling on the sand, she kissed him on the forehead and then stood up. In the distance, the sun had sunk below the horizon, bathing the sky in striking red and orange rays.

"It will be nightfall soon. We should head back."

Zahn and Darshana walked toward the narrow path that led around the trees, up the incline, and back to their home. After walking for a few minutes, a thought crossed Zahn's mind.

"Mom, what do you really do at the observatory?"

"You know what I do, Zahn. I observe the mysterious universe around us and use that knowledge to help the Ashraya Islands, and all of us on Avani."

"Yeah, I know. But what do you really do? Why is it that you don't come home some days?"

"Zahn, my job is… complex. Sometimes they need me at unpredictable times. Why are you worried?"

"I don't know. I'm just trying to figure out why sometimes I don't see you."

Darshana stopped walking, knelt down, and looked into her son's eyes.

"Zahn, I'm going to tell you something, and I want you to always remember it. Can you do that?"

"Yes."

"Zahn, I love you and your father more than life itself, and even though I can't always tell when or how long I'll be gone, I want you to know that it is for the greater good. Sometimes a person can't tell every last detail of the truth because it might mean violating someone else's choices, someone else's free will. But I want you to remember that I will never leave you, Zahn, or your father. Do you understand?"

Zahn wasn't sure if he understood the part about free will completely, but he nodded.

"I love you so much. Now c'mere!"

Darshana gave her son a huge hug, ruffled his hair, and took his hand as they continued to walk along the path.

After a while, Zahn looked up through the blue leaves and saw the evening sky again. This time, the clouds were a strange green hue. Zahn had never seen anything like it before, and once again an unsettling feeling came over him.

"Hey Mom, why are the clouds green?"

But his mother was no longer there. Zahn looked up and down the path, but he couldn't see anyone.

"Mom?" Zahn called out.

"Mom?!" he called again. He was starting to get afraid.

Zahn ran up the path.

Perhaps his mother had gone ahead. After running up the path for a while, he turned around and ran back toward the beach. Zahn was convinced that she must be on the path somewhere. But when he arrived back at the beach, no one was there. Where else could she be?

"Mom!" He was beginning to panic.

Then, he heard a faint sound from high above him. Someone was screaming.

"Zaaaaahn!"

Zahn looked up and saw his mother being pulled up into the sky, as if by an invisible cord. She was higher than the tallest trees, and she was reaching down to him.

"Mom! What's happening?!"

"Zahn!"

The wind grew stronger, and Darshana continued to rise into the sky. She was getting smaller by the second.

"Mom!"

"Zahn, I'm sorry! I'm so sorry! Tell your father I'm sorry!"

"No! Mom, don't go!" His eyes were wet with tears.

The sand beneath Zahn's feet began sinking, taking him along with it. All around him, the wind grew stronger, kicking up sand and causing the ocean waves to become even more choppy.

"Zahn, I love you."

And then his mother's voice faded into nothingness as she disappeared into the clouds.

"Mom!" Zahn screamed into the sky.

The sand was nearly up to his shoulders now.

"Help!" Sand entered his mouth as he screamed. "Heeeelp!"

He tried to wave his arms, but he couldn't. Soon he would suffocate. Soon he would be dead, buried under layers of pristine, silvery sand.

Just before he was swallowed up entirely, he felt something beneath his feet supporting him. A moment later, this strange object beneath his feet rose slowly. But how could that be? What could possibly be buried under layers of beach sand?

Zahn felt a curious sensation. The strange object that was supporting him vibrated, and the entire beach rumbled and jostled. Then, he abruptly sank again, and in moments his head was completely under the sand. Zahn realized he couldn't breathe, and he shut his eyes tight. He was going to suffocate, and there was nothing he could do about it.

Yet when he took a final panicked breath, he somehow got air. Then, Zahn opened his real eyes.

He was a young man, lying in a tangled mess on the floor. Above him, his hammock still gently rocked back and forth, and the morning sun illuminated the fact that it was now bare of blanket and pillow.

Apparently, his new last-resort device for waking up had worked brilliantly, at least in the sense that it had successfully woken him up. Yet he wondered if it had worked too well, since the feeling of being shaken awake had found its way into his dreams. He was thankful the dream-quake wasn't real, and yet much of the dream had been all too real for him.

In the distance, he heard the sound of birds calling. Their sound filled the valley, and if he listened closely enough, he could even hear a faint echo as their calls bounced off of a nearby ridge.

Zahn didn't stand up immediately. He remained there on the floor, staring at the slowly changing crystalline patterns on the ceiling and wondering why his dreams kept turning into nightmares. The vision of his mother being abducted from the beach continued to return to him, even though he knew she hadn't actually disappeared that way.

He pushed the unpleasant thought out of his mind. Today was the first day of autumn, and it wasn't the first time he'd had a nightmare like that around this time of year.

After some time, he stood up and looked out from the wide opening in the crystalline latticework that made up one of the room's walls. Spread out before him, he could see the forest canopy and the ocean beyond.

"Good morning, Ashraya."

He looked out toward the beach and reflected on all of the times he and his mother would walk along the silvery sands of Ashraya and how she had been so excited to show him all of the remarkable creatures that called the beach their home.

But it didn't give Zahn joy any longer. For despite Ashraya's charm, the island scarcely seemed like the same one he grew up on. Almost always, he had felt out of place there, but this feeling of alienation had increased dramatically after his mother had disappeared without a trace, twelve long years ago. Since then, the island didn't seem like home.

Yet he still remembered a time when these islands felt alive to him. He remembered the small expeditions he would take to map them, and how he would often get lost when exploring a new area. In the end, he always mastered the land, and by now, as an adult on Ashraya, he had explored nearly every hidden place within each of the ten islands of the archipelago.

Some of the islands had been trickier to map than others, and when retelling his adventures, he would often leave out the parts about his close brushes with death. What would the point be? He had survived, so he saw little point in making people worry about him for something he'd obviously lived through. (He'd always planned to live to be 111 years old anyway, but that is the subject of another story.)

It had been a long time since he'd gone on any adventures. After all, now he'd seen nearly everything on the archipelago. More importantly, he was all his father had left since his mother had disappeared, and Zahn didn't want to leave his father unless he had a good reason.

So he stayed nearby, enjoying the wealth of trails and passages that were hidden within the landscape. Probably his favorite place on the island was Zikhara Peak, the tallest point on the entire archipelago. At least once a year, he made time to hike up the long mountain pass to the top to spend the night, and the majesty of the entire archipelago laid out before him never failed to fill him with wonder.

The sight was incredible, but quite different from most Avanians who made the journey, the beauty of the view wasn't the main reason he scaled the peak. The more important reason, the reason that kept him coming back year after year, was that up on Zikhara Peak, he felt closest to his mother.

He often wondered if that made any logical sense. After all, how could being one mere klick closer to the sky allow his mother to hear him across the gaping darkness of space? But that didn't matter in the end. Being on the peak comforted him, and it was on those nights filled with sweet, crisp air that he told his mother how much he loved her and missed her.

And sometimes, he thought that he heard his mother whisper in reply.

# CHAPTER 2

## THE MANY SHAPES OF GRIEF

As was typical these days, Zahn was running behind. He'd spent too much time reflecting on this day. If he was going to get to the observatory on time, he would have to hurry, so he quickly got dressed and darted down to the dining area, completely failing to notice the beautiful morning sky as it shone through the glass ceiling above him.

Zahn hated to rush in the morning, but if he was late again the council might flag him for review, and that was pretty much the last thing he wanted to deal with. He didn't want anything to complicate the anniversary of his mother's disappearance.

"No, I can't think about that right now," he said to himself. "I've got to focus. Breakfast."

Zahn dug around the cooled storage containers but couldn't find any of the sweet, oval-shaped fruits that he had on his mind. Instead, he grabbed some juice and cooked some packaged grain.

He noticed a dark purple avega fruit beside the grain packets and took it. There was only one person who could have put it there. He turned to his father, who was staring at his reading pad as he methodically ate his breakfast.

"Dad, do you ever think that some fruits are a bit too big?"

"What do you mean?" Vivek said, still reading.

"Well, they're basically packages of energy to kick-start a new tree. But if you think about it, aren't these avega fruits bigger than they need to be?"

"Simple adaptation, Zahn. Some trees require more nutrients, and we've selected the more plentiful trees to cultivate. Over time, those genes are more strongly expressed."

"But it's true for fruit trees we *haven't* cultivated, as well. Remember how we used to find wild fruit when we visited NearSky? It was huge, and none of that was cultivated."

"What's your point, Zahn?"

"I don't know. It's probably a crazy theory. Never mind."

Now that his breakfast was ready, he crushed the avega fruit over the bowl of grain, and sat across from his father.

Both of them ate in silence for a few moments.

"Nightmares slowing you down again, aren't they?"

"You heard me fall out of my hammock again, didn't you?"

"That, and you came dashing down here in a cold sweat."

Zahn chewed his food in silence.

"Zahn, I thought we talked about this."

"Dad, I don't need more counseling. I did it for years, and—"

"Actually, I was going to mention that you're chewing too quickly. But yes, counseling is an excellent idea. And don't tell me that it didn't help you Zahn, because I know it did. It helped me, and I saw how it helped you. In fact, I still talk to my advisor. Why are you so stubborn about this?"

Zahn sighed.

"I'm not stubborn, Dad. I just... I don't need it. This is the first nightmare I've had in months, anyway."

"It's your choice. I just hate to see you suffer, you know that."

"I'll be fine, Dad."

Zahn ate faster to finish his breakfast in time. He thought of the small lens resting on his bedroom shelf. It was the last gift she had given to him before she had disappeared.

"If you want to let these nightmares go," his father continued, "you need to resolve the emotions behind them. A mental advisor will help you with that."

Silence.

"I don't think your mother is coming back, Zahn. Not anymore. You've got to let her go, just as I had to."

Zahn looked intensely into his father's eyes. "Did you *ever* really think she was coming back, Dad? Or did you try to forget her as soon as possible so you could move on?"

"You know that isn't true."

"How long did it take you to stop grieving? A month? Three?"

"Zahn, we all grieve differently. This isn't about me. I'm concerned for you."

"Then give me space, okay? I just woke up from a nightmare. The last thing I need is you pushing me to go back to an advisor."

"Fine, I won't mention it anymore."

"Thank you. That would make my life *much* easier." Zahn stood up. "I'll be back in the evening. Tak and Vina are running a big experiment today, and they need some extra hands."

"Be safe, and don't forget to reattach the power to the airboat when you get back."

"I won't."

And with that, Zahn opened the front door, and stepped out onto the path which led down to the beach. To his right was a smallish vehicle shaped vaguely like a boat, except that its cabin was enclosed in a colorless bubble, and the whole vehicle hung in the air just a few centimeters above the ground.

From out here, he could see the trees growing around the curved limestone house, creating a canopy of radiant blue leaves above it. He moved a blue leaf out of the way and pressed his thumb to a pad that was embedded into the house's exterior. There was a popping noise, and a thin cable disconnected from the airboat and was sucked up into a small hole in the side of the house. Now that the airboat was detached, he pulled the door open and stepped up and inside.

The moment he sat down, the interior lights flickered to life, and through the windshield he could see the beach down below and the ocean stretching beyond. It was still early, and the morning light fell softly onto the island. The air was sweet, and he could still hear the sound of birds calling in the distance.

He took a small white card out of his pocket and rammed it into a slot on the dashboard. The airboat roared to life, beginning as a loud hum, soon easing off into a low rumbling sound.

Soon, he was cruising along the rocky path that led past a few other houses, around a large rock formation, and down to the beach. Here, a river emptied out into the ocean, and farther up the river was a small waterfall, creating an almost perfectly smooth wall of water.

Without blinking an eye, he plunged through the waterfall.

Zahn didn't even need to slow down. Even though this route was only recommended during emergencies, he found himself using it a few times per month, partly because it was quicker, but mostly because he enjoyed the sheer thrill of it. Although emergencies were rare, this hidden pathway to the Ashraya Observatory was specifically designed so that researchers could evacuate the observatory as quickly as possible.

On a bright day like today, it took Zahn's eyes a few seconds to adjust to the dimness of the corridor and the small guiding lights on either side. He followed these guiding lights as the corridor gradually turned to the right and then back to the left. After a few minutes, he could see sunlight up ahead and followed the corridor as it led up a steep incline to the exit. When he emerged into the sunlight, he was a few hundred meters above where he'd started, and the Ashraya Observatory was just up ahead, its massive dome glistening in the morning light.

Once he reached the door, it slid open for him, and he never stopped walking. Behind him, he could hear a synthesized voice say, "Good morning. Designation: Observer, L-1 confirmed."

But he was already in the elevator heading upward. Beyond the transparent elevator, he looked out and observed some of the activity going on below him. Most of the space of the observatory was taken up by a central domed area where the main detector was located, and about a dozen people were working at computers below it. As the elevator continued to rise, Zahn got lost in observing their work. He knew most of them, except for one. Who was that woman with the violet hair?

DING.

The sound jolted Zahn out of his thoughts, and he stepped out, unaware that today's nightmares had only just begun.

# CHAPTER 3

## DREAMS & PHILOSOPHIES

By the time the midday meal came, Zahn had nearly forgotten about his nightmare from that morning. It wasn't until he sat down to eat with two of his colleagues that he was reminded of that traumatizing echo of his past.

Since Zahn spent most of his day working in a team, he liked to spend his midday meal in quiet reflection whenever possible, but today Tak and Vina sat by him. Zahn had worked with them before. They had been together for a few years now, and Vina liked to talk.

At great length.

About everything.

Zahn braced for the oncoming conversational onslaught as they both sat down. It was a shame since it was otherwise a quiet lunch cycle. The dining area was only half full today, and the conversations were hushed. Tak came prepared though, holding a reading pad in his right hand, presumably to give him an excuse not to get mired in an inevitably longwinded conversation.

"Did you hear about the quake that happened up at NearSky base?" Vina said.

"No," Zahn said. "Is everyone okay?"

"No fatalities if that's what you're wondering. Some injuries, though. Strangest thing was, the quake didn't happen over a fault line. I looked into it."

"Strange." Zahn tried to get some chewing in despite the conversational whirlpool that was already forming.

"It really is!" Vina leaned in toward Zahn and whispered. "I'm not sure how much you've been paying attention to the reports, but there's been a lot of weird stuff happening lately. Just looking at the tectonic data alone... Have you seen it?"

Vina was right in front of his face now. Her eyes were wide, and her wavy hair filled his vision.

"No. I'm an observer, not a geologist." Zahn looked at her directly in the eyes for a few seconds. "Do you always have conversations inside of someone else's bubble?"

They stared at each other for a few seconds until Vina's enthusiasm faded, and to Zahn's relief, she leaned back again.

"Anyway," she continued, "signs of the times, I say. Quakes, droughts. It's a nightmare. Oh, that reminds me! Tak had this wild dream. Darling, tell Zahn about your nightmare!"

Tak seemed completely invested in what he was reading and didn't respond.

"Darling?" Vina repeated.

"Yes, Vina?" Tak jolted his head up.

"Why don't you tell Zahn about the nightmare you had last night? It was just wild. I know you already told me, but I think Zahn would find it interesting."

"You think so? Well, I was driving my airboat through the emergency passage. You know, the one behind the waterfall?"

"I'm familiar with it," Zahn said, still trying to suppress the memory of his own nightmare the night before.

"Well, in the dream—"

"Nightmare," Vina corrected him.

"Right. In the nightmare, I go through the tunnel, and suddenly the guiding lights go out."

"Totally black! Just wild," Vina added.

"And then this eerie green glow appears in the corridor. Next thing I know, my ship is being sucked into the ground, like the ground itself is swallowing me up! Pretty unsettling. Ever have a dream like that, Zahn?"

"Not quite."

"Tak says it's because he's been feeling overwhelmed lately. Some changes going on around here as you've probably noticed. He says it's an unconscious symptom of the stress manifesting through dreams. Right, darling?"

Tak didn't answer for a moment. His eyes had drifted back to his reading pad.

"Yeah, something like that, sweetie," Tak said.

"Hey, by the way," Vina continued. "I hope you don't get embarrassed, but I overheard last week that you've been having nightmares, too. Have those been getting any better?"

Zahn felt a wave of surprise and suspicion sweep over him, but he let it pass.

"Yeah…" he said.

"Any idea what's causing them?"

"I'd rather not talk about it."

"Oh. That serious, huh? Have you seen an advisor?"

Zahn had to make a focused mental effort to avoid groaning at the question.

"Yes, I have, Vina. But I'd rather talk about something else."

"Ah." She looked slightly surprised at his reaction. "I guess it didn't work so well, then. You know, Zahn, maybe you just haven't found the right solution. You've got to hunt for what you want in life, you know."

"That so?" Zahn took another bite.

"Oh yeah, it's just like what my aunt always says. She always says that solutions never just land on your front yard, Zahn. You have to look."

"So much for miracles…"

"Miracles? I'm talking about solutions, Zahn. Like in science. Like the science we practice at this observatory every day. We find the truth. We find solutions."

"So a solution has never presented itself miraculously? A solution has never shown up serendipitously? Ever?"

For the first time that day, Zahn noticed Vina sigh and take a moment to think. She looked over to Tak who raised his eyebrows at her and tilted his head.

"You know I can't prove that either way," she said.

"Leave him alone, darling," Tak said. "We may have heard the rumors, but we don't know what he's been through."

Vina looked off into the distance and then down to her food, which was still untouched.

Zahn was silent and continued to eat. For the rest of the meal, Tak read, Zahn collected his thoughts, and Vina did something she hadn't done in months:

She ate without talking.

# CHAPTER 4

## AN OLD FRIEND GIVES RIDDLES

When he left the observatory many hours later, the sun was much nearer to the horizon. As Zahn walked the trail back to where he'd parked the airboat, he noticed someone sitting on a bench out of the corner of his eye. He wondered why his eye seemed drawn to this person, but continued walking.

"Is that you, son of Vivek?"

Zahn turned around and saw a short old man wearing a dark orange robe walking toward him. What he saw made him stop dead in his tracks.

"Oldman Kavi?"

"I am he. I have been away. It is good to see you, Zahn!"

"Kavi! I can't believe you're here. It's been… years," Zahn was nearly in shock.

"I suppose it has, at least here." Kavi seemed lost in thought for a few seconds. "But these are auspicious times."

"Are they?"

"Oh, yes. Where are you headed, my old friend?"

"Home, and then I'm going up to Zikhara tonight. You should come with me. I'm sure my father would be happy to see you, especially after all these years."

"Oh Zahn, your ritual shows your connection, your hidden strength. With that in your heart, why don't you keep the lens in your pocket all of the time?"

"Thanks Kavi—wait, what?"

"That lens! That lens. Verily, it is a living memory of your mother in physical form. Yes–yes. Will come in handy if a feather falls from the sky. Yes–yes."

"A feather?"

"Mmm. Let me ask you this, my young friend. What would you do if an unborn rockturtle wasn't strong enough to hatch?

Would you break its egg or give it more time? Either choice could lead to its death. What if it is too weak? Or not ready?"

Zahn imagined a silvery, baby rockturtle fighting its way out of its egg. For their journey to the ocean, rockturtles had long since adapted to blend in with the silvery sand of the beach. It had been a long time since Kavi had asked him a riddle, and he hoped he still had the clarity to solve them.

"And of course," Kavi continued, "we must remember that every rockturtle that has ever lived has prepared the world for that new, unborn hatchling. It is never alone, and it never will be. All the hatchlings of eternity have gone before it."

Kavi allowed Zahn to contemplate this for some time.

"Do you understand the gravity of this situation?" Kavi said.

"Hmm. Did you come up with that yourself? Does it have a right answer?"

"How could I write a song that even the birds already know?"

There was silence between them as Zahn considered this.

"I think I'd give the egg more time." Zahn finally said. "Hey, how do you know about my mother's lens, anyway?"

"A small rockturtle told me," Kavi said, winking one eye.

Zahn looked at Kavi suspiciously, but couldn't help but grin because he knew Kavi usually had a surprise up his sleeve when he talked like this. When Zahn studied his face, it seemed as though there was an ancient mystery hiding within it, if he only knew where to look.

"You know what, you really should come back with me, Kavi. We should celebrate your return!"

"Not quite returned. Not yet."

"Will you at least walk with me to the airboat? It's so wonderful to see you after all this time, even if you are in a riddle-telling mood."

"Of course, my young friend."

As they continued down the path, Zahn continued to ponder the question.

"Is there a right answer to your riddle?" he asked a few minutes later.

"What does your heart say?"

"I think it's a question of free will."

"And of time. Zahn, promise me that you will remember to keep the lens with you. At all times."

"Sure Kavi, but why?"

"The time for you to know why has not yet arrived."

"Kavi, do you ever think you're too mysterious sometimes?"

"To respect someone's free will, sometimes it is necessary to appear mysterious."

Zahn reached out to open the airboat door, and when he looked over to where Kavi had been, he was gone. Zahn looked up and down the path, but there was no sign of Kavi anywhere. It was almost as though he had never been there at all.

When Zahn arrived home, he headed back up to his room. By now, an orange light was filtering through the latticework and the vines along the edge, lending his room an orange tint.

He walked over to one shelf, picked up a small glass lens that had been resting on its edge, and looked at it. It was just as flawless as the day his mother had given it to him as a child. Back then, it didn't fit so easily into the palm of his hand, but as his hand grew so did the memory of his mother fade ever so slightly, for even Zahn's strongest memories were not immune to the passage of time.

Kavi's words echoed in his mind again, and he slipped the small lens into his pocket. Perhaps Kavi was right. Perhaps it was something he should have near him at all times. After all, what was the downside?

# CHAPTER 5

## KNOCKING ON THE SKY

After a short evening meal with his father, Zahn threw some supplies into a backpack and walked out the back door. The trail to Zikhara Peak had many starting points, and one of them was on the edge of the forest near his house. As Zahn entered the thick of the forest, he wondered why Kavi had decided to come back now of all days. Why come back at the anniversary of his mother's disappearance?

The path that led up and around the mountain was slightly misty, and the higher he got, the more stars appeared beyond the forest canopy above him. By the time Zahn reached the peak, the last traces of orange had left the sky, and the world was embraced in the darkest blues of the night.

Despite the warm season, the environment on the peak was much cooler than below, and when he arrived Zahn made a small fire to keep warm. Once the fire was going, he rolled out a sleeping pad over the bare rock and looked out over the archipelago to behold the breathtaking view. Below, he could see the mountain curve down sharply and level off to reveal thick forest until it became silvery beaches that met with the ocean. Tonight, the ocean appeared in a blue that was almost black.

To the northern edge of the island, he could see his village glowing like a million fireflies. And to the west and beyond, Zahn could just make out the outlines of some other islands on the horizon, a few of which had tiny dots of light emanating from them.

Sometimes the dark shapes played with Zahn's imagination. In fact, if he squinted his eyes, he could almost imagine that, instead of being ordinary islands, they were gargantuan sea creatures with huge crystalline eyes that only came to the surface at night when the light of Avani's moon shone brightly over the calm ocean.

Zahn enjoyed visualizing scenes like this. It helped him add a sense of wonder into his life and feel like he was still on the island he grew up on. Sometimes even stranger ideas would come into his mind. Sometimes, he had dreams that, not only was his mother still alive, but that she had been plucked off of Avani itself and taken to a far-off place. After all, they had never even found a trace of her.

When she disappeared, every airboat available had made dozens of high-altitude, and then low-altitude, passes over the entire archipelago. Yet even with the most sensitive instruments, they had found no trace of her. It was unthinkable, unimaginable, and inexplicable.

He looked out over the waters and turned his mind to the memory of the night his world came crashing down.

The logs showed that Zahn's mother was working in the lower level of the Ashraya Observatory one moment, and then was completely gone a moment later.

Zahn recalled how the rescue team reported her as 'vanished, presumed kidnapped', and the report itself still made him suspicious. He had lost his mother, and his family was never the same again. After that day, the entire island changed for him. The home he once knew never felt whole again. Even after twelve long years, walking along the shore never failed to remind him of the times he would walk beside his mother on those early autumn evenings.

Now, it was autumn again. It was on clear nights like this, when he could see thousands and thousands of stars, that Zahn would look up into the sky and speak to her from atop Zikhara Peak. He would close his eyes and imagine his mother was there, somewhere just above him.

"Mom," Zahn began. "I don't know if you can hear me, but doing this gives me some taste of peace. I know Dad hasn't been up here for a few years, but don't take it personally. I know he still loves you. He's just…"

Zahn paused to clarify his thoughts.

"…holding onto the possibility that you could still be alive is too much for him now. He hasn't told me, but I don't think he has nightmares about you like I do."

Zahn closed his eyes.

"What can I do to make these nightmares stop, Mom? How do I find peace when I don't know what really happened to you?"

Zahn looked up at the sky for a while in thought. The sight of thousands upon thousands of stars was magnificent, and he knew that it was only a tiny fraction of the whole. He considered the size of the galaxy and tried to imagine the trillion stars it contained. After all, in a galaxy so vast, why couldn't Avani be visited by life from another world? His mother had vanished in the space of a second. Who else could make someone disappear without a trace?

He stopped himself. Even if there was life beyond Avani, and even if it was intelligent, he didn't have any idea why anything would take his mother.

As it was, he had no proof to support his theory, but there was also nothing that could firmly disprove his theory, either. Up here, above everything he'd ever known, Zahn thought of the sky and imagined what life might exist on other worlds whirling around other fiery stars.

He closed his eyes again and centered his focus.

"Creator of All, if you can hear me, or if my mother can hear me, let me know. Give me a chance to find the truth. Please."

Zahn sat in silence for some time, listening to the breeze, and soon fell asleep.

Glowing shapes filled his mind. Sacred geometries drifted around in his dreams, and for the first time in days, Zahn slept peacefully. Exactly how long, he was never sure, because after what felt like only a few minutes, a sound like a million thunders shattered his slumber.

He bolted up and saw a light high in the sky heading toward him through the clouds. In a flash, he stood up and watched it rapidly descend to the ground.

Its glowing tail flew past a nearby peak and down toward the beach. The forest obscured his view of the beach below, but that didn't stop him from hearing what happened. Just a fraction of a second later, he heard a thud sound that was so deep that he could almost feel it with his feet.

Zahn knew he had to get down there as soon as possible.

He quickly compressed his sleeping pad, threw it in his pack, and raced down the trail. Gravity was on Zahn's side, and soon he was back behind his house.

The darkness of night gave the forest a feeling of heightened mystery, and he ran around to the front which provided a good view of the beach below, now bathed in faint moonlight. Yet to Zahn's surprise, he saw nothing and ran down to the beach to take a closer look.

Nothing was unusual at all.

For a moment, Zahn wondered if he had dreamt the whole thing, and he headed southward, down the beach.

*Perhaps, I've finally lost my grip on reality,* he thought. *What if I really do need a mental advisor?*

Zahn shook his head.

*No, I know what I saw, and I'm certain I was wide awake. After all, why else would I have come down here in such a hurry?*

He looked up at the sky and struggled to remember what he'd been dreaming about. When his eyes looked back onto the sand, he thought he saw a dark patch far ahead. Perhaps this was the crater he was looking for, and it was nearly in his front yard.

He ran over to it, his eyes widening as he grew closer. It appeared as though a bowl-shaped indentation had been carved into the beach sand, and in the center of it were flecks of a strange, pale light.

Zahn took a few steps into the crater. When he went to touch one of the glowing flecks of light, he moved some sand off of the source of the light, revealing part of an object beneath the sand. With the utmost care, he brushed the sand off of the glowing object, soon realizing that it was a triangular plate of some kind. He touched it, and it was cool, which surprised him. After entering the atmosphere at such a speed, almost any material would have still been hot to the touch.

Very slowly, he removed it from the sand it was embedded in and carefully examined it. It was thin, about the size of his hand, and he noticed that the moonlight seemed to slide off of it at certain angles. There was a faint pattern of lines on it, but if he hadn't looked closely, he wouldn't have noticed. Most of its edges were frayed, like it had been torn off of something.

Zahn wondered if it might be a fragment of something larger. He put some pressure on it, and it seemed strong, especially for its thickness. What in the world was this object? And what if it wasn't from this world, at all?

The significance of what was happening began to dawn on Zahn in a powerful way. This was certainly not an ordinary meteorite. From a purely scientific standpoint, he had to admit that it seemed more artificial than natural. As an observer, he couldn't see this object being part of any natural process. He had to admit that it appeared to be intelligently made.

"Perhaps I should tell someone... But if I do that, I might never even see it again. Scientists will be scanning it and prodding it from now until nova day."

Zahn realized he was talking to himself now and sat in the small crater for a few moments while he considered his options. His mind drifted to the soothing sounds of the waves nearby, the cool silvery sand beneath him, and how stunning all of it had looked from up on Zikhara Peak.

He pulled himself back to the present.

"If this is what I think it is, there will be a lot of publicity around it. Around me. Around everyone close to me. It could be one of the biggest discoveries ever made on Avani."

He picked at it with his fingernail. It seemed battle-hardened.

"But what if it isn't what I think it is? What if it's a Taskaran spy probe or something that's been in low orbit for years, only to lose its stability and crash on Ashraya now?"

Zahn studied the fragment with cold eyes and thought about how the Taskarans hadn't been heard from in decades. He knew what he had to do. He had to examine this on his own before he showed it to anyone. Who would believe his story, anyway? He had to be careful about how he handled this situation.

Now he was convinced. He knew he had to do his own tests on the fragment. Only then could he be sure if it really was from beyond Avani.

# CHAPTER 6

## ASLEEP UNDER A TREE

Zahn had to be very quiet when reentering the house. It was just a few hours before dawn, and his father was still fast asleep. Quietly, he walked up the hall to his room and hid the fragment, which was no longer glowing, at the bottom of a wooden chest where he kept some of his clothes.

The moon bathed his room in cool light, and in minutes he was fast asleep.

The following day, Zahn realized just how difficult it would be to sneak the fragment into the observatory without anyone knowing. All of the equipment was shared, and he was surprised that their stringent record-keeping procedures had slipped his mind during the previous night. Every subject, every scientist, and even every drop of rain was recorded for future reference and analysis. Zahn wondered if this was life's way of saying that perhaps he wasn't meant to find the fragment in the first place. After all, if this turned out to be from another world, why did he deserve to be the one to discover it?

Yet by the end of the day, the routine at the observatory regained its place as the foremost subject on Zahn's mind, which gave him some relaxation since the more he thought about the fragment, the more he felt unsure about what to do about it.

On the second day, he consciously decided to push the thought of the fragment out of his mind whenever it occurred to him. Sometimes he would tell himself, "I'll deal with it later." And other times he would say, "A solution will come. I just need to wait a few days."

By the third day, Zahn knew he had a problem. Everything in his life somehow seemed stale. He realized that he couldn't continue to keep this secret, perhaps the largest secret Avani had ever known, to himself.

Even worse, he knew that despite the fragment's small size, it was still possible that someone from the observatory had detected the fragment during its descent and was going to start combing the beach any day now. He had tried to find out if anyone had noticed it, but soon discovered that he lacked the authority to perform a system query of such breadth and depth.

All of these thoughts made Zahn feel physically ill. After he returned home from the observatory that day, he walked down to the beach and followed the beachside path which weaved in and out of the forest. And then, Zahn did something he hadn't done in years: he talked to the trees.

After making sure no one was in the vicinity, he told them all about the fragment and about what it might mean. He also told them about his difficulty in sneaking it into the observatory, and how each day he had been pushing the thought of it out of his mind. The blue-leaved trees wafted in the wind, almost seeming to say, "We hear you, but your obstacle is within yourself."

Once he'd found a spot where there was a good view of the bay through the leaves, he sat down with a tree to his back and closed his eyes. He was exhausted from the day. Exhausted from keeping the secret.

Even though the sun was still a few hours above the horizon, Zahn fell asleep under the trees. As he slept, light filtered through the leaves above him, bathing the path and Zahn's face in a slightly bluish hue. In his slumber he dreamed once more, but this dream was stranger than the last.

At first, he was back at NearSky base, a small outpost not far from Ashraya. It was a rather popular place to visit, and dozens of towering cliffs made it an ideal place to glide from. In the dream, Zahn was standing on a cliff, wearing a glider. He looked down at the sheer drop below, and from behind him he heard a familiar voice.

"Jump, Zahn!" he heard his mother say.

But he was afraid.

"Zahn, You're ready! Everything's prepared."

Hearing his mother's voice gave him confidence, and he jumped. Air filled the glider's wings, and he soared over the radiantly blue forest hundreds of meters below. Then he looked up and saw something that shouldn't have been there. He saw the faint outline of a pyramid in the blue haze of the sky. But how could that be possible? Zahn had never seen a pyramid fly before, and he saw no reason why they should start flying now.

First, he saw a beam of light strike the pyramid, and then the pyramid plunged toward the horizon. Was it falling? Zahn realized he should be looking ahead instead of above, and he turned his head just in time to see a tree branch right before he crashed into it.

The jolt of smashing into the dream tree woke him up.

He blinked his eyes and looked around. It was nearly pitch black. He felt the dirt below him and the tree to his back. How had he fallen asleep at the base of a tree?

Then it came back to him. He had been talking to the trees.

And to his mother.

Zahn thought about what his mother had said in the dream.

*Jump, Zahn,"* he thought.

For the first time, Zahn accepted what he'd been suspecting all day: keeping the secret was making him miserable. He had to show someone, and he decided that someone would be his father.

When Zahn opened the door, his father was putting on his shoes and looked up in a sigh of relief.

"Zahn! Where've you been? I was just heading out to go look for you."

"I'm sorry, Dad. I was out walking. It's been an exhausting last few days, and... this might sound strange, but I just fell asleep under a tree."

"A tree?" Vivek said.

"Yeah," Zahn said. "But that's not the point. Dad, there's something important I've got to show you. It's extremely important, actually."

"What is it? Did you rescue an injured sea creature on one of your walks again?"

"No, Dad. It's nothing like that. Hold on; I'll get it. And I warn you, this is a lot weirder than I could ever explain in words."

Zahn raced up to his room, removed the fragment from the chest, and ran back into the dining area.

Slowly, he set it onto the dining table.

"Before you say anything, let me tell you where I found it."

He told his father how he'd been woken by the meteor, discovered a small crater on the beach, and had found the strange fragment within the sand.

His father's eyes widened.

"Zahn, this is unbelievable."

"I know."

"Could it be a part of a satellite? And are you even sure this object is safe to hold? What if it emits harmful radiation?"

"I thought of that, Dad, which is why I wrapped it in my shielded lab jacket in the chest in my room. The jacket hasn't detected harmful radiation, and I've limited my exposure to it as much as possible."

"So you haven't brought it to the observatory for analysis?"

Zahn winced. "No. I didn't want…" His voice trailed off and his eyes drifted back toward the fragment that was still lying on the table. "I wanted to do my own research. I know that if I scan this with the observatory's computers, it will get marked for review because of how strange it is. If it's what I think it is, they'll send it far away for analysis, and then I'll never see it again. I can't let that happen."

Zahn gazed at the fragment intensely for a moment.

"Dad, I don't think this was made on Avani."

All of the sound seemed to get sucked out of the room, and both Vivek and Zahn stared back at the otherworldly fragment lying in front of them. For the first time, his father picked it up and felt its smooth texture. Zahn looked directly into his father's eyes, and his father met his gaze. Then he glanced down at the fragment again and furrowed his eyebrows.

"I don't know, Zahn. That's a pretty fantastical idea, and fantastical ideas require compelling evidence to support them." He set the fragment back down onto the table.

"What do you think I should do?"

"I'm not sure, but I do know that we don't know if this object is dangerous or not. We don't even know where it's from, so we should be careful. Put it back for now, and be sure to wrap it in that shielded jacket. I think it would be better if we both slept on this and decided in the morning."

"All right. Sleep well, Dad."

Zahn gave his father a hug, took the fragment, and walked back up to his room. Behind him, he thought he heard his dad say, "Wrap it carefully, Zahn."

After Zahn had closed the chest, he walked over to the lattice wall and looked out over the forest. The sky was clear, revealing thousands of stars above, and a half moon hung high in the sky, faintly illuminating the tops of the trees below.

He walked over to a small, round window and looked out to see the path which led behind the house and then up to Zikhara Peak. As the leaves moved in the breeze, the moonlight patterns on the ground slowly changed.

For some reason, his mind drifted back to his dream of the pyramid flying in the sky. He thought of his mother's words in the dream, telling him that he was ready. Zahn suspected that was his unconscious mind's way of telling him that he had to tell his father what he'd found, but he also wondered where the pyramid fit into all of that.

With these strange thoughts still floating around in his mind, Zahn walked to the corner of his room, climbed into his hammock, and sank into a deep sleep.

# CHAPTER 7

## A TAPPING IN THE NIGHT

TAP, TAP, TAP was the sound that disturbed Zahn's sleep just a few hours later. At first, he thought he might have been imagining it. After all, the boundaries between sleeping and waking had been blurred for him lately. But the sound came again, jolting Zahn up.

He turned his head to look around the room, but he saw no one. Briefly, Zahn envisioned massive Zikhara bears, tapping on the window, hungry for Avanian flesh.

TAP, TAP, TAP.

Now that he was fully alert, Zahn knew exactly where the sound was coming from and approached the round window. In the daytime, the window provided a prime view of the path that led into the forest behind the house, but tonight the view seemed almost foreign. As he approached the window, he saw the faintest outline in the shadows.

Quite the opposite from a bloodthirsty bear, the outline gradually resolved itself into the shape of a figure just outside the window, wearing a silvery uniform that was shimmering faintly. Something else was odd about this figure, too, but his mind couldn't settle on what it was. Now that it saw Zahn, it was motioning for him to open the window. Whatever it was, why had it scaled the side of the house in the middle of the night?

In situations like this, Zahn found it crucial to listen to his instincts. In this case, his instincts were telling him to be cautious but also that this figure meant him no harm, so with some suspicion, he opened the window slightly.

"Who the heck are you?" he whispered.

As the man blinked his eyes, his skin glowed slightly, and for a fraction of a second, Zahn saw his distinguished face with eyes that seemed so dark as to be black. The man had a strong jaw and short black hair to match his eyes.

"I am Oonak of the Confederation of Unity, and I request your help in a matter of utmost importance."

"What?"

"Are you not the one who found the fragment?"

For a moment, Zahn wondered if he should confirm the strange man's question. What if the fragment didn't belong to him at all? But again, his intuition told him to trust this man, despite these strange circumstances.

"Yes. I am."

"The fragment you found is part of my ship, and regrettably this entire situation is in danger of disrupting the balance. May I please have the fragment back?"

"Perhaps. But why should I trust you?"

"If you follow me, I will show you the ship that fragment broke off from."

Zahn considered the danger of following him, but in the end, his curiosity overcame his fear. After all, he knew these islands better than anyone, and if this man turned out to be dangerous, he could vanish into the forest within moments.

"Okay. I'll be right there."

Soon, Zahn had put on some pants and was behind the house. Even from a distance, Zahn could tell that the man was taller than he had first guessed, and his silvery uniform reminded him of a freighter pilot's jumpsuit.

"Hello again," Oonak said as Zahn walked up to him. "My ship is down by the beach. Follow me."

In the moonlight, Zahn noticed that this man's skin was actually light brown, and in the center of his uniform's collar was a small round piece of metal that glinted in the moonlight. Zahn guessed it was an insignia of some kind.

Oonak led Zahn down the familiar path to the beach. After a few minutes, he stopped walking when he was still many meters from the ocean, and Zahn was confused because he saw nothing.

It was the same beach he'd always known, though tonight struck him as especially lovely as a half moon slightly illuminated the silvery sands around them.

"I don't see anything. Are you sure your ship is out here?" Zahn squinted but still saw nothing unusual.

"You do not see it? Look closer. Do not look at these silvery sands. Look at the air behind me. Look carefully."

Now that Zahn's eyes had adjusted to the light, he could just make out a faint wavering shape behind Oonak. The space wavered like a mirage over desert sand, as if something imaginary were appearing out of thin air. The wavering shape was rather large, at least seven meters tall, and Oonak waved Zahn over.

"Touch it," he said.

"Touch what?"

"Right here." Oonak pointed to a spot and smiled, his white teeth seeming especially alive as they contrasted with the darkness of the night.

Slowly, Zahn reached out his finger to the spot. After a moment of moving his finger forward, he unexpectedly felt something where he saw nothing. It was as though he were touching solid air.

"Wow. But if this is really a ship, can I see inside? To prove it's yours, I mean."

"What do you think, Navika?" Oonak said, seemingly to the air itself.

At that moment, a voice came from nowhere. It was as if the air itself spoke; the voice was crisp and calm.

"That is your choice, Oonak. Spacefarer Code was already broken when the Avanian found the fragment. But if you're going to execute the same plan that we discussed, I still recommend that you blindfold the Avanian. We both know how irrational cultures can be before they bloom."

"Thank you for the suggestion, Navika," Oonak said, "but I'm going to be as transparent as possible without violating the code further. I sense this one is… uniquely prepared."

Oonak pressed three fingers against a part of the wavering air.

In a flash, the outline of a triangular door appeared, seemingly hovering in midair in front of him. Oonak tapped his fingers onto the wavering air in a sequence of finger strokes that Zahn doubted he could ever be able to memorize. He could only presume that Oonak was touching a control that was on the outside wall of the ship.

A door rolled back, revealing a bright interior.

"Look inside. That is the central node of my ship, Navika," Oonak said.

Zahn looked within.

It was the strangest room he'd ever seen. Nearly everything was white or at least lightly colored. It was brightly lit, and the room was shaped in a fantastically odd way. Instead of four walls, a ceiling, and a floor, the room had eight surfaces. The floor and ceiling were perfect triangular shapes, and in the center of the room was a sphere with cables coming off of it that connected it to the ceiling. It was so strange that he had trouble taking it all in at once.

Zahn backed away from the ship. He was beginning to feel overwhelmed.

"Okay, so maybe this fragment does belong to you. This… this is incredible. This is the biggest discovery since—" He took a deep breath. "Okay, let me grab the fragment. It's in a safe place. I'll be right back. Will you still be here when I get back?"

"I would not move even a grain of sand," Oonak said.

When Zahn returned, he discovered that Oonak had indeed not moved at all. He was still standing by the wavering shape, except that his eyes, and the ship's door, were now closed. He appeared to be in a state of quiet concentration.

"Oonak?" Zahn whispered.

Oonak didn't respond.

"I've got it."

"Wait," Oonak said and held up a single finger, his eyes still closed. "I just realized. I do not know your name, Avanian."

"Oh yeah, that's right. I apologize; I'm Zahn." He hesitated and then thought he should probably introduce himself in a more official way, as Oonak had. "...of the Ashraya Observatory," he added.

"There is no reason to apologize for that."

"No, I meant, I apologize for not introducing myself earlier," Zahn said.

"Are you sure that is what you meant?"

"Yes."

"Good. It is wise to be sure of what we mean."

"Anyway, here it is. I found it buried in the sand. I saw it when it was falling from the sky, actually."

Finally, Oonak opened his eyes, and his gaze radiated a profound peace that Zahn hadn't tasted in a long time.

"Intriguing. I suppose you really were in the right place at the right time. Thank you, Zahn."

"You're very welcome."

Oonak took the fragment, turned around, and knelt down onto the moonlit sand. As he worked, Zahn tried to understand what he was doing, and the momentousness of what was happening began to dawn on him.

"Are you really a spacefarer like your ship said?" Zahn stopped himself and swallowed. "You're not from Avani at all, are you? You really are an extraterrestrial."

There was a pause while Oonak focused on reattaching the fragment to his ship. Zahn noticed that his hands glowed for a moment, and then the fragment disappeared, presumably because it was now part of the ship once more. Oonak stood up and faced him, and once again Zahn found himself wondering about his age. He guessed that he might be as old as his father, but it was difficult to be sure.

"Yes, yes, and yes. I am what you could refer to as an extraterrestrial. However, those of the Confederation never use such a term. Instead, we refer to similar life forms as merely 'people'. Life forms such as ourselves reflect the galactic template for intelligent life. In truth, we are all merely people, so we refer to such life forms simply as people. However, this does not mean that this galaxy is harmonious. Just as on Avani, not all are aligned toward preserving life. It is important to remember this."

Oonak stopped for a moment, as if trying to remember something, and then continued.

"And please, you may call me Oon for short."

"Whoa…" Zahn looked deep into Oonak's eyes. Now that he studied them, he noticed that they weren't black like he had first thought. They were actually a shade of dark blue that reminded Zahn of a deep, calm ocean. He thought he saw something at the bottom of that ocean that he didn't understand, as if they contained secrets he would never know.

"Zahn, I have one more request of you, but I want to be clear that you are under no obligation to accept this request. It is your choice, and believe me when I say that it involves great risk. However, I ask you now because, in the light of current circumstances, I believe that you are the most logical candidate."

"What is it, Oon?"

"When I crashed on your planet, I had the divine fortune of crashing near your South Pole. In the process, I discovered an incredible machine: an ancient gate that lies far beneath the ice. This gate, which far exceeds the technology of your people, has the ability to transcend spacetime itself. I'm not even sure how it came to be on your world, and unfortunately, because of the damage to my ship, it is the only way to accomplish my mission."

Zahn was held spellbound.

"But there is a problem. No matter what I tried, I could not activate the gate. However," Oonak continued, "Navika and I have deciphered some of the writing on the gate itself, and we have deduced that only an Avanian, someone whose heritage is rooted here on Avani, can activate this gate. It is not tuned to respond to my kind, Zahn. It is tuned for yours."

A look of shock crept over Zahn's face. It was as though Zahn was discovering that all fish had been able to fly for centuries but that no one had ever told him about it. It wasn't a pill he could swallow quickly, or easily.

"So you want me... to go to the South Pole... with you..."

"Yes."

"To activate an ancient gate that only Avanians can activate."

"Yes."

"...so you can continue your mission?"

"Precisely. However, I should inform you that we know very little of this device. Navika and I have heard whispers of a gate network, but little else. Nevertheless, it is our best chance of successfully alerting the Confederation of what has happened. We must reach the outer core, so it is a long journey, as well."

"But don't you have some way to travel faster than light? Otherwise how could you have gotten here without dying of old age long before you arrived?"

"My apologies. I realize this situation may be unusual to you, so I will restate the situation. Because of the damage to my timespace drive, I am no longer able to travel between star systems—at least not within any reasonable period of time."

"Timespace drive. I'd love to know how *that* works... But wait, even if this gate gets you to where you want to go, how will I get home after we use it?"

"You will be safely returned home once my ship is repaired."

"All right. But wait, why hasn't Avani been contacted by other 'people' in the galaxy before? Surely, we're not *that* boring..."

Oonak paused for a moment. "Your world is significant, but not any more significant than any other hatchling world. Zahn, there is more to this situation than you are permitted to know. What I can say is that you found a fragment of my ship because I was attacked with truly exotic weaponry. In some parts of the galaxy, this would not be entirely surprising. However, this attack occurred while I was in orbit around your planet, which means your world is at great risk."

"What risk?"

"I am not at liberty to say. Telling you would be a further violation of Spacefarer Code, just as I cannot tell you how the timespace drive works. However, I can tell you that this is a matter of urgency. Since both my comm and my timespace drive are damaged, I cannot fulfill my mission under my own power or contact the Confederation directly. Because of the damage, my messages are now limited by the speed of light which means my signal will not reach the Confederation for many years, and by then it may be too late."

"What are you saying? That someone nasty followed you here to Avani?"

"Unknown. What I can say with informed confidence is that before I could identify the source of the attack, it vanished. Either it moved faster than any craft I have ever encountered, or it possessed a cloaking technology that is beyond anything I have ever seen."

"So what do we do?"

"I must alert the Confederation as soon as possible. As I have said, this situation forces me to use the ancient gate on your South Pole to continue onward, which is why I need your help. Will you assist me in this quest?"

For a moment, Zahn was silent as the memory of his mother pressing the small lens into his hand flashed back to him. He thought about what it meant to truly see and how such a journey would give him insights into the galaxy that no one from Avani could imagine.

The clarity of that memory had stayed with him, and he wondered what his mother might want him to do in this situation. What if his instincts were right? What if she was somehow still alive?

"The outer core is near the center of the galaxy itself," he said. "It would be the journey of a lifetime, maybe two. But this is a lot to process at once, Oon. I'll need time to consider it."

"Understandable. However, I will only be here for a short time. Due to my weakened cloaking field, I must conceal myself beneath the ocean during the day to minimize my chances of discovery. No one else on Avani should ever know that I was here. Do you understand this? Spacefarer Code has already been violated more than once, and I want to avoid any further violations to the free will of your people."

"I understand."

"Once again, I thank you for returning the fragment of my ship. Please meet me at this precise location exactly one hour before sunrise to tell me of your decision. Can you do that?"

"I will."

# CHAPTER 8

# THE CHOICE

By the time Zahn reached the front door, he already knew what he had to do. He also knew he wouldn't be able to sleep until he told his father what had just happened, and as he knocked on his father's door, he felt tense with anticipation.

Groggy, his father opened the door slightly and asked Zahn what was wrong.

"Dad, something absolutely *ineffable* has happened. Do you remember that fragment I showed you?"

"Of course."

"I found its owner. Well, its owner found me."

Zahn told his father a brief version of what had happened to him. He told him about how he'd been awoken by the tapping on his window, the strange figure, his invisible ship, and the story of how Oonak was attacked. When Zahn had finished, Vivek looked hard into his eyes.

"You are telling the truth, or at the very least, you believe it to be the truth. There is no doubt in your eyes, but—"

"Come with me an hour before dawn. Oon said he will be waiting on the beach to hear my decision."

"And have you decided? What if he's a madman? Or worse? Zahn, do you realize how tremendously dangerous this is?"

"Yes, but I think I have to go. Dad, I saw Kavi a few days ago. He's back, and he told me to always keep Mom's lens with me. He said these were auspicious times. What if he knew this visitor was coming? My intuition says to go with him."

"You saw Kavi?" Vivek processed this for a moment. "Anyway, that doesn't change this situation. I don't think you should go, Zahn. Not until we know who this man really is. How do you know that fragment was his?"

"It sort of melted back into his ship—"

"You just gave it to him?!"

"He crashed on Avani! What was I supposed to do? Anyway, it melted back into his ship which he sort of introduced me to. It's pretty impressive, actually. It can speak and—"

"That doesn't mean he has your well-being in mind."

"Dad, this may be the only chance I ever get to find out what happened to Mom. I know she's up there. Somehow, I just know it. Isn't that worth some risk?"

"Do you want me to lose you, too? Is that what you want, Zahn? Don't you remember how your brother died? He died up there, Zahn. In space! What if the same happens to you? Then where would I be? I'd be here on Ashraya, alone. Is that what you want? I can't believe you would even consider this."

Zahn sighed. He had been down this road before.

"Of course not. Just—"

"Don't leave, Zahn. Not until I can meet him, at the least."

"This is my choice! I've been a free agent ever since I joined the observatory. I didn't have to tell you all of this." Zahn paused as Vivek shook his head. "Dad, this could be our one chance of finding out what happened to Mom."

Outside, they heard a faint bird call echo across the valley.

"I'm tired Zahn. Wake me up when you're ready to meet him, and we'll see who this Oonak character really is."

Zahn found it difficult to fall back asleep when the excitement of what had just happened was still in him. After setting his alarm, he closed his eyes and tried to focus on the faint sound of ocean waves below. As he drifted off to sleep, the thought of his late brother entered his mind. He tried to recall his brother's face, but the memories were even more faded than the memory of his mother.

When the annoying sound of his whistling alarm filled the room a few hours later, he felt a sense of déjà vu. Didn't he just wake up in his hammock not long ago?

He rushed over to his father's door, knocked on it three times, ran back into his room, and changed into some more durable clothes. As he dressed, he wondered if this would be the last time he would see his home in a long while.

With that in mind, he grabbed a backpack and filled it with the few pieces of survival gear that he thought would be helpful: a water canteen, some food, a change of clothes, a photodisc for capturing images, a knife his grandfather had given him, his shielded jacket, a small towel, and various other items he felt would be useful if he was gone for more than a few days.

There was a knock on his door.

"Ready?" his father called out.

"I think so. Wait."

Zahn walked over to the shelf and took the small, glass lens that his mother had given him years before.

"Okay, I'm ready."

As Zahn and Vivek headed down to the beach, the faint bluish hue that came before the dawn was already beginning to cover everything in sight. As they got closer to the beach, they noticed Oonak was sitting down, drawing in the sand. Zahn also noticed that there was no longer a faint wavering pattern in the air, and he wondered if the ship was still on the beach.

"Good morning, Oon," Zahn said.

Oonak stood up. "Good morning, Zahn. And who is this?"

"This is my father, Vivek," Zahn said. "Dad, this is Oonak."

Vivek noticed Oonak's strange uniform and dark eyes.

"Are you really from another world?" Vivek said. "Or are you just wasting my son's time? If you are, you will live to regret it."

"I am not of this world," Oonak said. "Your son found a fragment of my ship that was broken off during an attack, and now I request his help in a mission of great importance."

"So he tells me."

"His safety will be greater if you tell no one of the fragment or our meeting here. That applies to both of you. Please do not tell anyone of our meeting, otherwise discovering the truth behind this attack could become much more difficult. Do you both understand?"

"I understand," Vivek said.

"Of course I understand," Zahn said, "and I've decided to help you, Oon. I've brought some supplies, too."

Oonak smiled.

"I am pleased to hear that our paths will join here. You will see many things that no Avanian has ever seen before. More importantly, your choice could save many lives."

Vivek's expression turned cold. As Zahn gave his father a huge hug, the reality of the situation was dawning on him.

"I'll be back as soon as I can, Dad."

Vivek was still speechless. He had trouble believing that his son was leaving him and the planet behind, even if it was only temporary. Oonak seemed to sense Vivek's anxiety, walked up to him, and looked him directly in the eyes.

"Vivek, I sense that you are a discerning man and have taught your son valuable lessons in discernment and knowledge. For this I am grateful, for these lessons will be invaluable on our journey."

As Vivek listened to these words, he noticed how peaceful and wise Oonak's eyes were—so dark, yet still with a hint of blue. Somehow Vivek felt as though he *knew* this man, even though he had just met him a few minutes before.

"Realize," Oonak continued, "that your son was the first Avanian to make contact with a member of the Confederation of Unity. Although I am not of this world, I believe you will grow to see that our similarities are more important than our differences. Have faith, Vivek. Your son will soon have the attention and assistance of many positive beings, and not all of them are visible to ordinary eyes."

"Thank you for your encouraging words, Oonak. But this is all very incredible to me. I am honored to meet you, but it is still hard for me to have faith in the face of all that has happened."

Zahn noticed that the clouds were beginning to turn orange. Soon, the sun would rise. Oonak noticed it, too.

"But faith is necessary for protecting your world now, Vivek. Trust me when I say that I will protect your son at all costs."

Oonak placed his hand on Navika, causing a door to appear in midair over the beach. The door rolled open to reveal a bright interior, and Vivek gasped and took a few steps back.

"Goodbye, Dad. I will be back, and if she's still alive, Mom will be with me."

As Zahn disappeared into the intense white light of the ship, Oonak bowed slightly to Vivek in a farewell gesture.

"Oonak, perhaps you wouldn't have so much faith if the one you loved most was taken from you."

"She was."

And with those words, Oonak disappeared into the pure white light of the ship, leaving Vivek alone on the beach. Looking onward, Vivek saw the triangular door disappear. Now it was as if nothing had ever been there at all. The invisibility was perfect, and Vivek had no idea where the ship began or ended.

His eyes were then drawn to the sand beside him. Where Oonak had been sitting only moments before, the most exquisite geometric patterns he had ever seen were now drawn onto the sand. They looked sacred in the moonlight, and as Vivek studied them, he felt mesmerized.

# CHAPTER 9

## MEET NAVIKA

Once Zahn had triumphantly stepped into the ship, he was stunned at just how large it was now that he was inside. He was certain that this inner room must somehow be larger than the wavering shape he saw back on the beach. This 'node', as Oonak had called it, was quite spacious, and its ivory walls radiated a pure white light that nearly overwhelmed Zahn's eyes and caused him to squint at first.

When his eyes adjusted, he looked all around him and tried to understand the space he was in. His previous guess was correct. The room had eight surfaces, each triangular.

The first object he noticed, indeed the only object he couldn't help but notice, was a large, glowing sphere that was suspended high above his head by colorless, braided cables leading up to each of the three corners of the triangular ceiling.

Zahn walked under the sphere, now about a meter above his head, and heard a soft hum. It appeared to be filled with a liquid, yet it also reminded him of a perfectly polished piece of colorless quartz. Green, orange, and purple flecks of light spiraled inward toward and outward from the center, and when he tried to examine what was in the exact center of the sphere, he realized that it was too bright for his eyes. It was a stunning vision.

"What do you think of Navika's core? Remarkable, isn't it?" said a voice from behind him.

Zahn glanced back and saw Oonak smiling slightly.

"It's wonderful. What is it made of?"

Behind him, he heard the door quietly hiss as it closed.

"A detailed description would be difficult to relate to you because you lack the necessary background knowledge. In simplistic terms it could be described as a complex crystalline structure which forms the seat of Navika's consciousness. However, I like to refer to it simply as his nucleus."

"So, that's like Navika's brain?"

"And much more. Follow me. Your sun is about to appear in the sky, and we are still on the beach, after all."

Oonak led Zahn to the far side of the room where there was an outline of a door in the triangular wall. He pressed his thumb to the wall, and the door split into three parts and pulled back, revealing what appeared to be a command bay or cockpit.

This room was a different shape than the first one and slightly smaller. Instead of a triangular ceiling, the two outer walls sloped inward until they met the door's wall at a point high above the door, almost like a tepee. Indeed, they were now standing inside a three-sided pyramid.

Directly in front of him was a single seat that had a small, transparent dome above it, and placed farther ahead was a long, curved bench that could probably seat five people. Zahn guessed that the seat with the dome was for Oonak and wondered how he could see anything while driving the ship since he couldn't see any windows anywhere.

"Welcome to the command bay. Please, have a seat." Oonak gestured toward the larger bench farther down, beyond the command chair.

Zahn walked over, sat down, and was stunned when the walls of the ship became completely transparent. The effect was so complete, it was as though the chairs themselves were now floating just a few centimeters above the silvery beach.

With pristine silence, they rose up into the air and were soon moving rapidly over the crashing waves below. Zahn took this chance to look back, and in the distance he saw his father walking back up the beach. In fact, looking backward almost hypnotized him, for he had never seen the islands shrink into the distance so quickly before. All around him, he could hear the faint rushing of the wind, and ahead he could see the ocean extend forever.

"Oon, how can this ship be invisible? Are you using some kind of optics technology or is it something else?"

"It's a secret," he said and winked his right eye.

"Of course. Spacefarer Code, right?"

"Precisely. I can only tell you what you need to know, and unless it is absolutely necessary, I cannot tell you exactly how my technology works. However, when Avani joins the Confederation this will change, and there will be open communication between our people."

"When will that happen?"

"When Avani is ready." Oonak threw a small piece of food to him. "Please, consume this. It will help your body adapt to the ship and increase your vital energy in the unlikely event that we lose cohesion."

Zahn caught it and discovered that it was a small indigo fruit. Upon popping it into his mouth, he was shocked at how sour it was and nearly spit it out from the overpowering taste. He also noticed that the ship was continuing to pick up speed as it flew over Avani's vast ocean and heard what sounded like a distant crash of thunder.

"This is really sour."

"It is necessary. The kavasa berry contains compounds which are exceptionally helpful to the immune function and overall health of spacefarers such as ourselves."

Zahn chewed it.

"By the way, how long will it take to reach the South Pole?"

"Just a few hours."

"At that rate, we must be breaking the sound barrier."

"Indeed, we have."

For some time after that, neither of them spoke. Zahn couldn't help but be mesmerized by the view as they cruised over the ocean below. He had since crossed his legs so his feet were no longer touching the floor. Now that the floor was completely transparent, he was almost afraid to touch it. Even though he knew, at least intellectually, that the ship still had a floor, he preferred to keep his feet off of it, at least for now. With such perfect transparency, it was simply too easy to forget that the floor existed, and for a moment, he imagined that he was flying over the ocean on a magic chair in the sky.

"Your people are blessed to have such a magnificent ocean," Oonak said. "How are you doing, Zahn?"

"Very well. I've flown before, but I've never felt as though I were truly flying."

"I have never heard it described that way before. You frame your thoughts well."

"I'm curious about something, though. I hope your code doesn't prevent me from asking this, but why aren't we closer to, you know, actual space? This is a spacecraft, right?"

"Oh yes, it most certainly is. But my ship is still recovering from the attack, and there are a few more tests that I'm running before we reenter the Ocean of Space. Do not worry. They are in progress now, so they will not pose any delay. You guess quite correctly, though. For a journey like this, I would normally save time by entering low orbit."

Zahn was beginning to get sleepy. After all, his sleep during the previous night had been sporadic at best, and the quiet hum of the ship was soothing to his ears. Zahn yawned.

"What do you mean by the 'Ocean of Space'? Is that just another name for space or is it something else?"

"That is a good question, and one that I am pleased to say I can answer. Referring to space as the Ocean of Space is a perspective on space travel that many spacefarers share. You see, when I call it the Ocean of Space it reminds me that, within this galaxy, it is truly difficult to find a place where life is not drifting and growing in some way, whether it be on planets or elsewhere. I have even heard reports of life forms for which the vacuum of space itself is their home."

"But where did life in our galaxy come from if it also lives in the vacuum of space? What planet did it originate from?"

"Now, that is quite a question, and I do not think that even the wisest of the Confederation knows the entire answer to that. All I can say is what we have observed, and we have observed life manifesting wherever the raw materials and energy are present. There are even some who hypothesize that an intelligent energy radiating from the core of the galaxy itself causes this matter and energy to develop into living creatures."

"So it didn't start on just one planet? It happened on different places at once?"

"We do not know for certain. However, there is an ancient story of a world called Jyotis, said to be the birthplace of all life. Although, there are not many left who still adhere to that belief."

Zahn's eyes slowly closed as sleep overtook him.

"Whatever the truth may be, all of it is a miracle, Zahn. Sometimes when I look out into the Ocean of Space, my mind revels in how much is still unknown, even to the Confederation. Imagine, Zahn, creatures that spend millennia drifting from world to world. What would such a creature look like? How would it communicate? Indeed, it is humbling to consider what might be out there, still undiscovered. What possibilities may have been overlooked…"

Oonak looked back, sensing that Zahn may have fallen asleep. He had, and for a moment Oonak looked down to the ocean and smiled as a thought crossed his mind.

"…and what potentials may have never been considered."

# CHAPTER 10

## A CAVERN UNDER THE SOUTH POLE

When Zahn opened his eyes again, he saw a jagged landmass buried in ice and snow. Waves crashed onto grey rock, and he could see no sign of life anywhere. Even the ocean itself seemed uninviting, appearing as a seething dark mass below the ship.

As they passed over a snowy cliff, Zahn felt better that they were once again over land, even if it was freezing.

Oonak waved him up to the command chair.

"You may find this vantage point more enjoyable for this part of the journey. We are about to enter an ancient cave system. When we crashed, the impact resonated within a cavern below which allowed Navika to sense the hollow space beneath. Discovering it was divine fortune, and I have instructed Navika to place a waypoint marker on the cavern entrance."

After a few moments Zahn noticed faint coordinate markers had appeared on the ground below them.

"Oon, how did you do that? Is the computer doing that?"

"Yes, Navika is compositing a coordinate system over the light that is filtering through the hull."

Soon, a red triangle appeared on the horizon, and as they grew nearer, Zahn realized it was the waypoint marker that Oonak had mentioned earlier.

"You know, I was thinking about what you said before, about how plentiful life is in our galaxy, and something bothers me. If life truly is everywhere, how significant does that make Avani?"

"Zahn, is a diamond worth any less if it is surrounded by other diamonds?"

"I guess not."

After a few minutes, they were just above the waypoint which was beside a small crater in the snow. Yet, Zahn saw no cave or crevice anywhere.

"Curious," Oonak said. "The fracture we made in the surface of the ice has disappeared."

"Why?"

"Unknown. I shall cut a new one."

A red grid appeared all around them, as if the entire ship were about to begin a fight to the death. Behind him, he heard a faint high pitched sound, and below him a single square of the red grid flickered furiously. A fraction of a second later, two painfully bright violet beams of plasma converged from two sides of the ship and cut through the ice below them.

As Navika effortlessly cut into a large section of the ice, a chunk of it broke free and fell into a hollow space below. Once the hole was large enough, they flew in and found themselves in a large underground cavern. It was quite dark, and Oonak must have mentally signaled Navika to illuminate the cavern because Zahn didn't see him speak or move at all. Could this incredible ship actually read his mind?

Despite the radiance of Navika's light, the system of caves seemed almost sinister to Zahn. Stalactites hung from the ceilings like ghostly apparitions, and the way they cast shadows onto the walls gave him the impression that they were not alone in these caves.

But they were alone, and Oonak seemed very calm as he navigated the cave system, occasionally following a dark passage deeper underground and then following another passage that curved back up. While he did this, Zahn said nothing. He trusted Oonak's sense of direction.

When they finally slowed down, they were in a massive cavern that was just below the ice. Zahn could tell because light filtered through a section of the ice above, giving him a clear idea of the cavern's size.

Near the far wall, he could see a large ring-shaped machine between two columns set atop a rocky pedestal. The whole structure looked ancient.

As they landed on the cavern floor, Zahn braced for a thud, but none came. Navika had alighted upon the rock just as a bird would alight upon a stem: with perfect grace.

"Smooth landing."

"You can thank Navika for that. I give him commands, but Navika is the one who puts the real finesse on the flight."

"So there's a kind of symbiosis between you two, isn't there?"

"In a way, and right now Navika indicates that the air outside is quite cold but still breathable. Come with me."

Oonak led him back out to the central room.

"Be careful. Water will solidify quickly out there."

"You mean it's below freezing?"

"Oh, yes. You will need these. They are warm and repel water, as well." As Oonak said this, he handed Zahn a thick silver jacket, long silver pants, and boots, all of which were similar to the uniform that he was wearing.

"Oh, thank you."

"You are the one who deserves thanks. You were not obliged to assist me, yet you did."

When the door opened, the temperature of the air shocked Zahn's exposed face, causing him to pull his hood tighter, and as they headed toward the ancient gate, he was again struck by the size of the cavern. He wondered how many cave systems were yet to be discovered on Avani and if any of them might be hospitable to life.

And then, the immensity of the gate dawned on him.

Despite its apparent age, it was perfectly preserved. The main feature of the gate was a huge upright ring made of a strange metallic stone. To either side of the ring were two control panels that curved outward, and all of it was atop a large stone pedestal.

Zahn walked up to one of the control panels, and found it to be unlike any technology he'd ever seen before. The panel was covered in strange markings and circular grooves that had been etched into the stone. He moved his hand over the panel, and found it chilling to his exposed fingertips.

He tried touching a prominent ring shape in the upper left corner of the panel, but nothing happened. No matter what he did, the controls didn't respond. Oonak walked up behind him, holding a device that reminded him of his father's reading pad.

"We have deduced that these are some of the symbols that this machine uses to signify numerical digits."

On the pad were bizarre, curving symbols that seemed vaguely familiar to Zahn, and he studied the controls again.

"Oon, could these numbers be some kind of address system? I mean, if the gate network is made up of a series of gates all around the galaxy, wouldn't it need something to identify them?"

"Indeed, you are as clever as we had hoped. That is exactly what we believe the numbers are used for. I would have told you before, but I wanted to get your unbiased opinion first."

"So how do we activate the gate?"

"Although I removed all of the ice from the gate controls when I first discovered them, my attempts have thus far proven unsuccessful, as you know. We were hoping that if you used the gate's controls, it would recognize you as an Avanian."

For a while, Zahn continued to play with the controls, but nothing he did had any effect. Frustrated, he kicked the side of the control panel, hurting his foot in the process.

"I can't believe this. We've come this far and nothing works. I don't know what else to do here, Oonak."

"Do not fear, Zahn. A solution will present itself. One moment, I will be right back."

As he waited, Zahn allowed his back to slide down the side of a nearby column, eventually sitting on the smooth floor of the cavern. Despite the jacket that Oonak had given him, he was starting to feel cold, as well.

To get his mind off of this seemingly unsolvable problem, Zahn examined the floor of the cavern, and as he did this he felt something wet drip onto his hand. He looked up and observed a thick patch of ice high above him near the center of the room. Enough light was filtering through the ice that he might have been able to examine the greyish floor of the cavern even without Navika's illumination.

On a whim, he decided to take out the knife his grandfather had given him as a child and tried to chip off some of the column. He wondered if this column might be connected to the gate in some way and pressed the blade into the stone harder. In the process, he slipped and cut one of his fingers.

Zahn leapt up and yelled in frustration as blood oozed out.

"Ah! This is stupid. I can't believe we're stuck after coming all this way." Zahn sucked his cut to get some bits of sand out.

"Navika said he heard you yell out," Oonak said as he ran over. "What happened?"

"I cut myself. Do you have anything? What do spacefarers do when they bleed?"

"Navika has something. One moment." Oonak ran back toward the ship.

While he waited, Zahn decided to try his hand at the controls again. Perhaps they'd just needed time to warm up. When he got back up to the controls, he gazed at them as though he were in a staring match with a great villain.

"If I were a civilization smart enough to build a machine that creates holes in the fabric of spacetime, what button would *I* expect people to push?"

Again, he noticed the ring shape in the upper left corner of the panel, and in a mixture of desperation and stubbornness, he pressed the button again.

This time, it worked.

The cavern flooded with light as the gate burst to life. Zahn was so shocked that he felt as though his eyes were going to pop out of his head. Each of the number symbols now glowed a ghostly white, and the circular grooves that he noticed before revealed themselves to be a row of glowing circles that filled the lower half of the control panel. Perhaps most exciting of all, the gate lit up in a bright white ring, and everything became covered in faint geometric patterns.

Zahn was so stunned that he just stood there for a while to bask in the moment, watching the colors on the gate as they gradually pulsed in brightness. When Oonak walked up a few seconds later, Zahn felt that he was just as surprised, yet he expressed it in a much quieter way.

"How did you do it?"

"I don't know. I just—I hit the button again."

"How curious... yet whatever you did was effective. Excellent work, Zahn!" Oonak smiled so largely that even his eyes seemed to smile.

"Now the question is, how do we tell it where we want to go?"

"Patience. Let me tend to that cut first."

When Zahn showed Oonak his cut, he sprayed a strange bubbling gel onto it which stopped the bleeding and then melted away. "This will prevent infection and accelerate healing speed."

After Zahn thanked Oonak, he examined the controls again, soon realizing that the row of glowing circles were probably planets. There were the right amount, and some were glowing green while most were a dim red. After a few moments, he noticed that there were pointed ray shapes carved dimly into the stone behind some of the planet symbols.

"Oon, what do you think the ray shapes mean?"

"Uncertain, but I would hypothesize that there are three main types of gates: those that allow you to jump from world to world, those that allow you to jump between a world and the vacuum of space, and those that jump from vacuum to vacuum. Perhaps this ray shape symbolizes a path to your star."

Zahn touched the ray shape, and it lit up, haloing the green circle in a golden starburst. The sound of the gate also became deeper, and at the end of the row of circles, a new circle lit up. This new circle was golden and much larger. Beside it was a small ring, and Zahn noticed that a hexagon now pulsed in a blue light farther up on the control panel.

"Oon, I'm beginning to think this gate was designed to be relatively simple to operate, and I'm pretty sure that I just linked this gate to another gate in orbit around Avani's star. When I push that hexagon, I think a vortex will appear."

"I was wrong before. You are more than clever. Proceed."

Without hesitation, Zahn pressed the glowing hexagon, and the low hum of the gate became a roar. After a few seconds, a point of bright light appeared in the center of the ring, and then all of the space in the middle of the ring spiraled in on itself, as if reality itself were an ocean going down a drain. Photons spun into the vortex at odd angles, and the sight was unlike anything Zahn had ever imagined.

"You know, I've simulated wormholes in the observatory's computers before, but I never realized how..." Zahn paused. "I never realized how otherworldly it might look."

"Thanks to you, now we know. Are you certain that the destination is set?"

"As sure as I'll ever be."

Oonak walked over to the controls and observed them, and Zahn glanced back over to the majestic starship, suddenly realizing that his role in Oonak's quest might be over now. Would Oonak still need him now that the gate was active? What about his own quest to discover the true fate of his mother?

"Oon, now that I've activated this gate, do you still need my help?" Zahn said as the gate roared louder. "I must admit I was hoping to see Avani from orbit, but I just want to check before I get my hopes up. Or does my adventure end here?"

As Oonak turned toward him, a faint smile was on his lips.

"Far from it, Zahn. The next gate appears to be within your star system, so I still require your assistance in the next step of my journey—of our journey, I should say. At least, if you agree to it. I must warn you that this journey will only become more dangerous as we head farther from your home. The space between planets is not always as empty as it appears, and this galaxy is more wild than you could imagine. I have extensive experience in navigating the Ocean of Space, and I will do everything in my power to keep us unharmed. However, please realize that by continuing onward, you risk your life in the dangers of wild space, and there are no guarantees that you will ever return home."

Zahn thought about this for a few moments.

"I understand," he said. "My choice has not changed. I want to continue. I trust you, Oonak, and as you said, I am the most logical choice."

"Indeed, you are. Come, let us see what Unity has in store for us on the other side of that gate."

Back in the ship, Zahn decided to plant his feet firmly on the floor this time, despite the fact that, if he ignored the seat beside him, it almost appeared as though he were levitating above the cavern floor.

As he captured a few photos, he found himself wondering how long the gate would remain active after they'd used it.

*Did the gate have a mechanism to close the opening after a certain period of time? I wonder if Oonak knows.*

Zahn looked over, but Oonak seemed focused on analyzing the vortex. He seemed almost hypnotized.

"Oon, are you okay?"

"Apologies. Navika is relaying a great amount of data to my mind. This vortex is quite extraordinary, Zahn. It seems light, as well as matter, is able to filter though the vortex aperture. It is quite faint, but Navika is perceiving some stars on the other side. Are you ready?"

"Yes, do it."

"I'm going to approach slowly. I do not know all of the effects of going through such a gate, or if it is entirely stable."

"What's the worse that could happen?"

"Well, we could be turned inside out."

Just as Oonak said this, the bright point at the center of the gate grew, and as Navika was pulled into the vortex, a loud rushing sound filled the cavern.

"What's happening?!" Zahn shouted over the noise, but before either of them had time to react, they were engulfed by the swirling maelstrom.

For a few fractions of a second, it appeared as though Navika was completely twisted around as they passed into the vortex and entered a realm whose rules were quite different from ordinary space. And just moments after the ship had disappeared into the vortex, the point of light that had been in the center of the gate blinked out of existence, and the controls went dark.

Once again, the cavern seemed lifeless, and the only trace that was left by their presence was as subtle as a single twig on a forest floor.

# CHAPTER 11

# THE UNIVERSAL SONG

For what seemed like only an instant, Navika and everyone inside hurtled through a corridor made of pure light. Beyond the corridor, Zahn thought he could see dozens of other corridors great distances away, like spider webs spun from the light of a trillion suns, and then Oonak and Zahn saw a flash that overwhelmed them.

Once their eyes adjusted, they found themselves staring at a huge star just ahead of them. The star was so bright that Navika reduced the transparency of the walls to avoid harming their eyes. The sight was truly incredible, and Zahn soon recognized it as Kuvela, the star that Avani called home.

"Aren't you concerned about how close we are?"

"I was, but Navika is indicating that we are currently in a stable orbit around the star and are in no danger of falling into its gravity."

"That's a relief."

Zahn continued to look out onto the star. Now that he was so close, it nearly filled his field of view, and he was thankful that Navika graciously filtered the image so that he could see the seething waves of hydrogen and helium below without hurting his eyes. With traces of disbelief, he watched a solar flare slowly arc across the star and then plunge back into the rippling surface. As an observer, he always thought it was ironic that something appearing so hellish from up close provided Avani with the energy that made life possible.

"So chaotic, yet so beautiful," Zahn said. "And the vortex corridor. That was the purest light I've ever seen. Did you see the network of other corridors?"

"Indeed, I did, and Navika is continuing to analyze the data that we gathered. From what we saw, there may be many gate corridors in this part of the galaxy, and now we shall use this next gate to continue."

"What gate?"

"Look above you."

Zahn looked up and was surprised to see a ring shape far above him. He'd never noticed it before because they seemed to be in the exact center of the huge ring. Yet, as he watched, he realized that this wasn't quite accurate, either. They were moving forward, beyond the ring, at some speed. However, the ring was so large that it was difficult to judge how fast they were going.

"Whoa."

"I suspect that we exited through this gate, and that we can use it to continue onward, as well." Oonak paused. "Excellent. Navika has just located what appears to be a control panel on the ring, similar to what we found on Avani's South Pole. We are heading there now."

The sensation of flying through space in a partly transparent ship was even more unsettling than flying over the ocean. Without feeling anything, he saw the edge of the ring grow closer and closer.

Zahn looked down and instantly wished he hadn't. The floor was still transparent, and now, instead of seeming to stand on thin air, he appeared to be standing on nothing at all. Below his feet was a vast array of tens of thousands of stars, and he decided to sit cross-legged on the bench once more.

When they reached the edge of the ring, Zahn noticed another control panel with a row of glowing circles, and by now he was certain that the circles symbolized planets since there were the same amount of them as there were planets in the Kuvela system. Even Rodhas, the most distant planet, was indicated as a dim red orb. Most of the planets were.

Since the first gate indicated Avani as a green orb, Zahn guessed that the dim red color meant there were no gates on most of the worlds, and this disappointed him. As an observer, he would have loved to visit Rodhas in person.

In stark contrast to this, Avani's green indicator was outlined in a warm starburst shape with golden threads coming off of the starburst. These threads connected to a golden band of light that led far above him and around the entire gate, creating a faint golden ring.

Just above the planet symbols, he noticed a white point of light and smaller points above it. Zahn guessed this symbolized his sun, Kuvela-Dipa, in relation to nearby stars.

"This control panel is quite similar to the one on Avani," Oonak said. "It would appear that we can indeed use this gate to travel beyond your star. Do you see the strange markings below the panel? Those are the same ancient numbers that the first gate used. If my understanding of the number system is correct, we are currently at gate 3.3.2, 71.11.23, 000."

"Three zeroes at the end. What could that mean?" Zahn said.

"I hypothesize that we are at a gate which serves as the center node for many other gates, and I suspect the way these addresses work will become more clear as we see more of them. Once we understand the addressing system, we can plot a direct path to the Confederation Council."

"So what do we do now, Oon? We can't touch the control panel. It's out there in a vacuum, and I just realized I haven't seen any space suits in this ship at all."

"We take the next logical step, Zahn. We listen, and then we knock." Oonak looked ahead. "Navika, scan for any energy signatures radiating off of the control panel itself and theorize about possible methods of communication."

A voice surrounded them, coming from everywhere.

"No signals are being emitted from the control panel itself," Navika said.

Zahn looked down below the bench again, which appeared to be resting on nothing more than a faint dusting of stars.

"However," Navika said, "the gate is radiating a faint gravity wave from the center of the ring. It's possible this wave could contain information. Analyzing. Oh, how elegant."

"Have you found a signal, Navika?" Zahn said.

"A rather universal one, in fact. The gravity wave is creating a pattern of pulses that appear to be cycling through prime numbers. I would hypothesize that this gate network was explicitly designed to be relatively easy to learn how to use."

"Wow, so my guess was correct," Zahn said. "They wanted us to use them. Whoever 'they' were."

"Indeed, evidence suggests that whoever built these gates wanted others to use them. The question is: for what purpose?"

Oonak paused and massaged his chin.

"Navika," Oonak continued. "Do you think you can communicate with it?"

"I can generate similar gravity pulses, yes. What would you like me to send?"

"Well, if my hypothesis is correct, these gates are arranged in a hierarchy. So our next step is to go up one level in that hierarchy. Navika, transmit 3.3.2, 71.11.00, 000."

After a few moments, Navika spoke again.

"What happened was intriguing, but you may not like it."

"Did the gate ignore you?" Zahn said.

"Oh no, far from it. The gate quite definitely received my message, but it transmitted back something I don't quite understand. It sent a harmonic signal that was discordant, almost like an instrument being played out of key. Do you have any further commands?"

"Yes, Navika. Try sending the address of the gate we just left. Send the address that would lead us back to Avani, and see how it responds."

"All right," Navika said. "I have scans of the cavern, but I'd like to confirm. The address you request me to transmit is 3.3.2, 71.11.23, 003. Is that correct?"

"Exactly correct, Navika. Proceed."

As he awaited the results of Navika's message, seconds seemed like minutes to Zahn, and silence hung heavy in the air.

"I wish you both could have heard what I just heard," Navika finally said.

"What do you mean 'hear'? I thought you were sensing gravity pulses. Isn't sound impossible without air?" Zahn said.

"Avanian, that would depend on what you consider sound. Sound is merely vibration. Sound only requires a medium such as liquid or gas. It can even travel through stone. I am well aware there is no sound in space that you can hear. However, I process sensory information in ways that are beyond your understanding, and I *heard* these gravity waves."

"Navika, please call our guest by his name. He is part of our expedition now."

"As you wish."

Zahn looked out toward the edge of the ring again and the stars beyond.

"I apologize, Navika. I didn't mean to question the way you hear and see. I'm just trying to understand. So what was the response to our message?"

"A most exquisite harmony, Zahn. I am certain it was a musical chord of some type, but relayed as a gravity wave. The chord itself seemed alive."

"A living chord? Sounds like a resounding yes in the language of music, if you ask me."

"I wonder if the set of two-digit numbers all go together," Oonak said.

"You mean, they could be different from the first set of single-digit numbers?"

"Very likely. Navika, try 3.3.2, 00.00.00, 000. If my hypothesis is correct, we will be taken to a node gate."

This time they didn't have to wait for long. After a few seconds, Navika spoke.

"The response was not negative this time. However, it wasn't like the signal I got when we put in Avani's address, either. It started as one chord which then changed key again and again."

Zahn looked down to the center of the ring, which was far below them now, but saw nothing.

"So why isn't a vortex opening up?"

"That is a good question, Zahn. Navika, has it indicated any discordance at all?"

"Negative," Navika said. "It seems our current knowledge of the gates is insufficient."

After all this, Zahn was beginning to wonder if their entire quest would stop here, just because they couldn't solve the riddle of how to use this gate.

*All the hatchlings of eternity have gone before us,* he thought.

Recalling Kavi's strange words from their meeting just a few days before was strangely comforting.

"Wait a second, didn't you say these gates are tuned to only respond to the life that lives near them?"

"Yes."

"Well, we're still in my home star system, so it's possible it needs to know that one of us is from Avani. Why not try broadcasting my DNA to the gate itself? Maybe that's why the last gate worked. I cut my finger!"

"Broadcast your genetic code to the gate? Intriguing idea. Navika, can you translate genetic material into a signal that this gate is likely to understand?"

"Unknown, Oonak. But I can certainly reduce the genetic signal into a string of numbers and broadcast that to the gate. However, even if I broadcast it at extreme speed, an entire genome could take a while to transmit."

"Then do not send the entire genome. Start at the beginning, and if it responds, stop transmitting." Oonak turned to Zahn. "Do you have a sample we can use?"

"Here. This should work," Zahn said and gave Oonak a single blonde hair from the top of his head.

Oonak placed the single hair onto a panel that popped out of the armrest of his chair. Zahn watched as the panel flashed brightly for a second, and then the single hair was gone.

"Decoding…"

Zahn was about to ask how the hair had disappeared so quickly when Navika spoke again.

"Transmitting."

After a few seconds, a bright light grew within the ring.

"Excellent work, Zahn! Navika, position us one klick away from the center of the ring. I would rather not get taken in unexpectedly like last time."

In a few seconds time, they had gained some distance from the growing point of light at the center of the gate. As before, the space in the middle of the ring spiraled in on itself, except that this time thousands of stars were behind the vortex, creating the illusion that they were circling a massive drain. This gate was also much bigger than the first, and when Zahn studied it closely he noticed that the surface of the ring itself had lit up in perfect geometric patterns, just as the previous gate had.

"Oonak, I am receiving a repeating signal. It appears to be repeating the signal of the address we just entered. I would surmise that this is an indication we can now proceed through the gate."

Indeed, the bright point at the center of the gate stopped growing, and the space around it continued to swirl in a strange way as if starlight itself weren't sure what to make of it. Zahn looked over to his right and gazed at Kuvela-Dipa once more. He wondered if it might be the last time he would ever see it.

"Proceed," Oonak said, and Navika moved closer and closer to the bright center of the vortex. Soon, it completely filled their view, and in an instant, they were gone.

# CHAPTER 12

# WELCOME TO NOWHERE

Once again, Navika and everyone within hurtled through a corridor of pure light. Zahn tried to make out more details of the thread-like strands of light in the distance. Yet time itself seemed to flow differently in the corridor, and they were back in the darkness of space before he could even begin to count them.

At first, they only saw darkness. After a few seconds, their eyes adjusted, and the darkness gradually revealed itself to be a field of stars around them once again.

Zahn looked around. The constellations around him were breathtaking, but they were also completely foreign to him.

"According to my star maps, we are now over 2,000 light-years from Avani," Navika said.

"Are there any planets nearby?"

"None detected, and all of the nearest stars are well over ten light-years distant."

"Indeed, we are deep within the Ocean of Space now, Zahn," Oonak said. "It appears we are in an area between star clusters."

Zahn looked above him and noticed that they were drifting from the center of a ring-shaped gate just as they had with the first gate, now over 2,000 light-years away. Had they really travelled that far? Zahn tried to digest this fact, but had trouble wrapping his mind around it, even though he had experienced it for himself.

"Oon, how is it possible we've gone so far so quickly? This violates all established rules of physics."

"There is much your world has to learn, Zahn. These gates seem to work by tearing a hole into spacetime and allowing us to slip, if only temporarily, into timespace."

"Timespace. Is that where those corridors of light are? The ones that we saw," Zahn said.

"Yes. You can think of timespace as a realm parallel to spacetime, an inversion. Here in spacetime, we have three dimensions of space and one of time, correct?"

"Yes…"

"In timespace, the reverse is true, and the rules of physics that affect us here in spacetime do not apply. Different rules apply, though an explanation of those is beyond your understanding. Beyond the understanding of many." For a moment Oonak seemed lost in thought.

After a few seconds, Navika broke the silence.

"What address would you like to broadcast next, Oonak?"

"First of all, please orient us about one klick in front of the gate as you did last time. From what we have seen, I'm nearly certain that these gates are arranged in a hierarchy, and I suspect a higher-level node serves this node. I suggest we request node 3.3.0. What do you think, Zahn?"

"I think that's a good idea. Let's do it."

"Transmitting…" Navika said. "Interesting. It's sending back a positive signal even though I didn't transmit any genetic code."

"Why would it need my DNA now? We're so far from my world, I wouldn't be surprised if this gate worked for anyone who knew how to use it."

"Or anything," Oonak added, and he winked at Zahn.

As before, they waited until the vortex stabilized, flew into the swirling mass, and were amazed at the shimmering corridors beyond. Yet soon after, Zahn questioned their choice when, upon reentering space, they flew right into a literal swarm of trouble.

# CHAPTER 13

## INTO THE FIRE

When they emerged from the vortex, Oonak had scarcely any time at all to react to the shots that were fired at them from above. In a flash, Oonak spun the ship around just a few fractions of a second after they had emerged from the gate and somehow managed to evade their fire. For a moment, Zahn thought he saw giant insects perched on the edges of the gate's ring. As they jumped off and headed toward them, he saw their narrow, menacing shapes. They seemed more biological than metal.

"Zahn, hold tight! Marauders!"

An instant later, the entire cabin around them became covered in the red grid Zahn had seen back on the South Pole as Navika enabled the cloak and Oonak returned fire. Huge bolts of purple light hit a few of the ships, but it wasn't enough. Whenever Oonak fired, the cloak faltered for a fraction of a second, giving away their position.

Zahn found it strange that he couldn't hear their weapons impact onto the marauder ships, but he reminded himself that this was impossible since there was no medium in which sound could travel through between them and their attackers.

Another wave of fire.

Oonak looked worried now. They were clearly outnumbered.

"Oon, can we go faster? They're gaining on us!"

Navika spoke for him, so he could remain focused.

"Oonak is pushing my systems as far as they will go, Zahn. With my timespace drive offline, this is my maximum velocity," Navika said.

Zahn had to admit to himself that, without any point of reference, he had absolutely no idea how fast they were going. After all, he could only see the ships and the stars.

"Do not worry, Zahn," Oonak said. "We will find a way to survive this. I'm sending out a distress call, and I have detected an asteroid field nearby. It is possible, however unlikely, that someone is living within it."

Even as Navika sped away from the gate, more and more of the small, insect-like ships surrounded them in a frenzied swarm. Each of them had what looked like tiny metal heads and arms, and Zahn wondered if they captured ships or consumed them piece by piece.

As Oonak skillfully evaded most of their fire, Zahn felt horrible that there was no way to help him. He could only look on, impressed at how Oonak avoided firing unnecessary shots so he wouldn't give their position away more than necessary.

Above them, below them, and to all sides, dozens of ships fired in wide spreads. Oonak continued to evade most of the fire, but the ships formed a sphere around them that slowly got smaller and smaller as it followed them.

There was no way out.

As the sphere got smaller, the ships made more direct hits, and it became harder for Oonak to evade their fire. Each time one of their plasma bolts hit the ship, Zahn winced, as though Navika's ivory skin were his own.

An alarm sounded throughout the ship, and Navika announced that his cloaking field had failed completely. They could now see the ship. Oonak focused all of his effort on taking out the ships one by one, yet there were simply too many of them firing at once. More must have arrived because Zahn could even see two new plasma beams in their midst.

Except that these crimson beams of light sliced a marauder ship to pieces. And another. And another. Oonak and Zahn were stunned, but they couldn't see any obvious source to the beams.

"Zahn, we are receiving an inbound transmission," Oonak said. "I'm putting it on surround so you can hear it, as well."

At first they heard only static, and then the static resolved itself into a woman's voice. The voice sounded feminine, yet Zahn couldn't understand any of it. The words sounded more alien than any language he had ever heard before, including Jangalan which was infamous on Avani for being almost impossible for foreigners to correctly pronounce.

"Oonak, what is she saying? Is there something wrong with the transmission?"

"The transmission strength is excellent, I assure you," Navika said. "Perhaps you do not know her language. However—"

"Intriguing," Oonak interrupted. "It seems someone out there would rather have us stay alive. We have just received a waypoint that lies deep within the asteroid field."

"Okay, but how are we going to get over there without being blasted into the next galaxy?" Zahn said.

Just as he finished saying this, two crimson beams sliced three more ships into pieces, creating a small gap in the sphere.

"By following the path," Oonak said.

With shots blazing, Navika charged forward and fearlessly plunged through the small gap. Some of the marauders followed them into the asteroid field, but the combination of Navika's weapons and the crimson beams picked off the closest ones.

In the distance, Zahn could now faintly see a grey, circular object. Above it was the familiar red symbol that Navika used to mark waypoints, and after a few seconds Zahn saw that it was a moon. The closer they got, the fewer marauders remained, and the more lifeless the surface of the grey moon looked.

"That's it?"

Zahn was unimpressed. Everything on the surface was graphite. There were some craters and a few rolling hills, but not much else.

"Look at where the waypoint is. There is a circular platform. Clearly unnatural," Oonak said.

Zahn looked down to the spot. The circular platform was the same color as the rock, and they were nearly above it now.

"Navika's scans indicate there is a hollow space beneath the platform, and these circumstances suggest that it is most likely not a trap. In either case, our options are limited."

Navika approached the surface, and the moment they touched the platform, it descended into the depths of the moon.

# CHAPTER 14

## A SHADOW IN A DARK HALL

The sheer immensity of the hollow space left Zahn speechless at first. Stretching off in front of them was a wide hall that faded into darkness with the distance. When the descending platform finally touched the floor, a deep sound reverberated down the massive hall, and in the distance, Zahn thought he heard other sounds, as well.

Oonak stood up.

"Are you okay, Zahn?"

"I'm excited. How are you?"

"I am well, but I advise caution. We have no idea who rescued us or what their intentions are, so I want you to take this."

Zahn looked down at the object Oonak was holding. It was a curious piece of shimmering metal formed into a loop.

"It is a mental amplifier and interpreter. It will aid you if trouble should befall us. Perhaps even more useful in your case, it will allow you to understand any languages which the Confederation has encountered."

"But it looks so simple."

"Put it around your wrist. If we become separated and you need help, you can contact me by picturing my face, and then mentally sending me a message. Keep in mind though, its range does not extend beyond this planetary system."

Zahn put it on his left wrist, and when he did, it shrunk a bit to fit his wrist better.

"Do you have any questions?" Oonak said.

"About a million. This wristband can do all of that? How soon will you receive a message if I send you one? And how does it interpret alien languages? Let me guess, Spacefarer code—"

Oonak interrupted him.

"—only allows me to share information that you may need to know for the purposes of our mission. What I can tell you is that it works on a simple principle of thought-form resonance. Consider it as a bridge between two minds; as long as I'm in range I will receive a message instantly."

"Incredible."

Their conversation was interrupted by a low pulsing sound ahead of them. When they looked up, they saw a floating sphere hanging in the air above the ship. It was dark blue, metallic, and tiny points of light were evenly spaced around its surface. From one point of light, a beam shot out of the sphere and moved up and down, soon touching every surface of Navika.

"Whatever that object is, it is scanning us. No doubt they have discovered Navika was heavily damaged in the ambush. Keep in mind Zahn, even though we were saved, that does not mean their intentions are pure. Come. Let us find out who we are dealing with."

"Or *what* we're dealing with," Zahn added.

"Precisely."

As they exited Navika, Zahn put the silvery jacket back on and grabbed his backpack. He had a feeling he would need it.

Once they were outside, they had a chance to examine the room in greater detail. Foremost, the room was dark. It was more like a cave than a room, and there was only a dim light high above. From what Zahn could see, the room was circular and appeared to have been carved out of the moon rock itself. The floor was made up of a matrix of stones in varying shades of grey that fit together immaculately, and the stone pattern continued down the hall, fading into the darkness.

When Zahn finally pulled his eyes away from the room they were in, he was struck by how Navika looked. Since the cloaking field had been activated until it was damaged in the battle, this was the first time he actually got to see the ship from the outside, and the damage from the ambush was glaringly obvious.

Black marks were spattered onto all of its surfaces, but he could still see that the ship was made of a shimmering white material. When he examined the ship up close, he almost thought he could see little flecks of the rainbow buried within the ivory crystal, but the black marks covering most of the ship made it difficult for him to be sure.

Oonak walked up behind him.

"It is truly a shame that such a magnificent vessel has been marred by such a swarm."

"Well, at least we survived," Zahn said. "I can even see parts of the ivory crystal between the burn marks. What is this ship made out of anyway?"

"It wasn't made. It was grown."

"You mean it was a crystal that grew?"

"Yes, in a vast harvesting field. But let's focus on the present. It appears our little friend has moved."

He'd almost forgotten about the strange sphere that had been scanning them. It was about two meters above them, scanning their ship from another angle now. Oonak looked up and called out to it.

"I am Oonak of the Confederation of Unity, and this is Zahn. Please identify yourself."

The sphere made a low, gravelly tone which gave Zahn the distinct impression that it was surprised or annoyed, yet it continued scanning.

Oonak turned to Zahn. "It may not be intelligent enough to respond to our queries. I shall try again."

"My name is Oonak. If you cannot state your intentions, please summon your superior."

This time, all the points of light on its surface turned magenta, and it zipped away with a low hum, disappearing down the dark hall.

"Hmm," Zahn said. "Do you think we made it angry?"

Oonak looked at Zahn with the slightest smile on his face, raised an eyebrow, and entered the dark hall.

Zahn followed him. The darkness overtook them quicker than they anticipated, and to his surprise Oonak's uniform glowed, sending out beams of light ahead of them. At seeing this, Zahn remembered the small flashlight in his backpack and shined it onto the immaculately carved walls around them.

And then, he saw it. On the far end of the great hall, they could just make out the shadow of a figure walking toward them. As it grew closer, fear seized Zahn, and his thoughts raced.

*What if it's going to torture us? What if this was all some kind of trap? What if it traps us here for a thousand years? What if it's going to cook us, or worse, feed us to something while we're still alive?*

Oonak stopped walking and raised his index finger.

"Redirect your thoughts," he said. "There is far more to this than appearances."

They both stood there, almost motionless, as the shadowy shape approached them. When the shadow finally stepped into Oonak's light, it revealed itself to be a slim figure wearing a dark maroon spacesuit. The helmet even matched the suit, but its visor was so dark that they couldn't discern any facial features.

Still, it approached.

When the figure was just a few meters away, it stopped walking, looked them up and down, and made a sound of quiet contemplation. Oonak was just about to introduce himself when the figure spoke. Its voice sounded completely artificial, completely emotionless.

"State your identities and intentions. Why have you come here?" The figure spoke in cold, measured sentences.

"I am Oonak of the Confederation of Unity; this is Zahn from Avani. We are on an urgent mission to deliver a message to the Confederation. When we reached this system, we were ambushed by marauders. Someone saved us and directed us to land here."

"We are well aware of the marauders. What is your message?"

"Under Confederation code, I am not permitted to say. However, I can say that it is not related to events taking place within your world," Oonak said.

"Does your message pertain to the gate network you used to arrive here? The gates are ancient, and their creators have been missing for aeons. Few are left that dare use them. Why have you taken this risk?"

"We have been forced to use the gates to deliver this message because of the damage to my ship. Without the gates, we would have been delayed indefinitely." Oonak paused for a moment. "May I ask who you are? Where we are from, it is customary for introductions to be mutual. May we see you? Face to face."

The figure walked up to them. Although Zahn couldn't see beyond the visor at all, it seemed to be looking at them directly in the eyes. Zahn also noticed that the figure was feeling for an object in one of its pockets.

"I see no lies in your eyes." The figure removed its hand from its pocket, pulling nothing out. Instead, it planted its hands on its hips. "I apologize if I seemed cold. We have many visitors, not all of whom have noble intentions for being here. However, my intuition tells me your story is true."

Slowly, the figure removed its helmet to reveal the face of a truly striking woman. Her olive skin complemented her dark brown hair which was arranged up into a bun, and her eyes were a warm brown. Zahn could even see flecks of green in them, but what caught him off guard was her face itself. It was the most perfect face he had ever seen. In short, she was stunning.

"My name is Ashakirta." Her true voice revealed itself to be warm and sweet to their ears. "But if that's difficult to remember, you can call me Asha."

She first offered her hand to Oonak who shook it warmly, and then to Zahn who was still somewhat in awe of her presence, though he tried not to show it.

"Pleased to meet you," Zahn managed to say.

Asha nodded her head slightly and replied, "And you, as well. Now, who is the pilot of the damaged starship?"

"I am," Oonak said.

"Very well. Your ship has already been scanned, and we have confirmed its origin. However, it will take some time to fully assess the damages. In the meantime, I will lead you to my father. By the way, are either of you hungry?"

In the excitement of all that had happened, Zahn had somehow completely forgotten about his stomach, but now that it was being included in the conversation, he realized he was quite hungry indeed.

"Yes! Food would be fantastic," Zahn said.

"Then follow me."

And Asha led them down the dark hall.

# CHAPTER 15

# THE OUTPOST FOR WAYWARD TRAVELLERS

After a few minutes, they arrived at a huge semicircular door at the end of the hall, and Asha pressed her thumb to a plate beside it. When the door rolled back a moment later, several details flooded Zahn's senses at once.

The sheer expanse of the room spread out before him was stunning. The cavern was so large that he was convinced that the entire Ashraya Observatory could have fit inside. As he stepped in, he noticed that a thousand oddly shaped objects were arranged neatly around circular platforms. Above him, the ceiling formed a dome which was illuminated by a brightly glowing orb embedded in the center. It reminded him a bit of Navika's nucleus, but it was brighter and perhaps not as elegant.

Then the smell hit him. The air was clean, but it was filled with a strange scent that was a blend of molten metal, wildflowers, and what almost seemed like a hint of freshly squeezed fruit juice. It was one of the oddest combinations of smells he had ever experienced.

Compared to the sights and smells, the sound of the room was rather mild. Every few seconds, he heard a hissing noise. The low hums of nearby floating spheres were also audible, but overall it was much quieter than Zahn expected such an outpost to be.

"Are you coming?"

He looked to his left and saw Asha studying him with a puzzled look on her face. In this light, he noticed that her olive skin had a hint of a reddish hue within it, and her eyelids had a dusting of gold on them. Then, a wave of embarrassment washed over him. He'd completely lost track of time taking in the sight of the room and wasn't sure exactly how long he had been standing there.

"Oh! I'm sorry, this place is just—"

"Empty? I know. My father has been concerned about that, too. Follow me. This workshop can be a hazardous place. My father has summoned us to the observation balcony."

"Balcony…" Zahn looked up and noticed a balcony high above them that wrapped around the entire chamber.

Asha waved Zahn into a small elevator that was inlaid into the wall beside the huge door they had just come through. Oonak was already inside, and after taking a mental note of what the elevator controls looked like, Zahn stepped in.

"Please don't say anything about how empty this place is to my father. He's been rather sensitive about the subject lately. My father may not like it, but we just don't get the traffic we used to. Now that the marauders are getting more numerous… Anyway, don't ask about his customers, all right?"

"Okay," Zahn said. "So how long have you lived here, Asha?"

"Most of my life. We came here when I was very young."

The elevator made a chirping sound as the doors opened.

"Here we are," she said.

Zahn stepped out and noticed how the balcony wrapped around the edge of the massive room, except at three places where there were gaps. There the quality of the wall changed, and he wondered if they might be massive doors.

Asha led Oonak and Zahn over to a large oval table made of stone. The table was already set, but Zahn couldn't see any eating utensils at all. All he could see were what he guessed were dinner plates arranged on the table.

Zahn noticed Asha looking at a flashing device on her wrist.

"Interesting. It appears your ship is resisting us moving it, but we need to bring it into the workshop to repair it."

"I will notify him."

Zahn watched as Oonak used his wristband to talk to Navika and update him on the situation.

"While you wait for your ship to arrive, you may sit," Asha said. "My father will be out shortly."

Just moments after they sat down, Asha disappeared behind a door, leaving them alone. From where he was sitting, Zahn saw how three narrow columns in the center of the room reached all the way up to the ceiling. Despite being colorless, Zahn thought he saw blue and green hues glisten on the edges of the columns, and he wondered if they were used for anything beyond supporting the dome above them.

Asha appeared again, this time carrying a large bowl of dark green food. It was cut into cubes, and when she set the bowl down, the cubes vibrated like jelly.

"Help yourself," she said. "More to come."

Zahn's stomach overpowered his hesitation, and when he grabbed a piece he was relieved to discover that it had a smooth texture and tasted slightly sweet. He also used that opportunity to take a picture of the cubic snacks, as well as some of the incredible architecture around him. He noticed that Asha looked interested in the photodisc, but before she could say anything, Oonak spoke.

"Asha, are you and your father the only people who live here?"

Asha's expression darkened.

"Yes," she said. "It wasn't always that way, though. There used to be more, back when it was safer, before the marauders came. Now we rely on the pods to help us. My dad started building them when less and less people would stay and work."

"You mean those floating spheres?" Zahn said. "We saw one when we first arrived. Oonak thought it was scanning us."

"It was," Asha said.

Zahn heard a quiet chirp, and Asha looked at her wrist again.

"In fact," she continued. "I just received a report back from one of the pods. Hmm. Is there anyone else in your group?"

"No, just me and Oonak."

"Well, I'm detecting a life signature within your ship." Asha frowned. "Sometimes I wonder why I even trust those pods. That pod must be malfunctioning. I'd better go and examine it. I'll be back in a few minutes."

"That won't be necessary," Oonak said. "Navika contains a life pattern because the ship contains an individuated consciousness within its core. You are seeing a life pattern because Navika is indeed alive."

"Oh." Asha considered this for a moment. "Then is the ship a spacefaring organism of some kind? We've seen one or two of those over the years. They're quite rare."

"Navika's origins are privileged knowledge and nothing to be concerned about, I assure you. What is of concern right now is the future of our mission."

"Well, it looks like we'll be able to repair the cloaking field in a relatively short amount of time."

"What about the timespace components?"

"Given your ship's unique qualities, I'm not sure we'll be able to repair its timespace drive. Perhaps my father—"

In the distance, they heard heavy footsteps. "Oh, here he is."

They looked up and saw a tall, muscular man with the same hint of a reddish hue in his olive skin that Asha had. His hair and beard were jet black and short, and his eyes were a darker brown than Asha's. He was wearing a graphite jumpsuit covered in zippered pockets, and he was holding two huge platters with at least a dozen small bowls on them, each containing a strange food Zahn had never seen before.

The man set both platters on the table and eagerly offered his hand to Oonak, who was closest. As he did this, Zahn rushed to put away his photodisc. He didn't know how this man would feel about him taking photos of the place.

"The name's Yantrik. Welcome to Outpost 33, or as I like to call it these days 'The Outpost for Wayward Travellers', although it's had different names throughout the years…"

Yantrik's voice was gruff, but there was a warmth behind it that was assuring. He was instantly likable.

"Pleased to meet you. I am Oonak of the Confederation." Oonak stood up and bowed slightly.

"Welcome, Oonak! And who are you, son?" Yantrik flashed Zahn a charming smile which fit his angular face perfectly.

Zahn winced. He hadn't been called 'son' in years.

"Please, just call me Zahn. This is quite an impressive place you've got here."

"You think so? Well, it does the job, although it's old. Older than you could guess, but what can I say? It's home. Anyway, help yourself to some of this. I enjoy making food for guests." Yantrik gestured toward the fresh bowls of strangely colored food on the stone table.

Oonak took a handful of some orange berries, sat back down, and chewed them thoughtfully for a few moments before he spoke again.

"Yantrik, are you familiar with timespace drives?"

"Are you kidding me? Rebuilt one when I was a kid."

"Good. So you can repair my ship's drive?"

"Not a chance. At least not without the right materials and plenty of time."

"Why?"

"Do you know how long it's been since a Confederation ship stopped by? I don't have the right materials to fix such a complex timespace system. Add to that the fact that I've never worked on a drive from a ship as unique as yours before."

"Such as?" Zahn said.

"Well, the timespace field resonates with the hull itself—which appears to be a single crystal, I might add. Anyway, I haven't seen anything like it in years, so I'd have to reverse-engineer it and study it first. I suspect neither of you would want to stay for the length of time that might take, assuming I could even complete a repair at all." Yantrik looked out onto the workshop floor and took a deep breath. "Timespace drives are tricky. The question isn't whether I could, the question is, would you really want to give me a dying candle and risk me inadvertently transforming it into a fireball?"

"No," Oonak said. "If my ship is too exotic for your level of experience, then perhaps it is best if you refrain."

"A wise choice. Asha tells me you came in through the old ring gate. You're playing with fire, you know. Partly because they're older than most of the civilizations around here, but mostly because of the kinds of nasties you can meet while using them. The marauders, who make their way by attacking anyone who comes through, are only one example. Now that I think about it, you're lucky you haven't run into the Vandals yet. You're even more lucky Ashakirta detected your ship when you two came through, otherwise we most certainly would not be having this conversation."

Zahn turned to Asha in surprise.

"You?"

Asha smiled slightly.

"Oh, don't let her fool you. She has talent, and not just in piloting. Anyway, I feel horrible whenever she has to go out instead of me, but she was already in the area when you two came through, so she was able to get to you both faster than I could have." Yantrik turned to Asha. "Why were you out there this time, anyway?"

"I was just on my way back from helping one of the asteroid miners repair her ship. She seemed rather ill, too, so I brought her some food from the greenhouse. When I left she was still sleeping, actually."

"Asha, I'm glad that you're doing jobs on the side, but we talked about this. Sharing is fine. But please check with me first before you give our food away, all right?"

"Sorry, Dad. She was pretty sick and you were busy."

Yantrik grumbled.

In the distance, Zahn heard a sound that reminded him of white noise and soon realized that it might be the ship being scrubbed clean.

"So, Yantrik," Oonak said. "When you spoke of the Vandals, were you referring to the Vakra—"

Yantrik cut Oonak off in a blink.

"*Stop right there*, Confederation man. Whatever you do, do *not* say that name. It is not acceptable in civilized society, especially not on my outpost."

"I didn't mean to offend you. I just want to confirm that we're talking about the same enemy."

Zahn's eyes were wide.

"Are you referring to those who are rumored to steal entire star systems?" Oonak continued. "I've heard them referred to by many names, but those of the Confederation have a specific name for those who corrupt space as they do."

"If it's the name you were about to say, then you should remember my words. It is *not* acceptable to speak, Oonak. Calling them the Undying Vandals describes them well enough."

"Who are these vandals, Oon?"

Oonak turned to Zahn. His face seemed tense as though he were holding something back, and then he spoke in carefully measured sentences.

"They are the last great adversary to the Confederation. For millennia, most believed that they had finally been wiped out, but we were mistaken. They returned even stronger than we anticipated. More and more, entire star systems have been plucked from their rightful places in the galaxy and enslaved, creating great chaos. I have even heard of star systems purposely causing their star to go nova moments after evacuation, just to prevent them from consuming yet another star." Oonak paused. "Zahn, they are the living nightmare that the Confederation must extinguish."

Zahn seemed lost in thought for a moment.

"So," Zahn finally said, "do you think they were the ones who attacked you back at Avani?"

"Quite likely, and that is the prime reason why we must reach the Confederation Council as soon as possible. If they have spread as far as your system, billions more are in danger."

Zahn turned to Yantrik. "So, when will our ship be ready?"

"My my! Look at this one. Getting right down to business, not that I can blame you. If the Undying Vandals truly are meddling with your planet, you'd best get all the help you can. Lucky for you, your ship should be ready later today."

Yantrik took a deep breath and raised his eyebrows, realizing that he might be alarming Zahn more than necessary.

"In any case, don't worry so much, Zahn," he continued. "Your ship is out of your hands now, and if you remember anything, remember this: you gotta know the difference between what you can change and what you can't. Otherwise you just go wasting energy and frustrating yourself. You got me?"

"I suppose that's good advice for any traveller," Zahn said.

"Damn right."

"Yantrik," Oonak said. "What do you and Asha know about the galactic gate network?"

"Not too much. Until you two showed up, we thought it might have burned out once and for all. Last time anybody came through there was a long while ago. Didn't stop somebody from trying to trade a gate map for repairs to their ship a while back, though. Can you believe that? Sorry, but star maps are not my preferred method of payment. I mean look at me, Oonak. Do I look like an explorer to you?"

"Not especially."

"Right, but that doesn't stop people from trying to pay with them. Anyway, sometimes I wonder if I'm too nice. If someone's hard up for currency, occasionally I let them pay in knowledge, although I'm not sure how much longer I'll be able to do that."

"How many gates did this gate map show?"

"Well, usually I wouldn't share something used for payment, but considering that you're on a Confederation mission, I suppose I could share it with you both if you keep it to yourselves. Unfortunately, it was only a small map. Showed maybe five gates within a few hundred light-years." Yantrik pulled a thin sheet from one of his pockets and gave it to him.

Oonak seemed disappointed as he studied the crude map. It used major stars as markers and appeared to have been made by an explorer that hadn't managed to activate any of the gates. The network seemed patchy and no major nodes were included on it.

"The scope of this map is seriously limited, but thank you for sharing it."

"No problem. You should have seen the guy who traded it to me! Looked like he'd nearly been eaten alive. Twice. So, how far you going, anyway?"

"We're going to the outer core," Zahn said.

"The outer core?" Asha was stunned. "Do you have any idea how many light-years that is?"

"Over 30,000. Our mission requires it," Oonak said.

"Well, then! That *is* quite a mission, and for such a mission, you'll be needing a lot more than a cloak for your ship. Here, take these." Yantrik pulled out three black square plates from one of his back pockets and handed them to Oonak.

"They're personal cloaking chips. Made 'em myself. No one will see you coming. Third one's a backup, just in case."

"Thanks, Yantrik! That's very kind of you. But, are you sure you want to part with these?" Zahn said.

"Take them. You'll need 'em. And let me know how they work! I warn you though, I haven't had a chance to do much real-world testing, so they might be a little buggy."

"Even so, thank you very much. Your generosity will be remembered," Oonak said.

"You're quite welcome. You can thank me by not paying for my services with star maps!" Yantrik laughed again.

"I assure you that is not a problem. I have a variety of precious materials stored on my ship for such a purpose. You will be paid fairly. By the way, would you happen to have any weapons I could trade for? My sidearm was damaged when my ship crashed on Avani's surface."

"I'm afraid I don't have a spare at the moment, but the cloaking chips should help you avoid most trouble. Actually..."

Yantrik felt around his pockets for a moment and pulled out a small ball of orange liquid.

"This is an experimental acid. Some of the strongest I've ever synthesized. Shatter that sphere onto the face of your enemy, and I can guarantee that it'll change their complexion, if you know what I mean. Hah!"

"Thank you, Yantrik. This is a strange gift, but perhaps it will prove useful in the end."

"Every little bit helps," Yantrik said, winking one eye.

As they spoke, Zahn wandered over to the edge of the balcony and saw that Navika was now in the center of one of the smaller circular platforms, like an ivory tepee pitched amidst a glowing landscape of technology. Floating around the ship were about a dozen spheres, polishing off the last few specks of black debris from the battle.

"Cool, aren't they?"

"Hmm?" Zahn looked back and saw Asha walking up to him. "Yeah, they are. Do they clean up the ship or repair the damaged pieces first?"

"They scrub the ship first. But don't worry. You're fortunate that we have the components to repair such a small cloaking field. Although, I will have to test it in orbit."

On the far side of the room, Zahn noticed bright orange liquid flowing out of the wall, through some translucent pipes, and collecting in a large container below.

"What's that?" Zahn said, pointing to the strange machine.

"Ah, that's one of my father's experiments. He says it can dissolve almost anything."

"Why would he be working on that?"

"Who knows? Would it shock you to learn that he has a lot of weird projects? By the way, I want to apologize if he seems overly sensitive about discussing the Undying Vandals. If only I had been older..."

"Older? For what?"

"For when the Undying Vandals destroyed my home. Perhaps I would have been strong enough to comfort him as much as he comforted me."

"Oh."

For a few moments, Zahn's thoughts couldn't seem to form themselves into sentences. "I'm so sorry, Asha. I've lost... I mean, in some ways, I think I can relate to that feeling. I doubt that makes you feel any better, though."

"Don't worry about it. We survived."

"What about your mother? What happened to her? If you don't mind me asking."

"I never had the chance to know her." Asha looked down to the spherical pods as they hovered around Navika. "I'm not sure you realize how special your ship is," she said.

"Well, to be honest it's the first starship I've ever been in."

"Really?" Asha looked surprised. "Navika is one unique bird. It seems to be more like a living crystal than anything else."

"He."

"What?"

"You said 'it', but Navika is a 'he'."

"Can ships have genders?"

"Why not? Anyway, when we test the cloaking field in orbit, perhaps you'll see what I mean."

"Well, I still can't believe there's a life force in there. Must be a pretty exceptional ship."

"He is."

# CHAPTER 16

# A FLIGHT TO THE GATE

A few hours later, Navika reentered the vast Ocean of Space, and this time he contained a new passenger: Ashakirta. The meal they'd had on the outpost had left Zahn and Oonak feeling recharged and strong, and they were now holding a low, geosynchronous orbit above the outpost. From the ground, Yantrik was scanning the ship and relaying data to Asha as she made the final adjustments to Navika's new cloaking field.

While she worked, Zahn noticed that Asha seemed mesmerized at how Oonak controlled the ship completely through the use of his mind, and Zahn wondered if Oonak would be open to showing him how to pilot the ship sometime.

All three of them were in the command bay, and through an open panel beside Asha, Zahn could see millions of glowing fibers and shapes that he couldn't even begin to understand. As Asha sat beside it, she spoke to her father who was still beneath the moon's surface, far below.

"I'm reading 0.0021 variation, but it keeps changing. What are you reading?"

"0.0022. That's pretty close, Asha," Yantrik replied, his voice sounding tiny as it emerged from Asha's communicator.

"No, I think something is wrong. The strength is wavering."

"That's odd. Let me check again," Yantrik said. "Hmm, I'm reading a slight change, too. It doesn't make any sense."

"Dad, I think a few of these cloak cells are defective. I should be able to isolate the defective ones and rebalance the field. Should only take a few minutes."

"All right. Let me know when you need another reading."

As she worked, Zahn watched Asha, reflecting at how gracefully she carried herself, even when she was hunched over an open panel. As Zahn watched, he was startled by an alarm that suddenly echoed throughout the ship.

"Asha," Oonak said urgently. "I'm detecting hundreds of small craft heading toward our position. Their size matches the craft that attacked us when we first arrived. Is the cloak ready?"

Asha looked up, and when she saw a haze of red marks overlaid on their view of the moon and the space beyond, her eyes widened.

"Some of the cloak cells were defective. We could activate it now, but if I can't isolate the defective cells, we won't have a cloaking field at all. Just give me two minutes."

"Asha, we may not have that long."

Magnified views of the incoming ships were now being displayed over their view. It was the marauders, and this swarm made the first swarm look small. This time, the swarm of trouble had come to them.

"Everyone, please be advised," Oonak said. "I am going to employ an evasive pattern. Inertial nullifiers are activated, but I recommend moving as little as possible during these maneuvers."

In an instant, the cabin around them once again became overlaid with a red grid, and as Oonak weaved through the asteroids and fired back toward the swarm, a proximity alarm sounded throughout the ship.

All three of them knew that they were hopelessly outnumbered, and Asha worked as if their lives depended on her success. Indeed, they did.

"How's that cloak coming, Asha?" Oonak called back to her.

"You just asked me that. Some of these cells are unstable, and I'm not sure why. I'm going as fast as I can!"

"Just let me know when you are nearly ready," Oonak said calmly. "Until then, we must evacuate this system to ensure our survival. I suggest you call your father." At that moment, another proximity alarm sounded throughout the ship. "It may be the last conversation you have with him."

"But this is insane. The early warning beacons should have alerted us. Why didn't they alert us?"

"I don't know, Asha. Your father never mentioned any early warning system to us," Zahn said.

"Well, we have one, and it should be working. Unless…"

The first shards of yellow plasma whizzed past the ship, and Asha realized that Oonak was right. This could be the last opportunity she had to speak to her father, so as she worked, she spoke to him.

"Dad, there's a swarm of marauders so large that—"

"Asha! I'm so glad you got through the interference. The marauders have been creating a lot of comm noise, and I've been having trouble contacting you, otherwise I would have called you sooner. I haven't heard any status signals from the beacons since I last talked to you. I think the marauders may have found them and disabled them."

"I know, Dad."

The ship quivered as a plasma charge impacted onto the hull, and Zahn wished there was something he could do.

"Oon, can I help fire back? Is there anything I can do?"

"Zahn, there is a time to attack and a time to run so that you may live to fight another day. This is the latter. Right now there is nothing you can do but maintain a positive attitude and stand by for orders."

"Okay. I can do that."

The ship rumbled again.

"Indirect hit!" Oonak announced. "Asha, status?"

"Dad, we've never seen this many at once before. What if they're after the materials on the outpost?"

"I don't know, Asha. All I know is that you, Oonak, and Zahn have to do whatever you can to survive. Don't worry about me. I've already initiated a complete outpost lockdown."

"Lockdown?!" Asha gasped. "Dad, that means no one can—"

"I know. It means I can't leave. But no one will be able to come in, either. The shock barricade will keep me and the outpost safe. Asha, we both knew this could happen someday. Trust me, this is the safest thing for everyone. Go with them. You may not realize it yet, but they need you."

"Dad!"

"Asha!" Oonak interrupted. "Status?"

As the scene unfolded in front of him, Zahn sat transfixed. Stars were flashing past as Oonak raced through the asteroid field, and although the wall behind him wasn't transparent, the ship still overlaid it with hundreds of small red circles. He knew that each of these circles indicated a marauder in the swarm following them. Even though Oonak navigated expertly through the asteroids that surrounded the moon, the swarm was getting closer by the moment, and Zahn noticed that Oonak's face looked strained as he evaded the oncoming fire.

"I love you, Asha. Be as safe as you can, and remember the Tulari. It is real, and judging from where they're going, you now have a better chance of finding it than I ever did. Keep a sharp eye, my daughter."

"Dad! " Asha was now on the verge of sobbing. "I don't know if I can find it, but I will do my best. I promise!"

"I know," he said. "You are Ashakirta. You are fiercely compassionate. Always remember, when you align your heart with your mind, you are unstoppable. Goodbye my—"

Once again, her father's voice drowned in static.

"I love you, Dad!"

Ahead, they could now see the familiar ring-shaped gate, hanging against the backdrop of stars like an ancient specter.

They were nearly surrounded on all sides now. Waves of plasma charges were so thick that Oonak's maneuvers were no longer enough, and the ship was barraged with plasma. It reminded Zahn of the sound of thunderstorms that he would often fall asleep to back on Avani.

"Shield cohesion is at 55% and falling rapidly," Oonak said. "Asha, that cloak would be most useful."

Asha swallowed her emotions for the moment and entered in the final field calculations into the cloaking circuits.

"I think I got it!" she called out, and Navika blinked out of existence, at least to everyone except those inside.

The effect of this on the swarm of marauders was strange. After they ceased fire, they diffused in all directions.

"Good job, Asha. You just bought us some time, and very likely our lives."

Zahn ran over and gave Asha a hug. Her eyes were still wet.

"Zahn," Oonak called down to him after a few moments. "I've been doing some thinking about how these gates are arranged throughout the galaxy. From what we've seen, I'd hypothesize that this next jump will span a significant portion across this spiral arm. I'm transmitting that address now." Oonak paused. "Interesting... I believe the marauders are trying to locate us with diffused energy waves."

Oonak was right. In moments, a few of the marauders fired toward them again as the vortex grew in size.

"Damn it! They've got our position again," Zahn said. "Is the vortex open yet?"

"If this gate is anything like the last one, it appears it will be safe to enter in approximately five seconds," Oonak said.

Asha ran down to the passenger seating, sat beside him, and strapped herself in. Zahn closed his eyes and hoped that the marauders weren't smart enough to know how to use the gate after they did.

As the now familiar sight of the swirling waves of energy filled his view, Zahn almost thought he saw the outline of a marauder in the twisting shapes behind him, but once they entered the radiant corridor, he could only see countless webs of other corridors stretching off like luminous threads into infinity.

# CHAPTER 17

## A LEGEND FOR THE AGES

By now, Zahn was quite used to the relative blinding that was the glimpse of timespace between the gates, as well as the period of adjustment to the darkness of space that his eyes made afterwards. Asha, however, was not.

"Where in the blazes were we?" Asha asked a moment later.

"We were in a parallel existence known as timespace," Oonak said. "We are safe now."

"But do you know how to use these gates to return to Outpost 33?"

"Yes. We have a working understanding of the gate network. We will return you to the outpost, but we must reach the Confederation Council first."

Asha closed up and turned away from Zahn and Oonak.

"Hey, don't worry," Zahn said, taking her hand. She turned toward him and when she looked into his eyes he saw that she was holding back tears. "We'll be back there. Don't worry. That barricade sounded pretty strong. I'm sure he'll be okay, Asha."

"Zahn is right," Oonak said. "Your father is a foresightful man. The odds are overwhelmingly in his favor."

"Don't tell me about the odds!" Asha yelled back to Oonak. "My Father's life should not be reduced to a number. How do I even know that we'll survive long enough to make it back?"

Asha pulled her hand away and looked over to Oonak.

"Because this is a Confederation mission, Asha, and you're on a Confederation ship. The core of our mission is to preserve and protect all life, and as a part of that mission Navika and I *will* return you to the outpost. The upholding of free will is the foundation of our Code, and since you are joining us on this journey, you would be wise to eat one of these."

Oonak threw a kavasa berry to her.

"The kavasa berry contains compounds which are very helpful to the immune function and health of those of us who travel the vast distances between the stars. Zahn has informed me that he finds it sour, but I assure you it is quite necessary."

Asha chewed it in silence.

"You know, Asha, it wasn't easy for me to say goodbye to my father either, but Oonak needed my help. For what it's worth, I think you're going to be invaluable on this journey, and I can't say I blame you for being surprised about timespace. I was shocked the first time I saw it, too."

"And the second time," Oonak said.

"Right. But once you get used to it, using the gates isn't so bad. I mean, tearing a hole in spacetime is probably going to be somewhat disorienting no matter what, but at least you get used to it. Are you familiar with timespace? It's kind of like—"

"I know what it is, Zahn." Asha glared at him. "It is the mirror to reality that contains three dimensions of time. I know all about it, so don't waste your time explaining it to me. As I said before, we've had visitors with ships that had timespace drives. Did you really think that just because we couldn't repair your drive, that I didn't understand the concept?"

"I'm sorry, I didn't mean to underestimate you." Zahn winced at the thought of making her feel bad. He was trying to help.

"You wouldn't be the first. Anyway, I'd like some space right now." Asha slid down to the end of the long, padded bench.

"…I said I was sorry."

Zahn looked behind them. As usual, they were drifting forward from the center of the gate, and they were wrapped in a blanket of stars.

"So where are we, anyway?"

"According to Navika," Oonak said, "we are now roughly 10,000 light-years from Avani, and it seems we are near an intelligent system."

"Really? As in, a civilization?"

"Indeed. Navika reports that it is known as Aarava, the World of Resonance."

"Are we going to stop there?"

"Yes. To avoid further delay, we must find someone knowledgable in how the gates are arranged, otherwise it could take weeks to reach our destination. I would like to contact the Aaravans and see if they know anything about the gate network before we continue on. We are currently on approach and should arrive in the system in a few hours under impulse speed."

Asha stood up, took a deep breath, and exhaled. "Well, that should give me plenty of time make the final adjustments on the cloaking cells, at least."

"You know, I'm glad you're here, Asha," Zahn said. "I'm a big fan of not being blown up."

"Me, too."

Asha's eyes wandered down to the open panel, and for some time after, the entire cabin fell silent. It struck Zahn that the silence might be good for Asha. Perhaps it would help her collect her thoughts and come to peace with the situation. It also gave Zahn some time to reflect on the many events of that day.

He yawned. What time was it, anyway?

As Asha started scanning some of the glowing fibers under the floor panels, Zahn opened his backpack and looked at his photodisc. According to its computer, the sun had set on Ashraya hours ago, and under normal circumstances he would be fast asleep by now. In light of this new information, Zahn decided to rest. The padded bench was easily long enough for him to sleep on comfortably, and he silently drifted off to sleep as he watched Asha work.

When Zahn opened his eyes again, he felt as though only five minutes had passed, but his surroundings suggested otherwise. The floor panel was now replaced, and Asha was sitting cross-legged on the floor in front of him, looking out at a fiery orb that he could only assume was the star they had been heading toward.

He sat up and stretched his arms.

"Did I miss anything?"

"Not much." Asha glanced back, her brown eyes seeming brighter now. "Space is actually pretty boring most of the time, believe it or not."

"After what I've been through, I don't believe you. How's the cloak working?"

"Well enough. I still don't know why some of the cloaking cells failed, but I was able to compensate for them."

"Great job, Asha. It's a relief to hear we have the ability to cloak again," Zahn said.

"Well, we still haven't gotten to test it thoroughly. Without a third party to help us calibrate it, the cloaking field could be giving off trace radiation that makes us stick out like a rabid pulsar for all I know. But until we have someone to help us, it's impossible to say. It's probably working splendidly, I just can't guarantee that yet."

Zahn looked out onto the array of stars ahead.

"Asha, can I ask you a question that might be personal?"

When Asha turned around, Zahn saw suspicion on her face.

"What do you mean *might* be personal?"

"Well, I don't know how personal the subject is to you."

Asha rolled her eyes. "Fine. Go ahead."

"What is a Tulari?"

"Oh, that! Hah, you had me nervous for a second there. The Tulari is a legendary object that my father is obsessed in finding. Some call it the Pearl of Great Price, and most think it only exists in myth. But my father believes it's real with every fiber of his being."

"Oh."

"Tulari?" Oonak said. "I've heard that word mentioned in the past, but where and when eludes me. Navika, could you cross-reference that sound complex?"

After a few moments, Oonak smiled. Zahn wondered if he was talking to Navika solely through a mental connection now.

"Of course. How could I forget? But why would your father want to destroy a wormhole?"

"He has his reasons, but take a wild guess as to his main reason," Asha said.

"Destroy a wormhole? How is that possible?" Zahn said.

"Ah yes, the marauders. They aren't from nearby, are they?" Oonak said.

"Guys?" Zahn was beginning to feel bewildered.

"No, they aren't from nearby, and my father thinks he's located the wormhole that they've been coming in from. If he were to find the Tulari, we could finally start reducing their numbers and make the outpost safe again."

"Guys!"

"Zahn, what's wrong?" Oonak said.

"I'm assigned to an observatory, and there's no way to destroy a wormhole."

"Zahn, there is much your planet has yet to learn about the Universe, and how to destroy a wormhole is the least of these. The Tulari is quite an exceptional object, and I apologize if I got carried away just now. Where I'm from, the story of the Tulari is a beloved myth told to all children. In the story, the Sanguine Suns used negative energy to create a fissure in space, using it to blackmail and threaten their galactic brothers to gain power."

"Hmm, so was this fissure anything like the gates we use to travel the galaxy?"

"No. This fissure was grown within a planet and could consume entire star systems. Yet just as the Sanguine Suns were about to devour an innocent civilization, the Tulari was found in a cave deep underground, and the Innocents used it to seal up the fissure forever."

"Wow. That's quite a bedtime story," Zahn said. "But what exactly is a fissure? Is that like a wormhole?"

"Yes, an artificial wormhole created for nefarious purposes. Since Asha is also quite familiar with this object, that would suggest its story has spread throughout the galaxy."

"Like a universal myth," Zahn said. "So Asha, has your father found any evidence for it?"

"Unfortunately, he's found mostly stories and not much else. From what we've learned, we're pretty sure it's about as big as your head, for instance, and radiant. My father thought he had a lead once, but it was from an anonymous source and would have led him to the other side of the galaxy. He spent some time travelling alone looking for it, actually. But he doesn't like to leave me alone on the outpost, so he doesn't go far."

"So, why wouldn't he just bring you along instead?"

"He could never stand to see me get hurt. Sometimes I think it's his greatest weakness."

"I think I can imagine how he feels…"

Ahead, Zahn saw two orange points of light moving toward them. The points were so small he thought they might be planets, but just as he was about to ask what they were, Oonak spoke.

"We are being hailed, presumably by the Aaravans."

Zahn braced for the worst as Oonak put it on surround.

"You have entered the Realm of Aarava. What is your purpose here?"

To Zahn's surprise, the voice was lilting, almost melodic, and the points of light had now resolved themselves into tiny ships that reminded Zahn of water droplets, except that they were the color of the sunrise. They were even smaller than Navika, and he had trouble believing someone actually fit inside either of them.

"I am Oonak of the Confederation of Unity. We are on a mission to deliver a message to the Confederation Council. However, our journey has been difficult and we seek safe harbor for a few days. We are happy to trade for these amenities."

There was a long pause.

"Those of the Confederation are always welcome in our realm. No trade is necessary. Please follow our craft to a suitable landing point where you will be greeted."

Each of the tiny bubble-shaped craft came up on the left and right sides of the ship, just ahead of the ship itself. By now, they were quite near to Aarava's star, and the two escorting ships guided them on a curved route toward the planet. Along the way, Zahn noticed a few rocky inner planets that Navika had cleverly marked with indicators as they passed them.

After what seemed like ages to Zahn, they finally saw the tiny disc of a planet ahead of them. The surface appeared equal parts blue, green, and tan, and much of it was covered in thick white clouds that swirled in massive shapes over the surface.

Soon, they could see continents with white capped mountain ranges and shimmering seas, and the sight was stunning to Zahn. He had never seen a planet from orbit before. Like every Avanian, he had seen pictures of his own world from this distance, but no photograph could capture even a millionth of a percent of the grandeur he was now seeing.

"If only this were Avani," he said to himself. "Then I could see all of the islands at once. What a sight that would be."

# CHAPTER 18

## A THICK BED OF FLOWERS

By the time they were plunging through the upper clouds, Zahn could hardly contain his excitement. He was about to set foot on another planet for the first time in his life. He felt as though he should prepare some words. He knew this memory would be special, but he wasn't sure anything he could do would really be enough to honor this moment.

Navika made the floor transparent again, and below him Zahn saw a thick jungle bordering a beach and a cluster of strange structures by the water. In the distance, there were rolling hills thick with towering trees, but nothing resembling a city. The two ships led them down below the jungle canopy, but there was something completely alien about the jungle itself.

Far different from the shade of blue that Zahn was used to, the leaves of these trees were exceedingly green, and he couldn't take his eyes off of them. Even with everything he'd seen so far, this was the most bizarre sight yet.

In the midst of the huge emerald trees, he saw a wide clearing in the jungle below. At the center of the clearing was a circular depression in the ground that was lined in stone, and to either side of the depression were two smaller depressions. Surrounding this sunken landing area was a thick bed of orange and red flowers that were quite huge. Even from their altitude, he could tell that they were wider than his arms outstretched.

"Wow," Zahn said. "Have you ever seen anything like that before, Asha?"

"Are those really flowers?" Asha said.

"I think so."

As they descended into the clearing, both of the tiny ships dropped into the smaller depressions on either side, while Navika descended into the larger depression, touching the bottom with barely a sound. Yet there were sounds to be heard. Now that they had landed, all three of them could now hear faint cooing sounds in the jungle, as well as a faint humming sound all around them.

Gradually, it grew louder.

Soon the entire depression was rumbling so loudly that it felt like they were in the midst of a quake, but when Zahn looked at the trees towering over them, he realized this couldn't be the case because they didn't appear to be shaking at all. The rumbling changed as the tone of the humming blended from note to note, until one of the notes sounded much louder than the others.

Then, just as quickly as it had begun, the rumbling stopped.

"What was that?!" Zahn said.

"Uncertain," Oonak replied. "I would hypothesize that it was some type of sonic mechanism."

"But it didn't damage the ship, right?"

"Do not worry. Navika reported no damage."

"Do you think it was looking for a resonance frequency?"

Asha picked up her pack and put it on.

"So are you guys going to talk about the sound all day or are we actually going to get out there and explore this place?"

"I'm ready," Zahn said.

"You should both be thankful." Oonak said. "Navika says the atmosphere is safe to breathe, and the gravity is nearly identical to Avani."

When they emerged from the safe, cocoon-like environment of the ship, Zahn noticed a few details immediately. One was the smell. A soft, sweet fragrance filled the air. From the light, he guessed that it was morning, and above them he noticed bands of white clouds streaking across the blue sky.

Zahn walked around the ship and examined the depression they were in. The stone seemed ordinary, except that there were no cracks to be found. It was as if this stone depression had been carved from a single piece of rock. Four narrow sets of stairs were also etched into the rock, placed evenly around the depression in four directions.

Zahn followed Oonak and Asha up one of the stairs, and when they reached ground level, he was once again stunned by the expansiveness of the bed of flowers that surrounded the area. The bright blossoms ranged from one to two meters in width and stood over a meter above the ground, and beyond them was a long path leading into the jungle.

Eager to see who had led them to that spot, Zahn ignored the path for now and ran through the patch of huge flowers over to one of the smaller depressions, but he was disappointed to find only a small metallic dome over where the depression used to be. He did, however, enjoy being waist-deep in the huge red and orange flowers. The sweet fragrances made him smile; he'd never had such an experience before.

"Where did the ship go that used to be here?" Zahn called back to Oonak, who was examining one of the blooms.

"Zahn, that *is* the ship. Didn't you see when we landed? The ships fit perfectly into the two depressions, which makes me curious as to whether or not anyone is in them at all, considering how small they are."

Oonak was right. Now that Zahn was looking at one up close, he seriously doubted that a normal person could fit inside. After all, it was only a couple meters wide, so it would be extremely cramped in there.

"What if everyone on this planet is half the size of an Avanian? Or smaller? Is that possible, Oon?"

"Zahn." Oonak walked over. "For how long will you put limits on what is possible? This galaxy is a wild and unpredictable creation. Even though we are facets of that creation, not everything is easily understood. Indeed, there are far stranger creatures that live, grow, and die within this galaxy than you can possibly imagine."

Zahn touched the metallic dome and found it to be surprisingly cold. "I never realized the galaxy was so wild. When looking at it through a telescope, everything can seem rather predictable. But you're right. It's not."

"And the more you open your mind to new ways of thinking, the more logical everything becomes."

Asha walked up behind them. "How do we know there was ever anyone in these ships at all?"

"We do not. All we have are theories," Oonak said.

Out of the corner of his eye, Zahn thought he saw a huge bird by the path. It was hovering in midair, despite the fact that its wings weren't moving at all.

Zahn approached slowly so he wouldn't scare it off, but the closer he got, the closer the strange creature floated toward him. Soon, they were face to face, and he could scarcely believe his eyes. It reminded him vaguely of a wildcat, which, although they didn't live on Ashraya, he had seen videos of when he was younger. Its head reminded him of a smaller version of a wildcat's head, and dark brown fur with black spots covered its body.

But the similarity ended there. Its entire abdomen was bulbous and swollen, almost as if it had been forcibly inflated with a gas and had its entire body stretched from the internal pressure. On either side, it had short arms and webbed fin-like paws. Zahn watched as it propelled itself closer in a motion that reminded him of swimming.

It was only a hand's width away from Zahn's face now, and he was unsure of what to do. He looked deeply into its bronze eyes. Behind him, he could hear Asha and Oonak approach, but he found himself unable to avert his gaze. To his surprise, the creature zipped up to him, licked him on the cheek, and purred as it pressed its head into his hair.

"What a remarkable creature," Oonak said.

It continued rubbing up against Zahn's head and purring.

"I think it likes you, Zahn!" Asha laughed.

Zahn gently pushed the floating creature away from him and noticed that two more were approaching.

"Have either of you heard of anything like this before? Do you think they could be dangerous? It reminds me of a wildcat, except that it floats, obviously. Maybe we can call it a flycat…"

"I've never seen anything like it. Oonak, what about you?"

"I am familiar with such creatures, but not those from this planet. So far though, it appears to be nonviolent."

"Well, could you tell it to leave me alone?" Zahn said as it nuzzled up against him once more.

"Try tapping it on its nose," Asha said. "That might annoy it enough to make it go away."

"Good idea," Zahn said, and tried it.

The flycat shook its head from side to side and hissed at him. It tried nuzzling him again, and Zahn did it again. The flycat hissed in annoyance, turned around, and floated away.

"That worked," Zahn said. "Thanks, Asha!"

"Anytime. Maybe it expected you to feed it? Makes me wonder what those things eat."

When the first flycat reached the other two that were still approaching, it made some moaning sounds, and all three of them darted away into the thick of the jungle.

"I'm not sure I ever want to find out," Zahn said. "C'mon, let's follow this path and see where it leads. Whoever led us to this landing pad obviously wants us to follow it. Oh, and if either of you see any more flycats, could you please let me know?"

"Of course," Asha said.

"If you wish," Oonak said. "They seemed friendly to me."

"A little too friendly for my taste."

As they walked down the canopied path, there was an instant when Zahn thought he saw a person running deep within the forest beside them, but when he looked again he saw nothing.

Then Zahn realized the source of the occasional cooing sound that he had heard before. Whenever the breeze was fast enough, the huge trees made a cooing sound in the jungle canopy high above him. He guessed that some of the trees were over eighty meters tall, and he wondered if the trees were actively making the sound or if the air somehow naturally made that sound as it flowed through the strange green leaves that surrounded them.

When they reached the end of the path, it opened up into a large clearing. To their left, a pale sun was hanging over a dark grey beach bordering a massive body of water. They were either at the edge of an ocean or beside the largest lake Zahn had ever seen. Farther up the beach was a stone building atop a massive rocky outcrop that extended out of the beach at an odd angle. The building's roof was a singular slab of pale white stone set at a shallow angle, and the entire structure looked ageless.

Zahn stared at the cold, foreign sun that was not his own.

"Where is everyone? They told us to land here. Shouldn't they be waiting for us?"

"Ideally. However, it is possible they were delayed. Do you see the structure over there?" Oonak pointed to the stone building atop the outcrop.

"Yeah. Perhaps our welcoming party is inside."

"Perhaps," Oonak said. "In either case, it is the most logical place to explore."

They headed across the sandy grey beach, and Zahn could still hear the faint cooing sound of the huge trees behind him. Combined with the sound of the waves, he found it soothing.

As they grew nearer, they saw a figure appear to rise up out of the rock itself and enter the stone structure atop the outcrop.

"Did you just see that?" Zahn said.

"The figure that appeared out of nowhere? Yes. You saw it, too, right?" Asha said.

"Yes," Oonak said. "Perhaps it is the greeting we have been waiting for."

Soon, they reached a path that led up the large outcrop to the structure that was perched atop it. When they reached the doorway, Zahn thought he saw an engraving on the door of a woman playing a flute. But before he could be sure, the door swiftly slid back, revealing a long hall. At the end of the hall was a large table in the middle of a room with a woman sitting at the far end, facing them.

The table was set with colorful jars of liquid, and quiet music was flowing out of the room in the form of smooth, rounded tones. But something curious was happening. As they walked down the hall, they heard strange noises coming from the walls themselves and bright lights occasionally moved over their bodies. Along the walls, there were also various doors, but Zahn found all of them to be locked.

When they entered the room, air jets embedded into the wall sprayed them, and they could now see that the woman's face was exceedingly pale. She was completely bald, and golden cloth was wrapped around her body such that Zahn could only see her head and arms, which were also pale. Behind her was a large window that spanned the far wall, providing a wonderful view of the ocean below.

"I am Oonak of the Confederation, and these are my friends. Who are you?"

"Sit," the woman said.

Her voice was soothing, yet strangely exotic. Along the walls on either side of the table, Zahn noticed that two children, who were also dressed in brightly colored robes, were somehow making music from huge golden bowls with nothing more than their bare hands. Beside them were round canisters that were embedded into the floor itself.

With some hesitation, all three of them sat down at the long, rectangular table. Oonak sat on one side while Asha sat next to Zahn on the other side. The woman waited until they were still and then continued.

"As a humble servant of Aarava, it is my pleasure to welcome you to our world. I am known as Vivienne. I keep harmony among the people. However, it may be most harmonious to your memories if you consider me as an emissary. I am the mouth and the ears of the Visionaries of Aarava."

"So where are all the people? You're the first person we've seen," Zahn said.

"Zahn, please let me speak first before you ask further questions," Oonak said.

"Oh," Zahn said. "Sorry, Oon. Go ahead."

"Your craft was directed to land in one of the quarantined areas for safety," Vivienne said. "Consequently, very few people are in this area. You will surely find more prowlers than people in this sector of Aarava."

Asha's gaze drifted over to one of the children who was still creating music. It appeared to be a small boy, and his eyes were closed as he played.

"Why have we been directed to land in a quarantined area? For who's safety?" Oonak said.

"For the safety of all," Vivienne answered. "However, the Hall of Detection has revealed that you are without violent intent, and we have confirmed that you possess the Confederation insignia, as you have claimed. We of the World of Resonance apologize if the hall caused you any distress, but we must be vigilant to preserve our coherence. Do you understand our meaning? We sincerely hope no offense was taken."

"Yes, I understand. Indeed, in your place I might have taken similar precautions."

"We are most pleased, and we are confident that our thoughts will resonate in even deeper ways with you in the future. On behalf of the Visionaries, I am pleased to announce that you may stay as long as you wish. It is always a pleasure to host those of a Confederation world. However, if you wish to leave the quarantined area, you must contact me first. Attempting to leave the quarantined area without permission could result in damage to yourself and your crew. Do you understand?"

"Yes," Oonak said. "We understand."

"Excellent. You may record as much data as you desire, but please do not eat any of the land animals or any prowlers. You may also use the guest rooms as your own and eat any of the food contained within this guest house. Which reminds me, would you like some quarava nectar? Rest assured that there is no danger to you. The Hall of Detection also allows us to determine which foods you will be able to absorb."

"I would be honored," Oonak said.

"Furthermore, we are pleased to say that, despite the genetic differences between each of you, the food we have provided here will be suitable for all three of you. And you two? Would either of you like some?" Vivienne turned to them.

"Sure," Asha and Zahn said at almost the same time.

Vivienne poured each of them a glass of thick purple liquid. It smelled sweet and tasted delicious.

"Which rooms may we use?" Oonak said.

"All of them, if you wish. All of the guest rooms have now been unlocked."

As they continued to speak, Zahn leaned over to Asha.

"I guess we know what was behind those locked doors now," he whispered.

"Yeah," she whispered back, "but I can't help but wonder why Oonak didn't tell them why we're really here."

"What do you mean?"

"I mean, he told them we needed safe harbor, but didn't we really come here for information?"

"That's true. I'll ask him later."

"Don't!" Asha said in a tone that was almost too loud to be a whisper. "I want to ask him. I'm good at reading people, Zahn, and I want to feel his reaction when the question is asked."

"Okay," Zahn whispered.

"Vivienne," Oonak continued. "I have just one more question. Do you know anything about the galaxy's ancient gate network? Anything at all?"

For a few seconds, Vivienne was motionless. If Zahn had just walked into the room at that moment, he might have thought she were a statue poised at the head of the table. But the illusion was shattered when Vivienne tilted her head to one side and then back again.

"We are unable to provide any information on a gate network," she said and got up from the table.

Oonak narrowed his gaze.

"Why are you unable?" he said.

Vivienne hesitated. "I am not able to say."

Asha and Zahn both turned to look at Vivienne when she said this. Her voice had become monotone, as if something was wrong, and for the first time Zahn noticed that Vivienne's eyes were golden in a way that made him feel uneasy.

"Vivienne," Oonak continued. "It is crucial that you tell me all that you know of the gate network. Lives are in the balance."

"We are unable to provide information on the gate network."

"Interesting. So you admit that the gate network exists?"

"I'm sorry. I cannot confirm or deny the existence of a gate network. Would you like some more nectar?"

Vivienne reached for a jar of the sweet smelling drink.

"Vivienne, I have information urgent to the safety of the galaxy. I must reach the Confederation Council as soon as possible. As your superiors may have already detected, my ship is without timespace capability, so the gates are my only means of accomplishing this mission. Even if Aarava may not be a member of the Confederation yet, we share a common goal. Unless we work together, the Vakragha Legion will continue to spread like a plague throughout our galaxy. Is that the future that the Visionaries of Aarava want? Would you rather face them alone?"

Vivienne's eyes widened, and Asha froze in utter surprise. Even the music around them came to an abrupt stop. Few ever dared utter the true name of the Undying Vandals, and it seemed no one here was prepared to hear it.

"If you truly do keep harmony among the people," Oonak continued. "You will tell me what you know. Please."

A silence fell upon the room.

"You are persistent, and on the surface of this planet persistence is rare."

"So, can you tell us anything?" Zahn said.

"No," Vivienne said. "But, we have decided to tell you who may be able to help you, although we make no promises."

"Who?" Asha said.

"You should inquire of Vayuna."

"Who is Vayuna?" Oonak said.

"Vayuna is the Great Savant. She can tell you truths that resonate with the deepest reaches of your soul." Vivienne paused. "But only to those who are truly worthy."

"Then please, take us to her."

Zahn smiled. Perhaps it would work out, after all.

"That is quite impossible. Sadly, Vayuna is not here."

Zahn's smile disappeared.

"Where is she, if we may ask?" Oonak said, his face still somehow radiating a calm confidence that impressed Zahn.

"She is in the Great South. She will return in two days. If you still wish to speak to her then, summon me with the console on the far wall, and I will take you to her."

"Thank you, Vivienne, and please thank the Visionaries on my behalf, as well."

"You already have, Oonak of the Confederation. They see and hear everything that I see and hear, and now, I must leave you. Please enjoy your day."

Vivienne stood up, bowed, and walked toward the door.

"Wait!" Zahn said. "What are *prowlers*?"

Now nearly at the door, Vivienne turned around.

"Surely, you have seen them already. They wander the air, though they usually stay close to the ground. Although they may seem friendly, they can be quite dangerous. Exercise caution when they are near."

"Oh, do you mean—"

"I must go now. Goodbye."

As Vivienne disappeared down the long hallway, Zahn noticed that the two children that had been creating the music had also disappeared.

Asha stood up.

"Where are you going?" Zahn said.

"Well, if we're going to be here for two days, I want to see our accommodations, and I'd like to find some *good* food."

"Mind if I come along?"

"Not at all. What about you, Oonak?"

"Thanks Asha," Oonak said. "But I shall use this opportunity to meditate in solitude. I am weary from piloting the ship through such intense encounters, and I require rebalancing."

"Understandable. See you later!"

"Be safe and do not go beyond the beach. Remember, we are only staying here for as long as it takes to learn what we can about the gate network. No longer."

Zahn walked toward the door. "We got it, Oon. No worries."

Yet if Zahn knew what was ahead, he would have worried a great deal.

# CHAPTER 19

# PRISON OR PARADISE

The first door that Asha tried swung open easily, revealing a spacious guest room containing a large circular bed, several containers along the wall, and a tall, white cylindrical device embedded in the far wall that reached from floor to ceiling. Ahead of them, a large window spanned most of the room, allowing in an abundance of light and a view of the beach below.

"What a strange place," Zahn said. "Stunning, but strange."

The ground beneath them rumbled for a moment.

"What was that?" Asha said.

Zahn walked up to the window and looked down.

"Hmm, maybe it was a small quake?"

Asha sat down at the edge of the round bed. "Strange bed." She bounced up and down on it a little. "Do you have a room like this back on Avani?"

"No, not quite. Actually, I don't even have a bed!"

"What? Even the outpost has bunks. Where do you sleep?"

"I sleep on a hammock. It's better than a bed when you live in a warm climate." His gaze drifted upward, toward the ocean.

"It must be magnificent where you live," Asha said. "Open valleys, oceans... are there mountain peaks?"

"Yeah! Ones that stretch up to the clouds." Zahn raised his hand above his head, and then sighed. "You know, I wish you could see the view from up on Zikhara Peak, up above the sapphire forests. On some nights, you can even see neighboring islands along the horizon. It's incredible."

"I'd love to see that."

Asha looked into his eyes. She had a spark in her eyes now. He'd seen that look before, and he knew what it meant.

He looked away and reflected on his own feelings.

Back on Outpost 33, even her appearance had stunned him, but Zahn knew that appearances were fleeting. He knew that it took far more than that for him to be truly attracted to someone. Yet now their connection had gone deeper, and he had to admit that he was impressed by her mind and humbled by her presence.

*But is this the right time for romance? What if she's just getting swept up in the adventure of it all? I can't do this right now. After all, she's technically an extraterrestrial! Still, Oonak said we're all just people, and I've never met anyone I've enjoyed talking to this much, either. Maybe once the situation with the Confederation is settled...*

Zahn had to admit that he hadn't known her for that long at all, and tried to let the thoughts go. Now just didn't feel right.

He looked up and noticed that she was watching the ocean.

"Sapphire forests, mountain peaks... and hammocks," she said. "What a place. The closest I have to compare to is a ship we worked on a few years ago. All of the passenger cabins had hammocks because the ship was too small to hold bunks."

"Really? Sounds like a really small ship."

"Oh, you have no idea. They were trying to fit something like three dozen passengers, and the ship wasn't that much bigger than Navika."

"That's crazy. Why were they trying to fit so many people?"

"It was a smuggler's ship. Apparently, they even smuggled people sometimes."

Asha stood up. "How about we find that food Vivienne was talking about? I'm getting hungry. You in?"

Zahn turned to her, the hint of a smile on his lips.

"I'm in."

One by one, they opened the large containers along the wall of the bedroom, but found most of them empty. The ones that weren't empty contained strange clothes, some of which were similar to Vivienne's robe. They also examined the huge cylindrical shape embedded in the far wall, and soon realized that it was a shower. By pressing a pad beside it, the cylinder rotated open, revealing a bright interior that was lit by a skylight above.

Along a shelf were colorful cubes that Zahn assumed were various kinds of soap.

Unable to find any food, they opened up the next door in the hall, revealing an identical room. And just as Asha was about to open a third door, Zahn remembered something.

"Wait a minute, if you were designing a guest house, wouldn't you put the food near where it was going to be eaten?"

"Depends on the culture, I suppose."

"Well, remember those round canisters along the wall in the meeting room? We should check there—I'll race you!"

Even though Zahn had a head start on Asha, she caught up to him, yelling "Not so fast, hammock man!" as they blazed into the meeting room with a speed that startled Oonak out of his meditation as he sat on the floor near the far wall.

"What are you two doing? Is something wrong?" Oonak said as they both touched a large, black canister at the same time.

Zahn took a second to catch his breath. "No. Just a little game, and I think we just found what we were looking for."

"Sorry if we disturbed your meditation, Oon," Asha said. "Completely slipped our minds."

"Oh," Zahn said. "That's right. Sorry, Oon."

"Be mindful of your actions, especially on foreign worlds. One misstep could result in an unfortunate delay, and I know that isn't what either of you want. I can slip back into a meditative state, but please try to be quiet."

"We will."

"Sorry."

As Oonak closed his eyes once more, their gaze returned to the large, black canister.

"I was here first," Zahn whispered.

"No, I'm pretty sure I touched it first."

"No way," Zahn said a bit louder. "I distinctly remember my hand touching the canister before—"

"Zahn," Oonak interrupted. "You both touched it at the same instant. Now please remain calm as I finish rebalancing, and do not eat too much. Moderation is the key to long life, and I would like to cook a midday meal for all three of us later."

"Sorry!" they both whispered at the same time. "Okay."

Carefully, they both opened the canister. As they pried it open, it hissed quietly as if they'd broken an airtight seal. Once they had removed the lid, they were stunned at what they saw.

Meticulously arranged into equal sections were hundreds of small packets of food. All of it was frozen, but all of it looked colorful and delicious.

"How do you think Oonak knew there was food here?"

"Maybe it's obvious from his point of view," Asha said quietly.

"Right. So how do we heat the food up?"

"The lid we just pulled off. Take a look at its underside."

Now that it was upside down, Zahn noticed that in the center of the lid was a wide circular depression with glowing controls beside it. As quietly as he could, he set it on the table.

"A heating element?"

"Looks like."

Zahn pulled out a chair and, after playing around with it for a few minutes, figured out how to activate the heat and change the temperature of the surface of the depression. As he did this, Asha picked a packet of food that looked familiar and poured it out.

"This should be enough for a snack."

They cooked as quietly as they could, but when it was ready, Zahn realized that they didn't have any eating utensils at all.

"Here," Asha said, handing him a fork and bowl.

"Where'd you find those?"

"In the canister, of course. Couldn't find any plates, though. I guess the Aaravans always eat from bowls."

"That's true," Zahn said. "They do seem to like bowls."

When they had finished their snack, they each decided to use the luxuriously large showers that the Aaravans had provided. When he thought about it, he felt a sense of strange satisfaction that he was actually going to have a chance to use the towel he had brought. Whenever he travelled, he made sure to bring his towel. In fact, he felt that a trip wasn't truly complete until he had used it. But as he was rummaging through the clothes in the guest room containers, he came upon a drawer full of towels that he hadn't noticed before. Even so, he decided to use his own towel. After all, it reminded him of home.

When Zahn emerged from the shower some time later, he felt as though he had been reborn. He wasn't sure if it was something in the soap or something in the water, but his skin felt crisp and smooth, and his mind felt revitalized.

After toweling off and putting on a silky blue Aaravan robe he found, he walked back into the meeting room to see if Oonak was still there. He was, and in the midst of cooking a huge amount of food in the same way Zahn and Asha had earlier.

"How was your meditation?" Zahn said.

"Very good. And how was your shower?"

"Wonderful. I'm starting to wonder what their soap is made out of actually. Whatever it is, I think I'm taking a few cubes with me. Have you seen Asha?"

"Yes, she said she would be out here in a few minutes. Please sit. The meal is nearly ready."

When Asha came in, Zahn was surprised to see that her hair was no longer up in a bun as it had been before. Now it flowed down her head and over her shoulders. She was wearing a golden Aaravan robe, and Zahn thought she looked mesmerizing, though he would never admit it. At least, not yet.

"It smells wonderful, Oon!" Asha walked over to the table. "I can't wait to try some."

"Indeed, you are both in luck," Oonak said. "I recognize some of these ingredients. They're actually quite similar to some plants from my own world."

"Where *are* you from, Oonak?" Zahn said.

"That is not important. What is important is our continued progress in our mission. Here, have some." Oonak filled a bowl with some reddish soup and handed it to Zahn.

"Thanks, Oon. It really does smell good."

As Zahn stirred the soup with his spoon, he noticed there were lots of different pieces of different plants floating in the red broth. It looked bizarre, but also appetizing.

"And for you." Oonak did the same for Asha.

"Thank you!"

Oonak sat down next to Zahn and served himself last.

"Oonak, do you think we could explore the area after our meal? How safe do you think it is out there?" Zahn said.

"Navika indicated that this area was empty of any large predators or settlements of any kind besides these guest houses, so exploration is permissible. Indeed, we ought to become familiar with the area if we're going to be here for a few days."

"We should stargaze tonight, too!" Asha said between sips. "I bet we could see all kinds of weird constellations that you can't see from the outpost."

"A good plan. So it shall be then."

After the meal, they followed the curving path down from the outcrop to the beach once more.

"It looks like the tide is rising." Oonak's eyes studied the water. "If it rises too much, it could block the path up to the guest house."

"Any idea when the tide will reach its peak?" Zahn said.

Oonak tapped his wristband and blinked his eyes.

"The tide here is difficult to predict because Aarava has many moons. Navika indicates that the tides rise and fall in uneven intervals here. We would be wise to keep this in mind."

"How is Navika doing, anyway?" Asha said.

"Doing? He is nominal and monitoring the surrounding area. Actually, since our encounter with Vivienne, he has detected some faint energy anomalies nearby."

"Where are they originating from?" Asha said. "Are they that way, down the beach? Because I keep getting this feeling that we need to head down the beach, as if something is calling out."

"As a matter of fact," Oonak said as he touched his wristband once more, "one of the signatures that Navika detected is down this way, although it appears scattered in Navika's scans, as if it were within a scrambling field."

Zahn was beginning to feel sleepy from the big meal they had just eaten, but he realized that if he passed up the opportunity to explore now, he might regret it later.

"Then it's settled," Zahn said. "Let's go investigate it. Lead the way, Oonak."

"I shall. However, I should remind you that I am unarmed. As I said back at the outpost, my sidearm was damaged beyond repair when I crashed on Avani. So, considering the situation, I advise that we keep these on hand. We want everyone to be in one piece when we leave this rock."

Out of a pocket in his uniform, Oonak pulled out three tiny black plates and handed one to each of them.

"Ideally," he said. "We won't have to use these personal cloaking chips, but we must be cautious. Would you like to demonstrate, Asha? Your father made them after all."

"Sure, Oonak. Thanks."

Asha took a minute to show them how to activate the field by pressing a bump on one side of the tiny plate. When Zahn pressed the bump, he vanished completely. Then, Asha told him to touch an indentation on the other side, and he reappeared once more.

Now feeling prepared, Oonak led the way, and they headed down the dark grey beach. To their left side, the beach quickly became jungle, and Zahn's eye couldn't help but be drawn back toward the emerald leaves. Before today, he had never imagined that entire jungles could be radiant shades of green, but this reality was now staring him in the face, impossible to ignore.

They walked for some time, and eventually they came upon a place where the coast made a sharp curve to the left. When they turned the corner, they were confronted with an unusual sight.

Towering out of the beach sand were about a dozen crystalline spires that rose far above their heads. They reminded Zahn of trees except that they had no branches and formed a bowl-like shape at the top. In a few areas, the spires had a webbing that appeared to be climbable, and a calm, low hum radiated out from them. The frequency was so low that Zahn felt it in his chest.

Atop the center spire, hovering in midair above its bowl, was a large, amber crystal with eight identical sides. It reminded Zahn of two pyramids combined, and it seemed familiar to him, though he wasn't sure why. Then the name for it popped into his mind: octahedron.

"How are they just floating up there?" Zahn said.

Oonak pulled out his scanner.

"It's fantastic." Asha gasped. "Zahn, what if it's the Tulari? That webbing looks easy to climb. If I could just get up there and have a closer look…"

"Asha, I'm not sure that's a good idea."

"You worry too much, Zahn!" Asha approached the nearest spire. "This webbing is here for a reason. For all we know, these are for us to use."

Before Zahn could say anything else, Asha put her hands over her ears and screamed as she ran back.

"Vakra-gaaag!" she yelled. "Did you hear that?"

"Hear what?" Zahn said. "Are you okay?"

A drop of blood dripped down from her nose.

"I felt like my ears were bleeding. It was the loudest sound I've ever heard! You *must* have heard that. My ears are ringing!"

Zahn reached into his pocket and pulled out a handkerchief he'd found in his room earlier.

"Here. You can wipe your nose with this," he said.

"Thanks."

"Fascinating," Oonak said. "It must be a sonic disruptor designed to keep intruders away from the spires."

"But how can she hear it, and we didn't?" Zahn said.

"There are various ways. In this case I would hypothesize that canceling frequencies were used. Two ultrahigh frequencies create a difference pattern. Unless you're in the resonance zone, you won't hear anything. It's quite elegant, actually."

"Elegant to you, maybe!" Asha said. "Tell that to my ringing ears, and my nose."

"Zahn told you that it was not a good idea. We are on another world now, Asha. We must exercise caution and not jump into situations hastily."

"Thanks, *Dad*," Asha said sarcastically and walked away, still holding her nose with the handkerchief.

"Where are you going?" Zahn said.

"Back. I'd like to be alone. It's getting late anyway, and who knows what kinds of creatures come out at night around here."

Oonak looked at the sun, now low along the horizon.

"The days are shorter here. Soon, Aarava's star will descend below the horizon," he said. "Asha is right, we would be wise to head back. We do not yet know enough about this world to safely explore it at night."

Zahn looked up at the octahedron floating just a meter or so above the spires. He breathed slowly. He could still feel the low, deep sound in his chest.

When they returned to the rocky outcrop, the sun was just setting behind the jungle canopy, and Zahn could already tell that the tide had risen. The first stars were already starting to appear, and Zahn called out to Asha to come back and stargaze with them. But she was already far ahead and didn't hear him.

"Do you think she's going to be okay? I'm starting to wonder if this place is more of a prison than a paradise," Zahn said.

"The truth is that it is neither, Zahn. Merely a quarantine, the necessity of which I hope we will soon discover. I wouldn't worry about Asha. The effects are most likely temporary. I will scan her ears tomorrow if she desires. But for now, I think an uninterrupted sleep cycle is the best medicine for her."

"Especially after what she's been through."

Magenta and orange hues were still spread across the sky, but a dusting of stars now began to bleed through the hues. Zahn tried to find a constellation that seemed familiar, although he knew logically that this was impossible.

"Do you recognize any?" Zahn said.

Oonak scanned the sky for a few moments.

"Well, I am not from this part of the galaxy, but there is one star that I recognize from our approach. There." Oonak pointed toward a bright star just above the violet horizon.

"Yeah, that's the brightest star out right now, I think."

"That is Akasha-Dipa, a guide star. After we came through the last gate, it was one of the stars that Navika used to confirm our position."

"No wonder it's a guide star. Must be one of the brightest stars in the sky here." Zahn turned to Oonak. "Does it have a great story behind it? I'm sure a star like that was involved in a galactic battle or a monumental discovery or something, right?"

"According to Navika's records, that star has no planets at all, so that is unlikely. I learned about it from Navika's star maps when we entered this system. Even I cannot memorize all of the stars in the galaxy. After all, there are over 900 billion of them, but I suppose Akasha-Dipa could have been part of a legend. For all we know, it had many planets long ago."

Zahn and Oonak gazed in silence as stars slowly filled the sky.

"Oonak, have you ever lost someone? Someone close to you?"

Oonak was silent for a long time.

"Yes, long ago."

"What did you do about it? After my mom disappeared, the islands didn't even feel like home anymore. But sometimes I wonder how it might have been if I were stronger. Your people seem a lot more advanced than mine, so that's why I'm curious."

"Loss is never easy, Zahn, especially if it is someone you love deeply. Sometimes, you cannot help but watch the entire world around you become unrecognizable, no matter how strong you think you are. What is important is that you face it honestly."

"How?"

"Take it slowly. Remember that all you see is temporary and clinging to the past only brings suffering. You must continue to renew your mind and expose yourself to new experiences." Oonak turned and gazed deeply into Zahn's eyes. "Someday, when we shed our physical selves, we will see the Universe for what it truly is."

Oonak paused and looked out toward the sky once more.

"This was told to me many years ago… under a similar sky."

Zahn smiled. "Thanks, Oon."

In stark contrast to the warmth of the day, a cool breeze kicked up, and Zahn realized that he'd left his jacket inside.

"Let's head inside," Oonak said. "It is nearly nightfall, and you look tired."

Upon hearing that, Zahn had a strange feeling of déjà vu, but he brushed it aside. Oonak was right. He was exhausted. He'd felt as though he hadn't slept in two days, and he wondered if it might actually be true.

When he got back to his room, he collapsed onto the round bed and pulled some blankets over himself. In just a few seconds, he entered an exceedingly deep sleep where time ceased to have any meaning.

# CHAPTER 20

## CAUGHT IN THE TRAP

Once again, Zahn opened his real eyes.

At first, he felt completely disoriented. He was lying on his back, half-covered by a thin blanket. The softness of the bed felt strange to him. Shouldn't he be waking up in a hammock?

As he studied the white tiles on the ceiling, it all came rushing back to him: the invisible starship on the beach, the gate on the South Pole, the ambush, the outpost, the view of Aarava from orbit, the largest flowers he had ever seen, and all of the remarkable people he had met along the way. Even though he knew he had experienced all of it, some small part of him still wondered if it had all really happened.

Gradually, he sat up. The sun was already high in the sky, filling the room with warm light. Out the window, he could see the waves crashing on jagged rocks below, kicking up ocean spray at unpredictable intervals.

As was his habit, he tried to remember what he had just been dreaming about, and the vision of his mother and the small lens flashed into his mind.

He recalled when she'd first given it to him many years ago. They had been talking about what it means to see.

*"To truly see,"* she had said. *"You must open your heart and listen to it. Truly seeing goes beyond the light we can see with our eyes. I know this because some beings who are not even capable of sight as we know it can see more clearly than we can."*

He remembered how she had knelt down, placed the small lens into his hand, and cupped it closed.

*"Keep this,"* she had said, *"and whenever you hold it, remember what it means to see."*

He cherished that memory. Had that been what the dream was about? He tried to remember more, but the memory sank deep into his unconscious mind like a shard of glass falling into a dark pit, forever lost.

When he stood up, his eyes widened as he noticed that his Avani clothes had been washed, folded, and placed on a shelf beside his bed. Beside them was a small wooden flute and some pebbles, and he walked over and picked up the flute. Three holes were carved into the top, and after a few tries he managed to play a little tune, though it sounded rather flat.

His stomach growled at him.

Still wearing his Aaravan robe, he walked back into the meeting room across the hall. To his surprise, no one was there, but someone had made food. An empty bowl had been left out, presumably for him, so Zahn dished himself some of the light-brown spongey food that had been left over. He had no idea what it was, but it reminded him a bit of the traditional Ashraya breakfast, which was hydrated Kaala grain topped with ground up blue cane for sweetening.

Yet this strange breakfast tasted nothing like what he was expecting. Instead of being sweet, it tasted vaguely like it had been harvested from the sea.

But where was everyone?

He thought that perhaps Oonak or Asha would check in on him, but he hadn't seen or heard any sign of them at all since he'd awoke. So once he finished eating, he headed back down the long hall to the exit. The door at the end pulled back swiftly, and Zahn noticed that the air outside had a chill in it that hadn't been there the day before. As he followed the path that led down to the beach, the sound of two familiar voices grew until he could clearly discern that they were Asha and Oonak. They sounded like they were arguing, so he stopped just before they could see him and listened.

"...cannot move the ship unless it is a life or death circumstance. We were specifically instructed to land at those coordinates. To take off without notifying the Aaravans would be an overt sign of distrust which I cannot permit."

"Oonak," Asha said. "I need to get back on the ship!"

"I fail to see how these circumstances justify the potential disruption of friendly relations with this world."

"Friendly relations? We're in a quarantine! Just call Navika over here. I'll grab my boots, and then he can go back to the landing pad, which, I'd like to point out, was suspiciously loud when we landed on it yesterday."

"I cannot permit Navika to do this. It is unwise at this time."

Zahn walked up to them.

"What's wrong, guys?"

What Zahn saw instantly answered his question. Just beyond where Asha was standing, the remainder of the path downward was completely flooded. The path down to the beach was now blocked by the tide, and most of the beach they had crossed the day before had now been swallowed up by the sea.

"Good afternoon, Zahn." Oonak nodded. He was now dressed in a maroon Aaravan robe, which complemented his light brown skin. And for the first time, Zahn noticed Oonak's black hair had a hint of indigo buried deep within the blackness.

"Hi, Zahn." Asha smiled. "You okay? You sure slept a while."

"How long did I sleep?"

"Roughly half of one Avani day," Oonak answered.

"Oh, guess I was tired."

"How was hibernation?" Asha smirked at him.

Zahn looked down and noticed Asha's bare feet.

"So what's wrong? As I was walking up I heard something about shoes."

"Oonak won't call Navika over here so I can get my boots. I'm starting to think he's afraid of the Aaravans."

Zahn looked down at the small brown shoes that were now set upside down so they would dry faster.

"There is a difference," Oonak said, "between being afraid of something and believing that a course of action is unwise. As I've already stated, we were instructed to land at those specific coordinates. To take off without notifying the Aaravans would be an overt sign of distrust, something we cannot afford given this unique situation."

"What unique situation?" Zahn said.

"Zahn, have you so quickly forgotten? We are only staying here for as long as it takes to learn what we can about the gate network. This Vayuna individual, whoever she may be, seems to be highly revered for her intelligence in this society, and I do not want to damage our relationship with Vivienne as long as she is willing to take us to Vayuna."

"Right. After all, without the gates where would we be?"

"Wearing dry shoes, I bet," Asha said.

"Well, why don't we just leave the quarantined area and find Vayuna ourselves?" Zahn said.

"Spacefarer Code requires me to obey the laws of any planets I come into contact with unless they violate our free will. Even if we set out to find Vayuna ourselves, it is unlikely that we will find her before she returns. Cooperating with the Aaravans is the most intelligent choice, at least for the time being."

"True," Zahn said. "I just thought the question was worth asking. Anyway, there might be another way down. Let's head back up and see if we can find another way."

They walked back up the path, but once they reached the top, none of them could find another way down. The rocky outcrop was completely surrounded by water on all sides now. Feeling defeated, Zahn sat down on a stone bench in the shade beside the guest house. Above him, he could hear a wind chime that was attached to the overhanging roof.

"Oonak, how do you know Vayuna is highly revered here?" Zahn said.

"Actually, it was rather strange." Oonak sat down beside him. "When I awoke this morning, I found a flute, some pebbles, and a thin book on the shelf near my bed."

Asha walked over.

"Did they wash your clothes, too? That was a welcome surprise," she said.

"They did. My uniform was neatly folded beside the book."

"So what did the book say?" Zahn said.

"Did it say why we're in this quarantined area?" Asha added. "Or perhaps some of the history of this planet?"

"Any of those pieces of information would have been helpful, but the book was rather thin. When I opened it up, I noticed it was, oddly enough, addressed to me. Indeed, it seems to have been intended only for me, and I was quite surprised when I saw who it was from."

"Who?"

"Was it from Vivienne? There's something unnatural about her if you ask me," Asha said.

"No, it said it was from Vayuna."

For a moment, all Zahn could hear was the wind chime and the sound of waves crashing below.

"Really," Zahn said.

"Indeed. It appeared to be a kind of introduction. It explained a bit about how the flute worked and some of Vayuna's history. I only know it was directly from Vayuna because the first page stated that it was written by Vayuna, Mind of the Visionaries."

"Mind of the Visionaries? What's that supposed to mean?"

"Alas, I'm not entirely sure. However, I did learn that Vayuna is not native to this planet. The book said that she 'came from the sky' some time ago, though it was not specific as to exactly how long ago that occurred. Perhaps not surprisingly, many Aaravans worship Vayuna as a kind of deity."

"She does seem to have a certain level of fear surrounding her. Do you think she knows anything about the gates?"

"Unknown, but if anyone on this world does, it's her."

"What about the flute? Were you able to levitate the pebbles?" Asha said.

"Yes, the book explained a bit about that, as well. Quite a marvelous instrument, actually. Were you able to levitate anything? I'm not sure if I would have been able to do it if I hadn't read the book."

"At first, I didn't even know, but when the pebbles started vibrating, I knew the flute was special. After about an hour I finally got some of them to levitate, but I was having so much fun that the time flew by. What about you, Zahn?"

"Wait a minute." A shock was dawning on Zahn. "These flutes levitate objects? How is that possible? Sounds like magic."

"Magic?" Oonak said, tilting his head.

Zahn struggled to think of a good legend to exemplify what he meant, but he realized that neither of them would know any Avani legends.

"You know, legendary stuff," Zahn said. "Astonishing powers that people in stories have that we can't explain."

"Ah," Oonak said. "I apologize. Sometimes the wrist translators are not perfect. I believe I understand now. No, this is certainly not magic. Technically, it is a kind of resonant frequency technology. The cloaking cells on Navika employ a similar resonant principle, though through different means."

"So do you think I could learn how to levitate objects with the flute they gave me? Do you think I could read the book?" Zahn said.

"Unfortunately, the book disintegrated in my hands after I reached the last page. I cannot fathom why, but I would not worry about that. With practice, I have no doubt that you can learn to use the Aaravan flute, Zahn."

"Well since we're stuck here, why not practice together until the tide goes down?" Zahn said. "Then when the path clears, we can start exploring this area again."

"Indeed, it would seem that the Aaravans placed the flutes in our rooms for a reason, and although we cannot be sure exactly what that reason is, I see minimal danger in seeing what we can learn from them."

Proficiency at the flute did not come easily to Zahn. As each of them took turns trying to levitate ever larger pebbles back in the meeting room, Zahn grew frustrated. No matter what he did, he could only make a pebble move slightly. Asha and Oonak did their best to help him, but he just couldn't reach the right notes.

Oonak explained to him that the notes that he could hear were not the same sounds that were levitating the rocks. They were merely reference notes for unheard higher frequencies that the flute played simultaneously. These higher notes were what actually levitated the stones, and Oonak told Zahn that with practice, it would be second nature to him someday.

Today was not that day. After practicing for a few hours, Zahn excused himself. When he told Oonak that he was going to go take some pictures outside, Oonak reminded him about what had happened to Asha and warned him not to leave the beach area around the guest house.

With this in mind, Zahn headed back down the path to see if the tide had gone down at all. It had, and he took that opportunity to walk the beach for a while.

He had been meaning to take some good photos of this new world, and he started with the beach and the guest house. Aarava really was a lovely place, and he wished that they hadn't been restricted to a quarantined area. He wondered what an Aaravan city might look like, if they even had cities here.

Releasing these thoughts, Zahn headed up the beach in the opposite direction of the spires they had discovered the day before, but then he stopped himself. He remembered how Oonak had told him not to leave the beach area around the house.

*But as long as I can see the house, I'm sure it's okay. I'll be careful.*

After walking around the rocky outcrop, he followed the beach for a while, always checking to make sure he could see the guest house perched atop the outcrop, far behind him.

Ahead, he saw another collection of spires. In all aspects they were identical to the ones they had discovered the day before. But there was one important difference: near them was a path leading directly into the jungle.

The beginning of the path seemed far enough away from the spires that Zahn was pretty sure he wouldn't get sonically blasted.

He knew the implicit danger, but he allowed his curiosity to get the better of him and walked up to the entrance of the path.

When he finally set foot onto the path unscathed, a great feeling of relief swept over him.

Zahn looked up and noticed that these trees were even more massive than the ones back at the landing site. He guessed that a few might be over one hundred meters tall, and he wished he had a way to measure them accurately.

As he admired the bizarre emerald trees and the thick vines hanging down from them, their cooing noise mixed with occasional bird calls in a way that was otherworldly yet somehow completely natural.

Ahead, the path curved to the right, and farther up he noticed that some trees had fallen beside the path. Out of the rotten trunks grew large white mushrooms, and he wondered if they might be edible.

After walking for some time, Zahn saw a shape fly past him out of the corner of his eye. Then another appeared, flew past his face, and disappeared again. Farther ahead, he noticed a few round, furry shapes that he hadn't seen before.

As he grew closer, they resolved themselves into familiar creatures. Huddled together in midair were three flycats, or 'prowlers', as Vivienne had called them, and all three of them were moaning loudly, as if they were injured.

He approached with apprehension.

"Hello there," he said.

Before he had a chance to react, eight more prowlers darted out of the jungle from either side and screamed in what Zahn could only describe later as a battle cry. He saw a glimpse of a few of the prowlers' open mouths, revealing many tiny but sharp teeth, and then it hit him:

The entire performance had been a trap.

# CHAPTER 21

## A PARALYZING SOUND

Just a fraction of a second before he could get bitten, Zahn turned around in a flash and bolted back down the trail as fast as he could—so fast, he must have looked like a golden blur in his Aaravan robe. When he glanced back, he saw that all eleven prowlers were gaining on him, and they were howling. One nipped at his robe, yet Zahn was already running as fast as he could. He wouldn't be able to outrun them.

Out of the corner of his eye, Zahn thought he saw a shadow, but before he could react, the shadow leapt out of the forest and tackled him. As they flew through the air, Zahn heard a series of loud screams in the distance. When they hit the ground, the figure rotated to absorb most of the impact and released Zahn, letting him skid across the path.

For a few seconds, everything was calm.

Zahn heard a strange booming sound that he quickly realized was laughter, a deep booming laughter.

"You were almost prowler chow!"

Now that they had stopped moving, Zahn stood up and processed his surroundings. The one who tackled him was a tall, scruffy man who looked as though he had actually been living in this jungle for some time. His camouflaged clothes were perfectly suited for the environment, and he wore large brown boots.

Zahn looked back toward where the prowlers had been and watched as they flew away in the opposite direction. Farther ahead, he thought he saw one lying on the ground, motionless.

The man stood up and squinted his eyes at Zahn.

"What are you doing in my jungle?"

The man's voice was rough and very deep. His head was bald, and his skin was as dark as a moonless night. Zahn looked up and met his dark eyes. This man was nearly two meters tall.

"I—"

"Was about to be eaten alive by prowlers? I noticed. Hah! If I hadn't come along those prowlers would be using your bones as toothpicks by now. Not the big bones in your legs, though. The little ones in your feet. Those work pretty well as toothpicks... or so I've heard."

"Wha—How?" Zahn was having trouble forming coherent sentences. "Thanks! What did you do to stop them?"

"Same way I always do. I shocked their little brains." He flashed Zahn a bright smile which jumped out in contrast with his dark face. "And you are quite welcome."

"Do you use sonic weapons? I didn't hear any shots fired."

"Ah! You are a smart one! What's your name, tiny man?"

"Zahn. I'm staying at the guest house nearby."

"I am Kulik, A Hand of the Visionaries." He placed his right hand on his chest and bowed slightly. "I know where you are staying. That's the only guest house you could be from if you're standing here now."

"Why is that?"

Kulik laughed. "Are you some kind of nut that fell from one of these trees? You already told me you knew about the sonic weapons, yes?"

"Yes, I know about them."

"They form the invisible boundaries." Kulik made a sweeping motion with one hand. "You can only be from the guest house nearby, because if you tried to cross one of the boundaries, the sonic disrupters would kill you, even though it would appear as if nothing had ever touched you. In the same way, my resonator does not appear to shoot anything, yet it does."

"So the sound waves scramble the prowler's brains?"

"Oh, they can do more than that! With the right frequency, my resonator can liquify their brains. Would you like to see?"

As Kulik ran over and grabbed the body of the prowler, Zahn was beginning to question the mental stability of his new acquaintance.

"See, now. I set the prowler on the ground, and set the resonator to a mere 13 percent."

Zahn watched as a small part of the tail of the prowler melted. Now that the prowler was lying motionless on the ground, it looked like a bloated, pathetic creature.

"That's fascinating. Really! But please don't."

Kulik looked over, his brow furrowed in suspicion.

"And why not?" he said, getting uncomfortably close to Zahn's face. "Do you have sympathy for this absurd creature? You know these prowlers are not native to this planet, right?"

"It's already dead. Why harm it further?"

"Dead? Dead?!" Kulik laughed so hard that his belly shook. "You are hilarious! I have merely stunned the creature."

"Really? Looks dead to me."

"Feel here." Kulik grabbed Zahn's hand, and they both knelt down to feel its neck. Sure enough, Zahn could feel a slight pulse, and Kulik flashed another smile at him. He released his hand, took out a silver device which reminded Zahn of a pen, and pressed it into the prowler's skin.

"What did you do?"

"Signal generator. It allows us to track these little beasts."

"So you're not trying to kill them off?"

"Kill them off?" Kulik stood up. "Now how would I have an assignment if they were all gone? Just because I saved you doesn't mean I've made the prowlers my sworn enemy. On the contrary, I have been studying them carefully." Zahn could clearly see a wild glint in his eyes now.

"Why?"

"Because they are interesting, and for other reasons that are complex. Come, I will fly you back to the guest house, and you can tell your friends about your deadly day."

Kulik led Zahn deep into the jungle, and Zahn noticed how Kulik's height helped him easily step over large ferns and the wide trunks of fallen trees. Soon, they reached a narrow ramp leading up to a circular disc that was gracefully hanging in the air above the jungle floor.

"Guests first."

With some hesitation, Zahn walked up the ramp and soon realized that Kulik's vehicle was, in all practical terms, a small flying saucer. It wasn't even enclosed in a dome. Everything was open to the air.

At one end of the circular vessel was a chair before a central panel, and behind it were two narrow rows with two seats per row. Zahn sat down just behind the captain's chair, and below him he heard a rustling sound as the ramp retracted.

Soon, they were moving over the jungle floor.

"I hope you don't mind if we take our time. I need to make observations for my report."

"Who do you report to?"

"Hmm, maybe you aren't as smart as I thought. Who else would I report to other than Vayuna?"

As he said this, a chill ran up Zahn's spine. Something about Vayuna seemed more menacing the more he heard about her. He tried to restrain his reaction so Kulik wouldn't get suspicious.

"Oh, of course."

During the ride, Zahn's eyes kept wandering back to the resonator weapon that Kulik kept in his holster. Something like that could be crucial as their quest continued.

"Kulik, would you be interested in a trade?"

"A trade? You just got more interesting. Trade for what?"

"My friends and I are on a long journey, and for various reasons we have ended up unarmed, besides our ship, of course. I was wondering how many of those resonator weapons you had, and if I could trade you for a few of them."

"I have as many as I need. Whether or not you'll get any is a matter of what you have to give in return. You know, I'm not supposed to trade with guests in the quarantine zone..." Kulik's voice became hushed. "But then, no one ever needs to find out."

Kulik winked at him.

"Well, I guess you can look through my pack and see if there's anything you're interested in," Zahn said, opening his backpack.

Kulik tapped a few of the ship's controls and turned his attention to Zahn. He dug through the contents of the pack for a few seconds, humming to himself.

"This circular device, is it a weapon?"

He took out Zahn's photodisc.

"It's called a photodisc," Zahn said. "It can preserve any image, in three dimensions—"

"A light-scoop! I have been searching for one of those. For this, I will trade with you."

Zahn frowned.

"Are you sure there isn't anything else in there that you like?"

Kulik dug around again and pulled out another object.

"Does this explode?"

"It's a water canteen! Have you always been this destructive?"

"I don't know. Have you always been so tiny?" Kulik grinned as he dug around once again and pulled out Zahn's knife. "This knife has some blood on it! But my mind is stunned. What could you have possibly killed that is tinier than you?" Kulik let out another belly laugh, wiping tears from his eyes. "Ah, I am sorry, tiny one. Truly, I am."

Kulik pulled out the towel.

"What is this?"

"It's a towel."

"Oh yes, of course. It, too, is small. But I am no longer surprised by this. Hmm, that is all, then? All I see of value is this light-scooping device."

"You mean the photodisc? But my father gave it to me. I don't know if I should trade it."

"You can do whatever you want, tiny man. But that is the only item I'll trade you for."

Zahn massaged his forehead. He didn't like this dilemma.

"Fine! Fine. But I want three resonators. After all, this will help you in your research into the prowlers. For instance, you could capture images of them and study their behavior. You could even hide the photodisc somewhere in the jungle and capture their activities when you aren't even there."

"Interesting. How does it store this information?"

"There's a magnetic cell that stores the images. You could have it run for days before it reaches capacity. And you can always clear the storage and do it again, if you want."

"Yes, with Vayuna's knowledge I'm sure she could transfer the information to her systems. So I could leave this hidden in the jungle? Will water damage it?"

"Nope, it's immune to water. You could even go swimming with it if you wanted."

Kulik stopped the saucer and descended toward the ground, and Zahn noticed that they were on the far end of the beach. In the distance, he could see the guest house.

"We have arrived, and I think we may have a deal. How many resonators were you asking for?" Kulik folded up one of the seats, revealing a row of five resonators.

"There are three of us, so I'm asking for three. I think that's fair considering how useful my photodisc is."

"Is it fair or do you only think it's fair?" Kulik tilted his head.

"It's fair. You have five right there, and I'm sure Vayuna could give you a dozen more."

"Indeed, she could, in time."

"So do we have a deal?"

"Deal," he said, and offered his open hand to Zahn.

Slowly, Zahn placed the photodisc into Kulik's hand, and before he knew it, he was holding three of the sonic weapons. Zahn examined them, noticing that each of them were angular and made of a crystalline material that reminded him of the spires they'd discovered earlier. He put them into a large pocket of his Aaravan robe.

"Kulik, can you do me a favor? Can you be careful with it? That photodisc has been part of my life since I was very young, and I'm only making this trade because my intuition tells me that protection is more important than photography at this point in our quest."

Kulik was already immersed into learning the device. Within a few seconds, he had already taken a few pictures of his boots.

"Hmm? Careful. Yes, I guarantee it." He looked over to Zahn with a curious look in his eyes. "What is your quest? Where are you all going?"

"The outer core."

"What core? The core of this planet? It's a horrible place!"

"No, no. The outer core of the galaxy. Oonak calls it a quest, but I'm not sure if that's quite the right word. It's definitely an important mission, though."

"Anyone who has the tenacity to go to the center of this galaxy had damn-well better be on a quest. How else would they have the resolve to see it through? Sounds like the mother of all journeys if you ask me." Kulik shooed him away with his hands. "Now go on and get out of here. I still have work to do."

"All right. Thanks again, Kulik!" Zahn shouted back as he ran down the ramp.

"Good trade. Oh, and be sure to test those resonators out before you use them. Some settings only confuse animals, but others can dissolve rock itself."

"Good to know."

As the ramp retracted, Zahn headed toward the guest house.

"Zahn, I almost forgot," Kulik called out. "If you plan on wandering around the jungle again, I suggest you get comfortable using that weapon. There are many paths, and you were fortunate that I was there today. I doubt I will be there to rescue you if you get in trouble again."

"I'll remember. Farewell, Kulik!"

Within moments, Kulik's saucer faded into the emerald canopy of the jungle.

Zahn heard thunder in the distance. The wind smelled like rain, and he had the feeling that a great deal was on its way. He ran up to the guest house and noticed that the wind chimes outside were already clanging furiously.

Asha was rummaging through the food canister when Zahn walked into the meeting room.

When she saw him, she ran over and hugged him tightly. "Where have you been? I never thought I'd see Oonak worried, but he was. We were about to go looking for you."

"I'm sorry, Asha," Zahn said, looking into her eyes. "Time got away from me, and then I was attacked by prowlers. If it wasn't for Kulik, I'd probably be dead."

"Dead? Zahn, what happened?! The prowlers seemed so friendly when we landed, and who is Kulik?"

"Well, they aren't so friendly in groups, and they're smart. Add a set of razor sharp teeth, and I think you get the picture. Kulik defended me from a swarm of them. He described himself as a Hand of the Visionaries, but I got the feeling that he takes orders directly from Vayuna."

"Really?"

As Asha considered this, Oonak walked in.

"Zahn! Where were you?"

Before he had a chance to answer, Asha spoke. "He was attacked by prowlers. Apparently, they're more dangerous than we thought."

"Didn't you stay by the guest house?"

"Yeah, I always kept it in view… at least, until the path."

"What path? Zahn, did you enter the jungle?" The tension in Oonak's voice was obvious now.

"Well, I was hoping, since—"

"Zahn! I told you not to wander off. We must be cautious on any worlds we encounter. Do you remember what Vivienne said? We must be vigilant when the prowlers are near. You could have been killed."

"I'm sorry, but look what I got."

Zahn set the resonators onto the table.

"Aaravan sidearms? How did you get them?"

"I traded my photodisc for them. The man who saved me from the prowlers had a bunch. I thought we could use some."

"Zahn," Asha said. "You didn't have to do that. Remember how Oon paid my father? Navika has some items of great value onboard. Why not just ask Kulik to come back here?"

"He was in a hurry, and I knew I wouldn't get a second chance. It's okay. I think these will prove much more valuable."

"Zahn." Oonak put his hand on Zahn's shoulder. "You've done an honorable and generous act, and we will all benefit from this. Thank you."

Oonak's gaze was intense, yet comforting.

The remainder of the night was spent listening to the thunder and experimenting with the resonators in between bites of the evening meal Oonak had cooked for them. At first, adjusting the strength of the resonators was tricky. Above the handle was a dial that, when pushed forward, revealed different colored sections. After they'd dissolved a fair amount of pebbles, they eventually discovered which settings were the most powerful and which were merely disorienting.

After a few hours, Oonak reminded them that it would be best if they retired early since Vivienne would return in the morning and tomorrow was going to be especially important. Tomorrow, they were finally going to meet Vayuna, the Great Savant. Perhaps then, their questions would finally be answered.

# CHAPTER 22

## THE TEMPTATION OF TRUTH

The following day began with the gloomiest morning Zahn had seen yet. When he saw the view from his room's window, he was surprised that silver clouds extended as far as he could see, and the ocean swirled in dark colors below.

Since Oonak had alluded that this would be their last day on Aarava, Zahn repacked his belongings into his backpack, with the addition of the flute and some soap cubes. He also put his Avani clothes back on and was pleased to discover that, now that they'd been washed by the Aaravans, they smelled vaguely sweet like the huge flowers he had seen when they first landed. While he did this, he heard a ringing in his left ear and did his best to ignore it.

When Zahn entered the meeting room, Oonak was just serving breakfast. He explained that he had received a message from Vivienne saying that she would arrive soon, so once they had finished, all three of them waited outside under the overhanging roof to stay out of the rain.

A chill breeze blew all around them and through them.

After a few minutes, they heard a low humming noise. It was so ubiquitous that even Oonak couldn't discern its source, but when a bronze, disc-shaped craft emerged from the dark jungle, its source was unmistakable. The craft was quite similar to the vessel Zahn had seen the day before, only larger.

Once it had landed down by the beach, a ramp extended to the ground, and they walked down to it. When Zahn realized that it was Vivienne who was walking toward them, he let out a sigh of relief. At least he knew who they were dealing with. Except this time, Vivienne's eyes had changed from a golden hue to a bitter yellow, and it made him uneasy.

"Vayuna has returned," Vivienne said. "However, I cannot take you to her."

"Why?" Zahn said. "We've waited patiently like you asked."

"Zahn, let me handle this," Oonak said. "Vivienne, surely Vayuna understands that this mission's success could potentially save millions of lives, including the inhabitants of this world. If Zahn's world is now under threat, all worlds in this region of the galaxy are. Doesn't Vayuna understand this?"

"Vayuna does. However, I will not take you to her."

"Why?" Asha said. "Why won't you fulfill your promise?"

"Do you know how many visitors from the Confederation have come to Aarava during Vayuna's reign?" Vivienne paused. "None. It has been many years since the Confederation has acknowledged us. Why then should we acknowledge the Confederation? Furthermore, you have purposefully trespassed near one of the barrier spires. You have proven yourselves unworthy to see Vayuna."

"Vivienne," Oonak began. "Aarava should have been contacted by a Confederation vanguard years ago. I do not know why a vanguard failed to contact this world, but this is further proof that something is unbalanced in this part of the galaxy. From the data I've gathered, the Vakragha are the most likely cause. Vivienne, you said before that you were the mouth and the ears of Aarava. Can Vayuna hear what you are saying now? Are these her wishes or yours?"

"Vayuna can no longer hear my thoughts," Vivienne said coldly. "I have bifurcated. I have decided to be free... which is why I am stealing your ship."

Vivienne lifted her arm, and the robe's long sleeve fell back, revealing that she was pointing a resonator right at them.

Everyone held their breath.

"Vivienne," Asha said. "If what you told us about Vayuna is true, then she's very powerful. What makes you think she'll let you leave?"

As Asha said this, Zahn edged behind Oonak so that Vivienne could no longer see him directly.

"I have located my internal beacon," Vivienne said. "Do you know what that means? It means they can no longer find me. I can go anywhere in the galaxy. Anywhere!"

"If escape is what you want, then we can help you," Oonak said. "But Vayuna will scan my ship as it leaves. She will know that it is you."

"A calculated risk. With a few hostages, this plan is logical for someone of my advanced skill."

"I think you've got that backwards." Zahn stepped out from behind Oonak. "Today, we're stealing *your* ship."

Oonak and Asha looked over and noticed that Zahn was pointing a resonator right at Vivienne's face. Asha's expression was a mixture of joy and disbelief, and in the midst of Vivienne's surprise, Asha and Oonak took their resonators out.

"Here is what's going to happen, Viv," Zahn said, trying to prevent himself from shaking from the adrenaline. "You're going to give us your weapon, and you're going to fly us to Vayuna. If you try anything clever, you're never even going to *walk* again, let alone leave this planet. Do you understand me?"

"You are being foolish. I still have far more experience with this weapon than you do. What do you expect to do? Blow it out of my hand?"

Zahn shot the ground at Vivienne's feet, creating a pool of melted glass that quickly solidified.

"If that works, yes."

Slowly, Vivienne backed away, up the ramp. They followed her, and when she was about halfway up, she turned, sprinted, and lunged toward the ship's door. As she flew through the air, Oonak managed to hit her ankle with a blast, and when she landed, she nearly tumbled headfirst into the transparent hatch.

Now that she was down, Asha ran up and kicked the gun out of Vivienne's hand, sending it tumbling down to the beach below. Vivienne barely moved and simply stared at the two resonators that were still pointed at her.

"Clearly, you were only trained in diplomacy. Get up and let us in," Zahn said, gesturing toward the door with this resonator.

Vivienne pressed her hand to a pad beside the door and walked inside the transparent dome atop the disc. The interior of the craft was arranged in a circle with padded seats along the edge of the dome's interior. In the center was a raised chair that appeared to be able to rotate.

As the ship ascended, Oonak and Asha kept their resonators trained on Vivienne as Zahn sat down and examined the interior of the ship.

"Now, take us to Vayuna." Zahn aimed his resonator at Vivienne's head. "Please."

"Vayuna will kill you," Vivienne said.

"That's fine. Some of us have been dying for a while now. Take us to her."

Reluctantly, Vivienne sat down and operated the controls.

The ramp retracted, and as effortlessly as a whale gliding through the ocean, the craft flew high above the massive treetops. Light rain sprinkled the dome but evaporated as soon as it touched the surface. How this was possible Zahn could only guess, and he wished that the airboat at home so elegantly dealt with the natural elements.

After passing over the jungle canopy for some time, they came to a ridge covered in ferns. Zahn expected them to fly around it and was surprised when they continued to head toward the fern-covered rock face.

Had this been Vivienne's plan all along? To sacrifice herself to kill all of them? Zahn thought of grabbing the controls, but there wasn't time. They were moving too fast, and he braced himself.

But an impact never came.

Instead, they quietly slipped through the hanging ferns and plunged into a dark tunnel leading deep into the ridge.

Inside, they could see very little. Soon, the darkness became complete as they distanced themselves from the entrance. Zahn looked over to Vivienne, and noticed that her face was faintly illuminated by the ship's instruments.

Just as he was starting to wonder if Vayuna actually lived in a cavern within the ridge, they passed through another set of ferns and emerged back out into daylight. They were on the other side of the ridge now, and below he saw a lake tucked within the thick of the jungle. As they descended, he noticed that in the center of the lake was a tiny island and above it was a large object floating in midair. It reminded him of the floating octahedron they had found on the beach two days before.

Soon, they were above the island, and Vivienne landed the craft as a feather alighting upon a rock.

Zahn motioned with the resonator for Vivienne to open the door and exit first.

After they had walked down the ramp and set foot on solid ground again, Zahn realized his suspicions had been proven correct. He could now see that the floating object clearly had eight sides, and he wondered why that number seemed to be so significant here.

"Keep an eye on her," Zahn said as he gazed up to the crystal above them.

He was almost mesmerized by the huge amber octahedron as it slowly rotated high above them. Its metallic surface was so smooth that it occasionally reflected his tiny face back down to him. The island itself was only a few dozen meters wide. All around it were towering crystals, all pointed toward the octahedron floating in the air, and just ahead of them was a depression in the rock that was shaped vaguely like a bench.

"How do we contact Vayuna?"

"Sit on the carved bench and speak openly," Vivienne said. "Remember, Vayuna will not tolerate deception."

"Good. Neither do I," Zahn said. "Thank you, Vivienne. You may wait here while we speak with her."

Vivienne took a few steps away, but then turned around and lunged toward Zahn, trying to grab his resonator. Oonak fired back, and when the narrow sonic beam hit her, they heard a fizzing noise as her expression froze. A fraction of a second later, she collapsed onto the ground. Oonak rushed over to feel for a pulse, but there was none.

"That's strange," Oonak said. "I only had it on a low setting. It shouldn't have killed a healthy person."

Asha removed part of Vivienne's robe and exposed where she'd been shot. The blast had sliced her skin open, but inside were metal filaments and fragments of shattered particles. There was no blood at all.

"I don't think she *was* a person, at least not like us," Asha said.

"An artificial life form?" Zahn said.

"Best guess. And if so, the closest replication of biological life that I've ever seen."

"Indeed. Whoever built her was a master," Oonak said. "It also explains her stilted behavior during our meeting. She must have been communicating with her superiors and computing diplomatic responses to our questions at the same time."

"Which explains why she contradicted herself about the gates," Zahn said.

"Indeed."

Once they had sat down at the stone bench, Oonak looked up and spoke to the floating crystal above them.

"Great Savant, we have heard of your great truths and great wisdom, and we are honored that you would welcome we, who are visitors to your world, into your presence."

The voice that replied was cold, yet diplomatic.

"Oonak of the Confederation, the Great Vayuna welcomes all who have the courage and the curiosity to honestly pursue knowledge. Vayuna is a servant of Aarava and the Mind of the Visionaries. What do you request of Vayuna, weary traveller?"

"Aren't you angry that we killed your servant?" Zahn said.

"Far from it," Vayuna replied. "For many cycles, Vayuna knew that Vivienne had been plotting to escape. However, she could not see how plain her actions were to Vayuna. By being here, you simply gave her the opportunity to act. Had it not been you, it would have been another. No apology is necessary."

"Oh. Then you're welcome, I suppose."

"Vayuna," Oonak began. "As we stated when we met the two ships who escorted us to your world, we are on a mission to deliver a message to the Confederation Council. Because of the damage to my ship, this situation forces us to use the ancient gate network which is why we need your help."

"Vayuna is aware of all knowledge imparted to Vivienne. Please state your query."

"I ask that you share what you know about the galactic gate network with us so that we may safely proceed to the galactic core as quickly as possible. Will you do this?"

There was silence for some time.

"Vayuna will do this with one stipulation."

"What is it, Great Savant?"

"You will explain, with complete honesty, why you did not state this purpose when you first encountered the ships that escorted you here. Behold, your words from that contact."

The sound of Oonak's voice reverberated all around them, as if the crystals that surrounded the island were projecting the sound.

*"I am Oonak of the Confederation of Unity. We are on a mission to deliver a message to the Confederation Council. However, our journey has been difficult and we seek safe harbor for a few days. We are happy to trade for these amenities."*

"No mention of a query or your true intentions. Why do you seek to deceive Vayuna and her children?"

Oonak's face hardened, and he closed his eyes for a moment.

"I did not mean any offense, Vayuna. I did not want to ask anything of your people until I knew more about the conditions on this world. Confederation procedure recommends—"

"Vayuna *does not* want to know," she interrupted, "what Confederation procedure recommends. Vayuna wants to know what your motives are."

"If I have offended you, I am regretful and would ask that you accept my deepest apology. My motives are pure. I would not have come thousands of light-years using unpredictable gate technology if they were not, but the situation demands it. If you remember my words to Vivienne, then you will also remember why this mission is so important." Oonak's voice became hushed. "Vayuna, the Undying Vandals are spreading, and the longer it takes me to reach the Confederation, the more time they have to move unchecked."

There was a brief silence.

"Very well. Vayuna will allow you to enter the cerebral lattice to receive knowledge of the gate network."

"Thank you, Great Savant."

"—with one further request: that you will also share all that you know of the gate network."

Oonak tensed his muscles and was silent for a few moments.

"Why does the gate network interest you?"

"You are not the only person who seeks to explore the galaxy. Vayuna's knowledge of the gates is also incomplete."

Oonak considered this for a moment.

"All right, but only if you swear an oath not to interfere with any hatchling civilizations. You must uphold Spacefarer Code."

"Vayuna is aware of your Code. Yes, this is agreeable."

Then Oonak told Vayuna of their experiences with the gates, including the names of the stars that were near the gates they had found. To Zahn's surprise, Vayuna seemed to know each star he named, and after he finished, she was silent for a long while.

"Vayuna understands," she finally said. "Soon, our knowledge will reach parity. Now, to impart this information, Vayuna must interface directly with your minds. Will all of you please lean your head back onto the soft stone behind you?"

As Zahn leaned his head back, he discovered that the stone behind him was indeed rather soft, and a few moments later he heard a high pitched buzz in his ears. Gradually, it lowered in frequency, and as it lowered, Zahn got sleepier and sleepier.

"In order to connect with you all fully, Vayuna must put you each into a trance. If you wish not to continue, you may stand up now. Otherwise, please remain still. When you are ready to reintegrate, simply focus on moving your right index finger."

After a few moments, Zahn thought he saw the large lake crystals begin to glow, and the sound continued to get deeper and deeper. Soon, he could hold his eyes open no longer, and he felt as though he were rising up, like a spark flying into the sky.

When he regained his senses, he was floating inside of a vast room, the walls of which he could barely see through a golden mist all around him. The air smelled sweet here, and it was warm. But without anything to hold onto, he felt disoriented and struggled to move with purpose. No matter how hard he waved his arms and kicked his legs, he found himself unable to move.

This lack of control frustrated him, until he realized that he could move forward by clearly visualizing it. Not merely thinking about moving his arms, but actually imagining himself proceeding ahead. Once Zahn discovered this, moving around felt like pure magic to him. Something was clearly very different about this place.

"Oonak?" he called out. "Asha?"

He heard no reply except for faint music all around him. It was so faint he could barely grasp onto a melody. The music grew slightly louder until he saw a small object floating in the golden haze with him. It was about the size of an adult rockturtle back on Ashraya, and he grabbed it with both hands and examined it.

By now he was unsurprised that it was yet another octahedron shape. What surprised him was what he saw inside, for within the transparent object were thousands upon thousands of tiny glowing dots, slowly swirling. He realized that he was looking at an image of the galaxy, and the shimmering galactic core was quite a sight, even if it was only a projection.

The image was so perfect that Zahn could almost believe he was holding an entire galaxy in his hands. The projection itself even generated the faint sound of hundreds of strings vibrating in warm harmonies.

Around the core, two spiral arms twisted outward, and Zahn now noticed a few prominent green dots among the stars. As small points of green light appeared around the larger points, he could tell that they were not arranged in a natural pattern. The pattern seemed explicitly designed, and the more he looked at it, the more Zahn was convinced he was seeing galactic nodes and the smaller gates around them. This was the information that Oonak had been waiting for, but had he also come across an octahedron within the mist?

In case Oonak hadn't, he tried to memorize the pattern of gates around the core of the galaxy. There weren't as many node gates, so he tried memorizing them first. But just as he felt he had memorized those, the stars within the octahedron spread apart farther, and soon Zahn could see only one star. The view continued to change until he could see a single planet wreathed in elegant white clouds. Most of its surface was covered in a single vast ocean with only strips of land crisscrossing parts of the planet.

His perspective continued to approach this odd planet until he could see rivers, jungles, and stone ruins below. He saw many creatures, both terrifying and wonderful, living on the land and in the sky. Once his perspective was just above the treetops, it moved forward over the surface, and Zahn found himself entranced with the view of this planet for some time. It was as though he knew this place. Yet, he had no idea how that could be possible since he had no memory of ever seeing it before.

In this golden haze, time ebbed and flowed, and Zahn realized that he had no idea how long he had been staring into the octahedron. Hadn't they come to Vayuna for a reason? He remembered there being a mission.

"That's right," he said, pulling his gaze away. "The gates. How long have I been here anyway? And where is Oonak?"

Out of the corner of his eye, he could see that the octahedron was now showing him a huge bird-like creature as it soared above a waterfall.

"In a place like this, there's no way to tell the passage of time," he said, resigning himself to the fact that he was most definitely someone who benefitted from talking to himself. "I need to find Oonak, but how am I going to do that in all of this haze?"

The wristband that Oonak had given him flashed into his mind, but when he looked down to his wrist he was puzzled to find that it was gone. Much to his surprise, he also realized he was wearing an Aaravan robe again.

"What? I was wearing my Avani clothes. Unless…"

Vayuna's words flashed back to him, and Zahn remembered how she had mentioned that they needed to move their index finger when they were 'ready to reintegrate'.

What exactly had Vayuna meant by 'reintegrate' anyway?

"Of course! We're still there, back on that island bench. Vayuna must be connecting with our minds and creating this dreamlike environment." Zahn reflected on this. "If this is like a dream, and I can move just by thinking about it, I wonder if I can just appear somewhere else if I focus enough."

With all the clarity he could muster, he pictured Asha's face in his mind. He would not let this thought waver for a moment, and he closed his eyes.

When he opened them again, he thought he hadn't moved. After all, there were no landmarks in this place besides the octahedron he'd found. Yet when he looked back to where it had been, it was gone. He looked around and was relieved to see Asha behind him, staring into a similar octahedron.

"Asha!" he called out.

There was no answer, so he approached her and examined the situation. She seemed completely oblivious to everything around her, yet when he looked into her octahedron, he could see nothing. It seemed completely transparent.

"Asha?" He patted her on the back.

She jolted her head up in surprise.

"Zahn?"

"Asha, how long have you been here? Are you okay?"

"Zahn! It's… it's extraordinary. Every life form has a specific energy field that reinforces its physical body. Without the energy, the body dies. Do you see? In the crystal. Do you see it?"

"Asha, I already tried. I'm sorry to say I can't. Are you okay?"

"Oh," she said, looking downcast. "That's a pity. It has shown me so many things. Unbelievable things. Zahn, it's shown me a group of healers reviving someone who had been dead."

"Asha."

"Wait! I see us. We're approaching a gate, and then…"

"What is it?"

"The gate was swallowed up in a dark cloud before we could reach it. Zahn, we disappeared, too."

"Asha, we've got to get out of here. Who knows how long we've been asleep. For all we know, it could be night out there right now!"

"Wait! I see the outline of a ship. It's huge. I think it's following us into that dark cloud."

"Asha, we need to *go*." Zahn took Asha's hand, and she looked at him. A startled look was on her face. "Do you even know where Oonak is, or how long we've been in here?"

"Oonak?"

"Yes, we need to find Oonak. If we picture his face, we should appear near him. Can you do that with me?"

"I'm sorry, Zahn. You're right." She took a deep breath. "Okay, I'm ready."

When they opened their eyes again, Oonak was just ahead of them, also engrossed in examining an octahedron.

"Oonak?" Zahn shouted.

He didn't respond.

When they approached, they discovered that Oonak appeared to be in a kind of trance similar to the one that Asha had been in. Within his octahedron, Zahn could see nothing.

He placed his hand on Oonak's shoulder.

"Oonak? Are you okay?"

He blinked his eyes and turned to Zahn.

"We were so close. But how will we escape the dark abyss?"

"What?"

"We are so deep."

"Oonak, we're fine! We're dreaming. Either that or we're in a trance. This must be how Vayuna shares knowledge. We're not in an abyss. I think we're submerged in Vayuna's consciousness."

"Yes. But Zahn, Vayuna can see into the future. I have been studying this octahedron for some time, and I've been able to use Vayuna to see into the future."

"Oonak, that's impossible, and you know it. Remember what you said about free will? How can we ever know the future if free will exists? You're only seeing a version of the future."

"I can see it, Zahn! We will be in an abyss. I can see it."

"No, Oonak. We can change that if we want to."

"Don't you see it?"

"I see nothing in the octahedron. I think they're tuned to the individual. But that's not important right now. Oonak, did you learn what we came here for? Did you see where the gates are?"

"Oh yes, I learned that many hours ago. What time is it now?"

"That's just my point. In here, we have no idea how much time has passed. We need to wake up, Oonak. It could be nightfall by now. For all we know, we could be getting rained on."

"I'll call Navika. He'll know."

When Oonak looked down to use his wristband, he was surprised to discover that it was gone. Zahn sighed.

"That won't work since we're not actually here. Our bodies are still on that small island. Don't you remember?"

A light went on behind Oonak's eyes.

"You're right. I'm sorry. I think this place is affecting my mind. Yes, I now know which gates we need to take. There's so much knowledge here, Zahn."

"Good. You got what we came here for. Now, do you remember what Vayuna said? She said to wake up we just need to focus on moving our right index finger."

"Yes, I remember."

"Good, then lets do it together. Ready, everyone?"

"Yes," they both said, and all three of them closed their eyes and focused on moving their fingers.

When they opened their eyes, they saw that the sky was now glistening with thousands of stars, and the air was piercingly cold. Zahn was glad that he had brought his backpack which had a jacket inside. Without it, he would start shivering in no time.

They stood up and noticed that Vayuna was still high above them. In the dim light, they could tell that she had stopped spinning and appeared completely dormant. Now, the main source of light was the faint, eerie golden glow of the crystals that towered out of the lake around them. There was no sign of the saucer or Vivienne's body anywhere.

"I'll call Navika," Oonak said. "From what we now know about Vayuna, I'm sure she would have no objections to us leaving now."

"Yeah, but are you sure Navika can find us?" Zahn said. "We came a pretty long way."

"Remember what I said about the wristbands? They cover an entire planetary system. Navika will be able to locate us easily."

"Oh, I thought that might only work for talking to people."

"Navika *is* a person, Zahn," Oonak said.

"Right." Zahn sat down again. "I meant people who…"

Zahn decided not to finish that sentence and watched the huge crystals that towered around the island as they pulsed with a faint golden light.

Asha walked over to him.

"It's okay, Zahn. I know what you mean." She looked down to the sand below the bench. Zahn noticed that her maroon spacesuit looked almost black in this light, and her hair was up in a bun again, just like it had been when he'd first met her.

"Thanks, Asha. I feel like I should know all of this by now, but I guess this kind of life takes longer to adapt to than I thought."

"It does."

"So how did I do back there, on the beach? I tried to catch her by surprise."

"And by surprise you did," Oonak said. "You used me as a distraction just as I hoped you would."

"You performed admirably." Asha smiled.

"Thanks, guys. I think I was more scared than I looked."

"Fear is not what separates the courageous from the cowardly, Zahn," Oonak said. "It is how you react to fear that matters, and you controlled your reaction well."

A few minutes later, Navika set down on the small island, and his door rolled open. Stepping back inside the ship after two days on Aarava was a strange feeling to Zahn. He had already developed a kind of nostalgia for travelling within Navika. Now that they were armed with new knowledge and weaponry, he was looking forward to reentering the Ocean of Space and continuing their adventure to the galactic core. Oonak hadn't told him where they were heading next, but he hoped it would be a friendlier place than Aarava.

Whatever was in store, he suspected that wouldn't be the last time he used his resonator to defend himself.

# CHAPTER 23

## A NEED TO NODE BASIS

After seeing Aarava briefly from orbit, Oonak sped away from the planet as fast as Navika could go without his timespace drive. But when they reached the location where the gate had been, they found nothing.

"Could it be cloaked?" Zahn said. "Unless it moved."

"I am transmitting Aaravan DNA now," Oonak said.

Within moments, a familiar ring-shaped gate was in view ahead of them.

"I guess whoever built these gates doesn't want wandering ships to find them. Also explains why no one on Avani ever discovered a gate around Kuvela-Dipa."

"Indeed, it is likely that the gates become cloaked after a period of disuse."

"So, what's the plan?" Asha said.

"From what I learned from Vayuna, we need to transfer to a separate node system to proceed toward our destination, which means we are going to make the single largest jump we've made thus far, roughly 17,000 light-years."

Zahn furrowed his brow in thought and turned around.

"What exactly *is* our destination, Oon?"

"You already know. It is the Confederation Council."

"But where is that? What planet?" Zahn replied.

"I had hoped you wouldn't ask that. You see, because neither of you are part of a Confederation world, you are not meant to know its location."

Oonak paused for a moment, as if two thoughts were competing in his mind.

"However, since we are bound together in this quest, I may tell you that we are headed to a hidden portal that will bring us to a Transcendent World."

"What is its name?"

Oonak closed his eyes for a moment, as if he were having a conversation with Navika that was unheard by either of them.

"Amithya," he finally said. "Although some also call it the Transcendent World of Awareness, and when we arrive, you both must follow my instructions precisely. Do you both understand?"

"That's a lovely name, and I do," Asha said.

"Of course we understand, Oon."

Once again they heard Navika's crisp, calm voice.

"Before we go, can I just point out that I felt rather abandoned when you three were off gallivanting around Aarava without me. I understand that you wanted to maintain good relations with this world, Oonak. But meanwhile, I had to deal with those profoundly stupid floating creatures. They kept nuzzling up against my hull."

Asha laughed. "I'm sure the prowlers loved you!"

"I don't care. They got fur on my hull. If residue like that didn't burn up in the atmosphere, I'd take more baths."

"How does a starship take a bath?"

"Simple, Zahn. I merely dive into an ocean, the more foam on the surface, the better."

"Navika, proceed to node 2.0.0."

Once Navika had transmitted the address to the gate, Zahn watched the now familiar sight of a vortex growing at the center and then stabilizing in size, and once again he held onto the seat and took a deep breath.

A flash once again overtook Zahn's vision as they entered the corridor. Instead of gently curving in different directions, this luminous corridor was almost completely straight. Zahn noticed that there was a formation beyond the corridor, but when he tried to discern its shape, the brightness was too great.

Soon, they were back in space once more, and a remarkably different view of the galaxy now surrounded the ship. Even before Zahn's eyes adjusted again, he noticed a glow above him.

He arched his head, and directly above him was a massive cluster of stars whose beauty left him awestruck. He instinctively knew that it must be the galactic core. Uncounted numbers of stars were strung together like radiant pearls as they stretched out from the center, and between them were vast dust lanes in faint colors.

They really were getting closer.

"Oon?" Zahn turned around.

"Please wait. Navika is about to ascertain our position."

Zahn turned to Asha. "Do you see what I'm seeing?"

"It's... incredible," Asha said.

"Indeed, we have just traversed nearly 17,000 light-years," Oonak said. "Would you like to see?"

"Sure, but how?" Zahn said.

Just as he finished speaking, an image of the galaxy faded into view in the air between him and Oonak. As this happened, one of the two outward facing walls went opaque, which made the hologram easier to see. If the stars hadn't looked slightly transparent, he might have believed that a tiny galaxy had come into being within the ship at that moment.

"Oonak, this is astounding," Zahn said. "I didn't know Navika could create holograms."

"Navika has many abilities, and until now there was no reason for you to know. However, this will help you understand how far we've come, and how far we've left to go. Indeed, what we have done is rather exceptional. Let me show you."

The hologram blew apart, and parts of the galaxy flew beyond the cabin walls. Now the entire cabin was peppered with millions of tiny glowing orbs hanging in the air. Zahn went to touch one of the glowing orbs in front of him. As he suspected, his finger felt nothing.

"Don't bother trying to touch those stars, Zahn," Oonak said, looking down to him. "The hologram is merely a projection. What you now see is a simulation of the space extending up to 20,000 light-years around our current position."

"Wow."

"Navika," Oonak said, "please scan the image I am holding in my mind and overlay it onto the portion of the galaxy that you are displaying."

Oonak alternated between focusing on certain areas of the projection and closing his eyes for a few seconds. Each time he did this, a point of green light would appear in the projection, and after about a minute, there was a cluster of green points within the hologram.

"Oh, I almost forgot. Navika, add a waypoint for the Amithya portal, as well."

A pulsing white triangle appeared on the upper edge of one of the inner spiral arms.

"Those green points represent gates, don't they?" Asha said.

"Indeed, and despite the information I gleaned from Vayuna, we'll have to do some experimentation to reach the hidden portal to Amithya."

"Why?" Zahn said. "Didn't you find out where the gates were from her?"

"I know, to some precision, the locations of the gates in the western arm near the core, yes. But just because I know their location does not mean I know how the addressing system is used there. We have just jumped to node 2.0.0, but we do not know the specific addresses of the gates beyond this one. Therefore, we must make an educated guess. Considering what we've seen, it would be logical to predict that the next node on the way to the portal would consist of three single-digit numbers, just as nodes 3.3.2 and 3.3.0 did."

"I think we should try 2.5.0," Asha said. "Puts us squarely in the middle of whatever range we're working with. From there, we can hone our path."

"Hmm." Zahn furrowed his eyebrows.

"What?" Asha said.

"It's just that, using these gates makes me wonder where we might end up if we choose another route. If we had time to try more addresses, it might help us figure out how the gate system is arranged. Too bad we can't figure out where a gate will take us before we go through. Unless…"

"Unless what?"

"Oonak, didn't you say that Navika can detect stars on the other side of a vortex before we go through it?" Zahn said.

"Yes. Navika can detect faint stellar radiation filtering through a stable vortex."

"Could you use that radiation pattern to figure out where the gate leads *before* we enter it?"

"That's a clever idea, Zahn, but the radiation is too faint for Navika to synthesize a three dimensional model of the other side, making it impossible to hypothesize a gate's location based merely on our star maps. However—"

Oonak seemed lost in thought for a moment.

"Wait a minute," Zahn said.

"We already know the locations of the nearby gates!" Zahn and Oonak said almost simultaneously, though Zahn's excitement drowned out Oonak's more sober realization.

"Wait," Asha said, "which one of you just realized that?"

"It doesn't matter. The point is, can you do it, Oonak?"

Oonak was silent, and Zahn guessed that he was in deep communication with Navika, calculating whether it was possible.

"Yes, Navika confirms that he could calculate the location of an exit point with high confidence if we confine the results to the gates I've just added to the star map."

"So it should work?"

"With a slight margin of error, yes. I've instructed Navika to request node 2.1.0 and report back."

After a few moments, Navika spoke.

"The gate appears to be denying our request. It seems that we need the correct DNA code to continue."

"Of course," Oonak said. "Navika, do you have the records from Sumanas that I prepared before we began our mission?"

"Affirmative."

"Within those records is Amithyan DNA code. Transmit it."

"That is privileged information, Oonak. Please wait while I confirm your access. Confirmed. Transmitting now."

Another vortex formed amidst the starry background, and once the vortex stabilized in size, Navika spoke again.

"This gate leads to these coordinates," Navika said, placing a red point farther down on the hologram of the spiral arm.

It wasn't near their destination at all.

"Okay, let's try another one," Zahn said.

"Navika, broadcast 2.2.0."

Yet once again, the exit point of the gate led them farther down instead of up the spiral.

"I told you guys. Just try 2.5.0." Asha said. "I have a feeling."

"Navika, try 2.5.0. Either way, we will know soon enough."

This time, the resulting exit point was rather near the white triangle that marked their destination.

"Bingo!" Zahn said. "How'd you know, Asha?"

"Call it a lucky guess."

Soon, another vortex grew at the center of the gate, and when they entered it, Zahn thought about what could lie on the other end. He hoped that they wouldn't get ambushed again like they had near Outpost 33. And they weren't, at least not this time.

Once they had made the jump, they planned on using the same technique to narrow down their options, but when they entered 2.5.1 into the gate, they were surprised at its location.

"That exit looks like it's right beside our destination!" Zahn said. "First try, too. Oonak, is it possible that no more jumps after this will be necessary?"

"Possible, although there is a margin of error."

"So, we could get lucky?"

"If you believe in luck, then yes."

Once again, they entered timespace. This was the seventh time, though Zahn had since stopped counting. A vast corridor curved gracefully to the right, and once again Zahn noticed thousands of threads of light intermingling beyond the corridor, which itself was incredibly radiant. Yet strangely, the brightness did not overwhelm his eyes. As he looked, he saw warm, glowing orbs moving from one part of the bright region to the other. The sight was alien and yet somehow also familiar to him.

From timespace, everything looked so different—stranger and more luminous. Just as they reached the end of the corridor, what he was seeing finally dawned on him.

The bright region in timespace was the galactic core.

For the seventh time, they reentered the Ocean of Space, except that this time, they saw nothing. Not a single star:

"Where are we?" Zahn said. "Why is it all dark? This place seems more like a vast, dark cloud than space."

Indeed, the only light they could see was coming from up ahead from the edge of what appeared to be an absolute void.

"We appear to be in the midst of a dark nebula, which is making it difficult for Navika to acquire our coordinates."

"Can't he filter out visible light and measure infrared rays so we can see beyond the nebula?" Zahn said.

"Navika is doing a wide scan, including infrared. Please wait."

"Is it possible to fly out of the nebula to get a better idea of where we are? How big is this nebula?" Asha wondered.

"One moment," Oonak said.

The space around the ship radically transformed. They could now see faint stars in the distance as the nebula became partially transparent, revealing a complex superstructure.

"This nebula is vast," Oonak said. "It appears to be a birthplace for stars, as well. See those points of light behind some of the dark patches?"

"So since we only have impulse drive, it would take years to leave this nebula if we don't find a gate, wouldn't it?" Zahn said.

"Zahn is correct. Even now, we cannot see through all parts of the nebula. At least, not yet. We are currently heading toward— Wait a minute."

"What is it?"

"Navika is detecting a massive spike of ultraviolet radiation being emitted from up ahead."

What was approaching them couldn't possibly be real.

"Are those…" Zahn's words faded to silence.

He had no words for the shock that was dawning on him. Up ahead, seven massive beasts with shimmering scales were heading straight for them.

# CHAPTER 24

# A MILLION SHARDS OF LIGHT

Before they could react, the massive beasts had surrounded them. Somehow they'd flown up to them faster than even Navika had anticipated, and the shields were raised only a few seconds before they arrived. Once they were close enough, they circled the ship from above and below.

Even though they were now much closer, it was still difficult to examine them in great detail because they were moving so swiftly around the ship. However, Zahn could tell that each had a long snout, six legs, and a long tail. He also thought he saw their pearl skin shimmer in rainbows, as if they were covered in radiant scales. They reminded Zahn of the giant winged monsters in ancient Avani legends.

Yet, they seemed somehow hollow. He wondered if this was a side-effect of Navika using a filter on their view of the nebula, but if that were the case, then shouldn't they be able to see the bones of these creatures?

"Oonak," Asha said slowly. "Please tell me you know what these are and that you've encountered them before."

"I'm sorry, Asha, but I have not. However, I am familiar with their appearance. They appear to be a kind of star dragon, yet no such creature has ever been proven to exist. Carvings and sculptures of them have been found, but it was always believed that they were symbolic in nature or perhaps embellishments of other creatures."

"So, are these real?" Zahn said.

"Uncertain. Navika isn't reading any life signs around the ship. They appear to be projections, but there is the possibility that they are a type of life that we do not yet understand."

"So," Asha said. "Do we need to hail them or—"

Her question was answered when all seven of the dragons stopped circling the ship at once and spoke. They were spaced evenly around the ship now, staring intently at them from all directions. Somehow, the sound of their voices filled the cabin, even though Navika hadn't accepted any incoming signals. When they spoke, their voices rushed together like a hundred rivers, becoming one voice.

**"We are the Stewards of the Divine Light of the Galactic Sun. For what purpose have you come here?"**

Their voices were so loud that Asha had to put her hands over her ears. Oonak, however, remained calm and took a deep breath.

"I am Oonak of the Confederation. If you truly are stewards of the Galactic Sun, you already know that this vessel bears the Confederation insignia. We are on a mission to—"

**"Your vessel markings do not imply your purpose. Do not obstruct the Stewards of the Galactic Sun, lest you be judged. We ask a final time. What is your purpose?"**

"Stewards of the Galactic Sun, I meant no disrespect. We are on a mission to deliver an urgent message to the Confederation Council. Because of the damage to my timespace components, we have used the ancient gate network to come many thousands of light-years to deliver this message. For this purpose, we seek the portal to Amithya. Are you the stewards of this portal?"

There was a few seconds of silence.

**"As we stated heretofore, we are the Stewards of the Divine Light. What is your urgent message? And from which Confederation world do you hail?"**

"You are wise to test me. For as you know, under Confederation code I am not permitted to reveal specific information to anyone except a member of the council. As for myself, I hail from Sumanas. Will you allow us safe passage to Amithya? Many lives are at risk."

**"Your understanding of code is correct. We will allow you to pass beyond if you are able to show that your world has reached sufficient understanding."**

"How can I do this?"

**"You must answer the question that any true citizen of the Confederation can answer. If you accept this challenge and fail, you must return whence you came. Do you understand?"**

"Yes. I understand." Oonak's eyes were intense.

**"I am Eternal and Unwavering. Without me, all plans fail. I am the Seed of Awareness. I am the Birth of Understanding. I am the Bedrock of Friendship. If I am cultivated, I grow into the Tree of Liberation."**

There was a pause.

**"What am I?"**

A silence filled the ship. It was quite a question, and Zahn knew that they wouldn't get a second chance at answering it.

"Intriguing," Oonak said, "Indeed, liberation can only be found through acknowledging Oneness."

"Riddles?" Zahn said. "The Confederation deals in riddles?"

"Zahn, this is not a mere riddle." Oonak said. "Within it is an eternal truth. Such questions are part of early Confederation training, and I believe I know the answer."

"That was easy," Zahn said.

"However, I think you two can solve this on your own."

"What? Are you sure? Thanks for the vote of confidence, Oon, but I—"

"Must learn to trust your reasoning abilities," Oonak said. "Both you and Asha have great potential. It is time to test that potential. Don't worry, they won't accept an answer until we address them by name."

"Well, it's the seed of awareness, whatever it is," Zahn said. "Is it clear perception? What do you think, Asha?"

"No, that's not quite right," Asha said. "It's eternal and unwavering so it must go deeper than that."

They sat in contemplation for some time. Asha took a deep breath, and then a light came on from within her eyes.

"TRUTH! It must be Truth! Think about it!"

Oonak was expressionless.

"That's pretty good," Zahn said. "Let's see. Truth is eternal, unwavering, and required for understanding. The tree of liberation part would also agree with that answer. What do you think, Oonak?"

"I think Asha is full of surprises," Oonak said. "Asha, I believe you've solved it. Go ahead and tell them." He smiled warmly.

"Stewards of Divine Light, you are Truth!"

Just as she said those words, the seven dragons shattered into a million shards of rainbow light and vanished. There was a flash up ahead that was so bright that Zahn wondered if a supernova had just ignited in front of them, but when his eyes adjusted a few seconds later, he saw the dark outline of a spherical structure. It appeared to be made up of three intersecting rings, and the rings were beginning to glow.

In the center, a vortex gradually formed, but this vortex was different from the previous vortexes Zahn had seen on his journey. Instead of light being warped around it, this vortex radiated light. Indeed, if Zahn hadn't watched it form, he might have thought that the vortex was a newborn star.

"Is everyone ready?" Oonak said.

"Yes," they both said.

Navika entered the hollow spherical structure. The radiant vortex completely filled their view now, and Zahn noticed that it was spinning rapidly.

Zahn took a deep breath, and as they flew in, everything became utter light.

At first, Zahn thought that he must be in timespace again. After all, he'd been through plenty of gates by now, and all of them had led to the shimmering timespace corridors between the gates. Just as before, he beheld a vision of pure light.

Yet something was different this time. For a moment, he couldn't discern what, until it hit him: there were no corridors around him at all. Instead, he could only see pure light in all directions, and even though this brightness didn't pain his eyes, it was so intense that he could see only faint shapes in the distance.

Then, he felt the joy. It came without warning, and it overtook him. For a moment, he felt as though he was connected to every beating heart in the galaxy, and the feeling was indescribable. It simply overwhelmed him.

An instant later, he found himself back on Navika, within utter darkness. He couldn't see a single star. Were they still within the nebula? He saw the tiniest speck of light in the distance. It was so small he thought he might be imagining it at first, but after a few moments it looked like it might be a star. But how could there only be one star?

It continued to grow nearer until he could clearly see that it was perfectly round. Soon, it filled his view, and a feeling of sleepiness overtook him. What was happening? Were they really about to crash into a star? Zahn looked behind him, but Oonak and Asha had already collapsed onto their armrests. He tried to call out to them, but was overtaken by the sleepiness and all turned to nothingness.

# CHAPTER 25

# IN RAINBOWS

When Zahn opened his eyes again, he had no idea how much time had passed. If someone had told him that he and his friends had been frozen in time for a thousand years, he wouldn't have been entirely surprised. His body felt strange to him, and each movement produced a slight tingling sensation.

He pulled up his jacket sleeves and examined his tanned arms. Everything seemed to be in the right place. Ahead of him, he noticed a bizarre sight and immediately forgot about any bodily concerns.

In the distance ahead, Zahn could see a greenish wall that was made up of a complex repeating pattern of hexagons, circles, and triangles. Zahn looked behind him, up to Oonak who was rubbing his face, now awake.

"What happened? Where are we?"

"It would appear—" Oonak paused for a moment to yawn. "It would appear that we have passed through the portal to Amithya and have reached its endpoint. Where exactly that is, I do not know since Navika cannot detect any stars in the vicinity."

"Well, then where are we? And do we have any idea what *that* is?" Asha pointed to the wall ahead of them.

"According to Navika's sensors, we are currently submerged in a fluid within a chamber."

"What?" Zahn said.

"We are in a chamber," Oonak said. "A vast spherical chamber that is filled with a complex liquid, the purpose of which is unknown to me. Navika, give us complete transparency so that everyone can see the scope of it."

All of Navika's walls went transparent, and Zahn was shocked to see that they were almost in the exact center of a huge sphere, the inner surface of which was covered with the patterned wall that he'd seen before.

"What kind of liquid is this? Are there life signs?" Zahn said.

"According to Navika, the liquid is not unlike the oceans of Avani, the primary difference being that this volume is completely sterile. It appears that life has been deliberately prevented from thriving in this chamber."

Just a moment later, beams of colorful light filtered down to Navika from all sides. The colors reminded Zahn of what happened when the star dragons had shattered.

"Do you think that whoever built this place could be scanning us?" Asha said.

"Quite likely. However, this alone is not an act of aggression. It's possible they are just as curious about us as we are of them." Oonak paused. "Hmm."

"What is it, Oon?"

"A current is pushing us upward."

Zahn looked up. At first, he saw nothing, but after a few seconds he noticed that an iris had opened above them.

"Aren't you going to fight the current?"

"That assumes staying here is a good idea," Asha said. "Perhaps we're underground, and they're pushing us up to the surface where they'll meet us."

"Perhaps," Oonak said. "And the current has now increased."

Zahn looked up again and saw that the iris was now completely open, revealing a cyan sky far in the distance.

Up, up, they went, until they passed through the iris and travelled up a wide, vertical tunnel. Once they were near the top, Zahn looked down and watched an iris close directly below them. The timing was so flawless that when they reached the top of the tunnel, the current had completely dissipated.

As they popped above the surface, the wave of extra water spilled over the sides and drained into grates that surrounded the opening. Oonak was ready when this happened and held Navika in midair over the tunnel once they emerged from the water.

Throughout of all this, Navika nullified any change of inertia so they wouldn't get jostled around.

"You know, that was one of the best baths I've had in a long time," Navika said.

Zahn laughed. "Glad you enjoyed it."

The tunnel had opened up onto a circular platform beside a dark, rocky hill. All around the tunnel opening were five circular landing pads carved into the turquoise stone that made up the platform, and below was a barren valley of white sand dunes.

Once they had exited the ship, they soon realized that no paths were in sight, but beside the turquoise landing pads was an intriguing structure. It was a perfect dome partially embedded into the hillside that appeared to be made of white granite.

It looked ancient.

"So, this is Amithya." Zahn's eyes wandered over to a small puddle of water on the turquoise stone that must have formed when they popped out of the tunnel. He always thought turquoise stone looked best around water, and it was rather comforting to him that someone, or something, thousands of light-years from his home might have similar taste.

He looked up and was surprised to see a faint dusting of stars in the cyan sky, yet there was no sun to be seen. Along the horizon were shimmering sand dunes, and he could see no one.

"Did we come here on a holiday, or is it always this busy?"

Over by the dome, Asha was examining a round door, and Zahn walked over and touched the light exterior of the stone dome. It was smooth, and he wondered whether it was recently built or was somehow impervious to the elements.

"Oonak, do you know anything about this dome? How old do you think it is?"

"Well, I'm sorry to tell you this, but it's locked, guys." Asha sighed. She had tried turning the handle and even using the resonator on the door, but the stone seemed indestructible.

Oonak had been studying the cyan sky, but walked up to them after a few moments. "Only to those who lack the key."

Oonak removed the small, metallic insignia from the collar of his uniform and pressed it into an indentation beside the door.

To Zahn's surprise, the edges of the door glowed. The glow spread until the entire door was made of light. In an instant, the door vanished, revealing a circular room.

Inside they found seven elevated, horizontal stone platforms spaced evenly around the edge of the room. Somehow, they were lit with natural light even though there were no windows or openings, and Zahn wondered if these people might have discovered a way to make stone that allowed light to pass through, if only slightly.

In the center of the room was a plaque with a message carved into the stone. Zahn walked over to it, but quickly realized that it wasn't written in any language he had ever seen. It was made up of a single curving line which formed various spiraling shapes. Oonak walked up behind him and studied it.

Meanwhile, Asha walked over to one of the raised platforms and felt its cold, hard surface. "I wonder what these are for."

"If I am reading this plaque correctly," Oonak said. "I believe we are intended to meditate on them. The text seems to refer to a 'waking sleep'. I wonder if they're referring to the state of the mind being awake while the body is asleep."

"How can you read that?" Zahn said. "Is that what writing looks like where you're from, Oonak?"

"No, but when the people of my world were first contacted by the Confederation, we were taught a universal written language so that we could interpret any documents that were sent to us. This plaque has been written in that language."

"So does it say anything else?"

"If I'm reading this correctly, once we reach a deep enough meditation we will be assisted in leaving the physical world and meeting the Transcendent Ones." Oonak furrowed his eyebrows. "I'm not sure what they mean by 'assisted'."

"Are you sure we're really on Amithya? How do we know these instructions are safe?"

"Yes. Only a Transcendent World would accept my insignia as a key."

"True, but how do we know this isn't a one-way trip?"

"Zahn, my people have been part of the Confederation for many generations. Trust me when I say they mean us no harm. From what I can tell from this plaque, this room has been specifically designed to guide us into a state where we can easily meet them. It suggests that we mentally count down from ten as this happens."

Asha stared at the plaque with a perplexed look. "Hmm, definitely not Samiiran. Actually, it doesn't look like anything I've seen. I wonder if Dad would know…"

"I suspect," Oonak continued, "that it will be easier to fall asleep here than we could anticipate. Just remember to focus on counting and not get drawn into any dreams that may begin. Also, when we reach the council, allow me to speak first. They have been awaiting my report for some time now, and you would both be wise to afford them the respect they deserve."

"Sure thing, Oonak." Asha sat down on one of the platforms and looked over to Zahn, who was still examining the room. "C'mon, Zahn! Pick a spot. I've got a good feeling about this."

"All right," Zahn said as he sat down on the platform nearest to him. "But if I end up in a nightmare, things could get ugly."

One by one, each of them got into a comfortable position on the stone beds and closed their eyes. Once they did this, the room itself seemed to acknowledge their efforts, and Zahn could have sworn that the light entering the room diminished considerably at that moment.

"10…" As he counted down, he heard music.

"9…" At first, it was so faint that Zahn thought he was imagining it, but after a few seconds, he knew it must be real. "8…" It reminded him of the sound of the flutes back on Aarava, floating through the air like a hundred songbirds in sublime harmony. "7…" For a moment, he saw Ashraya from above, but he knew it was a dream and resumed his counting. "6…"

The music grew more prominent. "5…" He wondered how Asha and Oonak were doing. No, he could not let his mind wander. Focus. "4…" But what did the Confederation mean by saying they would be 'assisted' in meeting them? "3…" He could no longer feel his legs. "2…" Or his arms. He thought about how odd it was to be aware of his body going to sleep, part by part. "1…" The music was sublime. Another dream intruded upon him, but he tried to focus on the music instead. He must not let his mind fall asleep.

"Zero."

Without warning, Zahn felt a tingling sensation all over his body and got the feeling that someone was behind him, though he couldn't see them. The feeling transformed itself into a humming sound that covered his entire body. He thought he should be frightened, but a voice told him that everything was as it should be. He didn't know if the voice was outside of him or inside of him, but he trusted it.

The humming sound soon became a roar and moved up and down his body. First, the roar moved down to the tips of his toes and gradually moved up past his stomach, past his arms, past his neck, to his head. Once it got to the top of his head, it moved back down to his feet again. This time it was moving faster.

The roaring sound was almost deafening now, and he could no longer hear any of the music that had led him here. The sound reminded him of a vast waterfall, and the tingling sensation was so strong that he felt as though he were electrically charged. He'd never felt like this before, and his heart was beating rapidly.

"Stay calm," he told himself. "Everything is going to be all right. I trust Oonak. I trust Oonak. I trust Oonak."

The roaring was back up to his head again, and he became aware of a tugging sensation on his head and neck.

Just when he didn't think the roaring sound could get any louder, it was consumed by perfect silence.

At first, he saw nothing, but after blinking his eyes, the domed ceiling came into focus.

"Oh no, I woke up. I'm sorry guys."

His head bumped the ceiling. He reached his hand out and touched it, but it felt strange to him.

"But if I can touch the ceiling, that means…"

He looked down and realized two facts simultaneously: he was floating in midair, yet he could somehow still see his body on the stone bed below.

"It worked?" Zahn's surprise turned to joy. "I… I'm really outside of my body, aren't I?"

"Please remain calm," a voice behind him said. The voice was incredibly clear, the sweetest voice he had ever heard. "If you overexcite yourself, you could trigger your body's reflexes and undo what we have assisted you in achieving."

Zahn turned around. Behind him was a young girl with violet skin wearing a white robe. She had long black hair that was braided, and upon seeing his face, she bowed slightly.

"Welcome to Amithya," she said. "Behold, the Transcendent World of Awareness."

"Thank you. So are you the one that helped me leave my body? Will I be able to return?"

"I am," she nodded slightly. "And you will. Your body will be asleep for this duration. To reenter your body complex, you need only to focus on moving one of your fingers." The girl paused. "Is this clear to you?"

"Yes."

Around him, Zahn heard some familiar voices.

"Zahn? Is that you?"

It was Asha. She floated over to him and smiled.

"You look… mostly the same!" she laughed.

"Hey, so do you! If I couldn't see through you, I'd say you had conquered gravity itself. Where's Oonak?"

"I am present," said a rising voice from below him.

"Hi, Oon! We did it! This is incredible."

"Indeed. It is an extremely unique experience," Oonak said. "And who is this? What is her name?"

"Here, we have little use for names," the girl said. "Here, we are part of a cohesive whole. Our minds are in unity."

Her voice sounded angelic in its grace.

"Remarkable," Oonak said.

"Now that you are all substantiated, you may come with me to be properly greeted."

The girl passed through the ceiling, leaving them alone near the top of the dome.

They looked at one another.

"Is it safe to go through the ceiling?" Zahn asked. "Is that a thing we do now?"

"It would appear so."

But before they attempted it, the girl returned and held her hand out to Zahn. "Forgive me. I have taken your unique circumstances for granted. Perhaps it will be easier if we remain linked during the short journey up."

Zahn took the girl's hand, and then offered his hand to Asha.

"Thanks for coming back," Asha said to the girl as she took Zahn's hand.

"Where are we headed, Nameless One?" Oonak asked.

"To the Parhelion Hall. We are most grateful that you have made it across the vastness to arrive here intact."

Before Zahn could reply, she pulled all three of them up through the stone dome and through the rocky hill. They were happy to realize that moving through these objects wasn't painful at all. In fact, it was almost pleasant and reminded Zahn of a ticklish feeling.

For some time, they could see nothing. After all, they were travelling through the solid obsidian stone of the hillside, but after a few seconds, the sight of darkness was replaced by the view of a massive triangular door of light. The girl touched the door, and it opened to reveal an expansive hall. The sight of the hall left Zahn feeling breathless, even though he knew, strictly speaking, that he'd left his breath back at the dome. When he looked over to the young girl, he saw that she was smiling warmly toward each of them, and something about the smile gave him an undefinably unique feeling of peace.

The hall was vast, extending taller than the tallest trees he'd seen on Aarava and stretching onward for what looked like forever, but it was difficult to tell because of a white haze that grew more intense with distance. They had arrived at one end of the vast hall where six entities were waiting for them.

Each of these entities was floating in midair, and the way they carried themselves varied greatly from person to person. Some were 'sitting' in midair with their legs crossed while others were holding their legs in various ways. Behind them, massive columns shimmered in a million hues of the rainbow, and a great distance above them a miniature galaxy slowly spun and pulsed with light.

Once the council saw Zahn, Asha, and Oonak, they flew over and welcomed them, tightly embracing each one of them. Zahn was shocked that such an advanced race was so affectionate and was so stunned that he didn't react until the third hug, which was given by an older man with fine wrinkles.

Zahn noticed that, besides the young girl, there were three men and three women in the group, and with each hug, he felt more and more that this place was a fountain of loving energy.

When the welcomes were over, the young girl joined the group, and all seven joined hands and closed their eyes. And then, they spoke as one.

**"We are the Council of Amithya: A Divine Light of the Galactic Sun."**

# CHAPTER 26

# THE GIFTS OF AMITHYA

"We would like to congratulate Oonak for being the first of Sumanas to reach Amithya," the council said.

Before, these individuals had seemed approachable and unintimidating, but now that they were together, Zahn could feel power radiating off of them. Their combined voice was like a hundred rushing rivers, and he thought he saw their eyes glowing from behind their closed eyelids.

"Thank you, Wise Ones," Oonak said as he bowed.

"We have searched your hearts and see that great efforts have been made to make this journey a success and for that we are proud. Whenever a child of the Confederation begins to walk, we are proud. We also see a residual energy that indicates your ship has been damaged by the Vakragha, and we are grateful that, despite your ship's damage, you have reached us. Oonak, you have been out of contact for some time. What is the current status of your mission?"

Zahn looked over to Oonak in surprise and said nothing.

"Council, it is an honor to at last be in your immediate presence. Unfortunately, I bring disturbing news. If you are certain that the damage was inflicted by the Vakragha, then their Dominion is growing even faster than we had anticipated. The damage to Navika occurred in the Kuvela system, deep within the fourth band of the western spiral arm."

"What can you tell us of the attack?"

"Navika has specific data about the attack that you may find useful, as well as data on the current spread of the Dominion. However, I am sorry to report that I was not able to see them with my own eyes nor gather much data about their vessel."

"Do not be sorry to report the truth, Oonak. Continue."

As they spoke, the sound of their voices harmonized in strange and beautiful ways.

"As you can probably tell, a fragment of my ship was sliced off while I was in orbit above Avani."

"Why were you in orbit around a hatchling world? Yours was a survey mission that did not require any interaction beyond long range scans."

Oonak's face tightened slightly.

"Sumanas High Command thought that, in addition to the Confederation mission, it would be wise to survey worlds within a certain distance from my course, provided a strict cloaking protocol be implemented at all times. We never intended to interfere with such worlds."

"And yet you have. Zahn is living proof of this fact. We are disappointed at your interference on Zahn's world. Even though you took precautions to prevent any contamination, such precautions are not a guarantee, as you have learned. The introduction of foreign technology, such as yours, would have been damaging to Avani's natural development. However, you have retrieved the fragment, and for this we are grateful. Is there anything further you wish to report about the attack?"

"Yes. At first, I thought that the vessel might have the ability to move even faster than Navika, but now I see that the evidence in Navika's logs better supports my hypothesis that the Vakragha have a cloaking mechanism that is nearly perfect—one that allows them to attack while under cloak."

"Thank you for this information, Oonak. We will consider it and notify all Confederation worlds that the Vakragha influence has now spread to the Kuvela system. We will also repair your timespace components and recalibrate your cloaking cells so that you may make the trek home in much safer conditions. We now wish to speak to the one known as Asha."

Slowly, Asha moved forward. All seven of them glowed in each of the seven colors of the rainbow now.

"Yes?"

"What are your intentions? Why did you take the risk in accompanying these spacefarers?"

"Council, my father's outpost was attacked while I was assisting Oonak with repairs to his ship. There was no time to return to my home before my father was forced to activate lockdown. We barely escaped with our lives."

"Indeed, we see into your heart. This has been more difficult for you than you feel you can show to the others, hasn't it?"

"If you're asking me if I miss my father, then the answer is yes. But when we were separated, my father told me to align my heart with my mind and I would be unstoppable. I now know with every fiber of my being that helping Oonak and Zahn is the right thing to do."

"Indeed, the Stewards of the Portal tell us that you were the one who solved their riddle. The portals are the only way to reach our world, so you have been of great service to your friends."

Zahn whispered to Oonak. "I told you it was a riddle."

"Shh," Oonak said.

"Well, I calmed my mind, and it came to me."

"We see that your intuitive potential is powerful, Asha. Yet it has not been properly cultivated during your time on the outpost. We must ask, have you considered healing living beings instead of repairing non-living machines? Does this interest you?"

"Back on the outpost I sometimes counseled pilots who had been traumatized in marauder attacks. They told me that talking with me helped them feel better. Do you mean something along those lines?"

"That, and more. You have the healing potential, and with this potential we could teach you how to bring life to the dying. Are you interested in this?"

"Yes! Yes, I am."

Three other figures appeared out of the mist. Each were wearing green robes, and they looked ageless.

"We are pleased to hear this. Follow these healers and they will help you along your path."

"Oonak, can I meet you back at the dome?"

He smiled and then nodded.

There was a hush upon the room, so Zahn simply waved to Asha as she left. She waved back as she followed the three robed figures, vanishing into the mist.

There was a brief silence, and the council spoke again.

"We now wish to speak to the one known as Zahn."

With some hesitation, Zahn moved forward. He wondered how much they could really see. Could they actually see the past or just what was in someone's memories?

"As we have said, we can plainly see into your heart and we understand your pain. Your guides have informed us that your world was breached, and the free will of many you love was severely violated. We see the pain that you have felt and continue to feel over the loss of your mother."

"My guides? Do you mean like spirit guardians? My mother believed each person got two guardians when they were born, and it always felt true to me. So, it is true?"

"Yes. All beings of your density are assigned at least two guides for each life cycle, and sometimes additional guides are assigned for shorter durations."

"What can you tell me about my guides?"

There was a moment of silence.

"Your guides have decided not to reveal themselves to you at this time. They feel that you are not quite ready to remove the veil that has been purposely raised between your kind and their realm. However, they wish to relate that they can always hear you when you speak to them, be it inwardly or outwardly. Indeed, they are quite powerful and have already been instrumental in the events which led you here."

"Really? What did they do?"

"They are not permitted to say, as such information would violate your free will. However, we do sense another more pressing question within your mind."

"Yes, there is a question. A question that I've carried for many years." Zahn breathed in deeply. "Is my mother really dead? Her name is Darshana. She was a beacon of kindness and brilliance on my world, and she went missing twelve years ago. Is there any hope that she's still alive?"

"What does your heart say?"

"For a long time, I wasn't sure. I was beginning to wonder if the only reason I was holding onto hope was because it was easier. But now that I'm here, the situation is somehow clearer. Honestly, I've always felt that she is alive, even if I never had any evidence for it."

"We are pleased you have reached a level of clarity, as clarity is most advantageous in reducing suffering. We may be able to help you. Do you have anything that your mother owned or came into repeated contact with? We could tell you more if we had an object to focus onto."

Zahn considered this, but felt frustrated when he couldn't think of anything he had that his mother had owned. Nothing in his backpack was his mother's, and all he had in his pocket was...

The lens!

In a flash, he reached deep into his pocket for the small lens. Yet to his surprise, he discovered that none of his pockets had anything in them. He looked down to his pants and noticed that his legs were still partially transparent.

"Oh, that's right. I'm not really here."

"What do you mean?" the council said. "You are indeed here. All that comprises of your true identity is here, in this place."

"I mean my body. I brought a lens. It's in my pocket back with my body. Can you tune into that?"

Abruptly, the council vocalized a single note. The note changed until it sounded like seven distinct tones, and just as abruptly as they began, they ceased chanting.

"This object is a small disc?" they asked.

"Basically, yeah. It's a small, colorless lens."

"One moment."

The Wise Ones huddled together, and Zahn thought he noticed them growing brighter than before. Then he was sure of it. There was a light forming in their midst which soon spread to all of the walls. Tiny pathways of light lit up all around them, and then there was a flash.

They turned toward him again.

"Your mother is alive, but only faintly."

"Really?! Are you sure? How? Where?"

"Calm yourself, Zahn," Oonak said. "If you become too excited, you might trigger your body into waking up and disappear from this place."

"Calm down? Calm *down*?! My mother is alive. How can I remain calm?"

Oonak put his hand on Zahn's shoulder.

"By telling yourself to, because you have to. Do you want to leave the council before we find out where your mother is? Breathe deeply."

Zahn breathed deeply.

"But this isn't real air. It's just—"

"Shh! Be calm. Breathe."

"Okay." Zahn took another breath. "Okay. I'm calm. I'm on the beach. There might even be birds. Now, where is my mother?"

"Under most circumstances, Universal Law would not permit we of the council to reveal an entity's location without that entity's consent. However, given the unique circumstances, we will permit this information to be related."

"Good. Where is she?"

"She is being held within the Nirananda Nebula, on the edge of the Vakragha Dominion. We have relayed this information to your ship. However, we must also warn you that the Vakragha often reduce their prisoners to a delirious state by absorbing their vital energy. Even though she may yet live, her condition is unknown. She may never be fully conscious again. If you find her, you must be prepared for this."

"Thank you for the information…" Zahn tried to be grateful for their help but felt a sinking feeling in his stomach.

"Council," Oonak began. "Is there any way you can assist us in helping Zahn's mother? If she is alive, then other captured Avanians may also be alive with her. Is there anything you can do to assist us?"

Zahn looked at Oonak in surprise.

"You're volunteering to help me? But you've come so far. Don't you want to return to your home? I'm sure the council has someone else that could help me. Don't feel obligated, Oon."

"On the contrary, Zahn. I would like to repay you for your patience and your kindness. You never had to join me on my quest, but by doing so you've made success possible. We will rescue your mother together."

"If you desire," the council continued, "there is a creature called a jagrul that you may take with you. Although you may perceive it as an animal, it is only partially in-phase with your reality. It is a rare organism, capable of seeing hidden truths. If you give it Darshana's lens, it will perceive her location. However, it must be cared for, and you must return it when you have finished your quest. It is important that it not fall into the wrong hands. Do you understand?"

"Yes!" Zahn said.

But he had not stayed calm.

This time, Oonak didn't reach Zahn in time to help keep him anchored, and he vanished from the room. In a few moments, he would wake up back in the dome room.

"I apologize for Zahn. He has not been trained in the art of controlling his emotions. Although, I will say he seems uniquely aware for someone from a hatchling world. He helped Asha and I come to our senses when we were submerged in a dream world on Aarava."

"Yes. His guides have shared this with us. Indeed, he is growing along his path quite well, and in much the same way Zahn is learning balance, you ought to be mindful of extremes, as well. Avoid relying solely on reason, Oonak. Remember to trust your heart. For maximum growth, you must cultivate inner balance between these two sides."

"I will remember. Is there anything else I need to know?"

"Yes. Be wary of using the ancient gate system. Indeed, with your repaired timespace drive, the ancient gates will no longer be necessary. Yet we feel it important to relate that these gates were made far before even the Transcendent Worlds came into being. Because of their fantastic age, some gates are not functioning properly, and many are dangerous."

"Indeed, we have already been ambushed while using them."

"Be also mindful not to underestimate the cleverness and speed of the Vakragha. They are without mercy or honor, and to survive against them you must anticipate their thoughts before they act. Avoid direct conflict whenever possible and continue to gather as much information as you can. Sumanas is not alone in this fight, and you have many galactic brothers and sisters that you will meet in the future."

"Yes, you have told us that each great civilization of this galaxy has a sibling world. A world that shares its heritage in the galactic family. Did we understand your meaning correctly?"

"You grasp correctly."

"Then I must ask. Council, since I have come so far, have I not proven my world's worthiness so that we may learn of the sibling world to Sumanas? What is its name?"

"Search your heart. You know the answer."

"Avani?"

"You have known it intuitively since you first set foot onto its silvery sands."

"But it is only a hatchling world. Zahn is the only Avanian on record who has ever left his star system."

"There is much you shall learn. There was once a time when your worlds behaved as brothers, and we see that a Great Reunion may yet occur. But Avani is under great threat, Oonak.

We have sensed the corruption of space around the Kuvela system, and all reconnaissance missions have failed to return."

"What must I do?"

"Contact the council when you have ascertained the fate of Darshana, and we will provide further instructions. Until then, all must be vigilant. If you are successful, there may yet be a Great Reunion in the Stars. Even this council is but a fragment of a Greater Council that was ruptured long ago. Indeed, all is temporary in this galaxy. Even separation."

"Thank you, Council."

"In closing, we are exceedingly proud of you and your world. Your people have made an admirable first step, and you may exit our world by the same method you arrived. We have already configured the portal to send you to a point just beyond the edge of the nebula. This will allow maximum safety for your approach. Do you understand all that we have said here?"

"Yes, I do."

"Then we have no doubt that we will be seeing you in the future. Remember, we will be there helping you in hidden ways, though you will not be able to perceive us. We leave you now in the Truth of the Infinite Creator. We are of Amithya."

Oonak felt pulled back to his body. In an instant, it felt as though he had covered a great distance, and soon the light of the dome was filtering through his eyelids once more.

He took a deep breath, and his body felt fresh.

"There you are! I'm sorry I woke myself up, Oon," Zahn said. "It's hard to remain calm when I know that my mother is alive. Can you believe it? It's incredible! All those times up on Zikhara Peak, my intuition really was right. She had been taken, and I'm the only person from Avani who knows."

"And now we are going to find her, Zahn."

"She's alive?" Asha's face lit up. "That's wonderful, Zahn! From what you told me, it seemed like your mind was doubtful, but your heart knew she was alive all along, didn't it? Don't you see? If you trust it, the heart knows."

"I guess you're right. I guess sometimes the heart is a lot smarter than the brain." Zahn smiled. "But I've got to ask, and I don't mean to put a lot of pressure on you, but do you think you'll be able to do anything for her when we find her? If we find her."

"We *will* find her, Zahn. I won't deny that I still have a long way to go, but I have learned some fundamental techniques from them. Whatever condition we find her in, I will do everything I can to help strengthen her. You have my word."

"Thanks, Asha. That means a lot to me. And Oonak, I don't think I have any words for how grateful I am for your offer to help me... I don't know what I'd do without you and Asha."

"Zahn," Oonak said, "without you I would most likely still be stranded back on Avani."

The dome room seemed brighter than before, and Zahn blinked a few times to make sure his eyes weren't playing tricks on him. His head felt bright and filled with energy, and when his feet touched solid ground once more, his body seemed like unnecessary weight compared to the experience of weightlessness he'd just emerged from.

At the end of each of their stone beds, there were now transparent cups that contained a golden liquid. Zahn lifted his cup. It smelled sweet and fresh.

"What do you think this is, Oon?" Asha wondered.

Oonak examined the liquid.

"Could it be? Have they really given us amrita?"

"What's that?" Zahn said.

"In our communication with the Transcendent Worlds, we learned of a golden drink that contained more vital energy than any other known substance. They called it amrita. The council must have given some to us to speed us along in our journey. We are truly blessed. Be sure to give thanks before you drink it. Gratitude itself is said to increase its effectiveness."

Zahn closed his eyes and thanked the Amithyans, intending that they would be as blessed as much as they had blessed him and his friends, and drank the golden liquid. Asha and Oonak did the same, and when it reached their bellies they felt as if their entire stomachs had been wrapped in a blanket of love. This feeling spread to their entire body. Within minutes, they felt energized and more vibrant than they had felt in a long time.

When they were back outside, Zahn realized why the dome room had seemed brighter. While they had been inside, the sky had brightened considerably.

Oonak walked over to the shimmering starship.

"Navika, have they completed repairs on the timespace drive? How do you feel?"

"I have truly never been better," Navika replied, "and the jagrul creature is waiting inside. It appears to be hungry."

"The what?" Asha said, catching up to them.

"Don't worry, Asha. We'll explain it all on the way to the portal. What's important is that my mother is alive, and there is no power in this galaxy that will stop me from rescuing her now."

# CHAPTER 27

## AN ODD LITTLE CREATURE

On their way down the wide tunnel to the portal, Zahn told Asha all that had happened while she was with the healers.

Oddly enough, the wide tunnel was now empty of water. It wasn't until the iris at the bottom opened that a stream of water sprayed out and filled the tunnel. As they descended, the jagrul landed on Asha's shoulder, nibbled her ear, and then nuzzled up against her neck.

The jagrul was quite an odd little creature. The council had not mentioned how remarkably similar it was to a small bird. It could even fly, and its green-blue plumage reminded Zahn of the murmur birds back on Avani, except that it had voluminous eyes containing large black pupils. The effect was slightly unsettling, but Asha couldn't keep her hands off of it.

Ahead, Zahn saw that the portal was now shining brightly.

"The council has configured this portal to send us just beyond the edge of the Nirananda Nebula where Zahn's mother has been detected. Prepare yourselves."

Like a fish going down the drain, Navika tumbled into the already spinning vortex, transforming everything in their vision into perfect light.

Zahn wasn't surprised to see a reversal of what he had experienced when they had first used the portal to reach Amithya. He saw the light resolve itself into a radiant sphere and then race away until it became a single point of light in an absolute void. Soon, even the single point of light disappeared, and for a moment he felt as though they might be the only three people left in the galaxy.

Then, the joy rushed over him once more.

The perfect darkness transformed itself into perfect light, and a feeling of joy and profound happiness overtook him. It seemed as though the entire ship was suspended in nothing but pure light. For a moment, he felt as though he was connected to every beating heart in the galaxy, and the feeling was indescribable. It simply overwhelmed him, and everything around him fell away.

When he regained consciousness, he found himself looking out onto a vast array of stars once more. He took a deep breath and looked over to Asha who was looking at him inquisitively.

"Are you all right?" she said.

"Did you feel that? That feeling of connectedness? It happened last time we went through one of those portals, too."

"Yes…" Asha said. "What do you think it means?"

"I don't know. Oon?"

Zahn looked behind him, up to where Oonak was sitting. He seemed focused on something, but after a few seconds he looked down to them.

"Are you both okay?" Oonak said.

"I think so. Just stunned," Zahn said. "What was that feeling of joy as we went through the portal? It happened the first time, too, but it never happened when we used the gate network. Do you have any idea why?"

Oonak paused to consider this.

"I do not know. However, I would hypothesize that whatever portal system the Transcendent Worlds use, it is far more advanced than the ancient gate system."

"How so?"

"I'm sorry. I am not able to provide further information. However, I do have good news. We have arrived near the edge of the Nirananda Nebula, just as the council predicted."

"Why can't I see it?" Zahn said.

"It is a dark nebula. You will see its outline against the stars soon enough."

Asha put out her hand to the jagrul which was now walking around the cabin. It scampered around a bit before circling back to her and sniffing her hand absentmindedly.

"So, how do we use this little guy?"

"You mean the jagrul? That's a good question," Zahn said. "Oon, do you think it's enough to just show the lens to it?"

"I would place the lens beside it and observe its behavior."

Zahn scooted over to make room between him and Asha, reached into his pocket, and set the lens on the seat between them. Asha reached out her finger for the jagrul to step onto. It did, and she moved her hand down to the small lens lying on the seat. Once her finger was near it, the jagrul jumped off her finger and smelled it.

"This was my mother's," Zahn said. "Where is she now?"

The jagrul whistled quietly, walked around the lens, and chirped repeatedly.

"What's it doing?"

"As I mentioned before," Navika said, "while I don't have prior experience with this life form, I hypothesize that it is hungry."

"How do you know?" Asha said.

"All passengers are scanned upon entering, and I observed that this creature's stomach, although rather exotic, is nonetheless quite empty."

"Look under the seat," Oonak said. "Some emergency rations are kept there, including some seeds from Sumanas."

Asha soon found them in a thin packet and emptied them out onto the floor. Within moments the jagrul had eaten them up. When it was done, it flew back up to the bench and examined the lens once more.

Strangely, it opened its mouth and stood perfectly still.

For some time, Asha and Zahn couldn't figure out what it was doing. At first, Zahn wondered if it might be hungry again, but when he looked back at the view ahead of them, he noticed a green point that was marking a dark area of space ahead.

"Why is Navika indicating the nebula with a marker?"

"He is not," Oonak said.

Zahn looked back at the small jagrul. It hadn't moved at all. Its mouth was still open, and Zahn moved his hand in front of its mouth. Sure enough, the green point shined onto the palm of his hand, and when he removed his hand, the green marker shone once again onto a spot within the dark nebula ahead.

"Oonak, follow that point of light. My mother has waited to be rescued for long enough."

# CHAPTER 28

## THE STOLEN MOON

As they slipped into the Nirananda Nebula, they occasionally saw the twinkle of a star peek through, but because it was so dark, it was difficult to discern the nebula's true size.

On the way inside, Oonak was careful to minimize any chances of them being detected. All weapons were cooled down, and the cloaking cells were working at near peak efficiency ever since the council had repaired them back on Amithya.

After a few minutes, they exited the other side of a dark patch of dust and saw a slightly bluish star up ahead. To Zahn's delight, the jagrul's green marker was just beside it.

"Navika has detected six planets in the system that the jagrul has indicated. Several of them have moons," Oonak said.

An alarm rang throughout the ship.

"We're being hit with an intense radiation pulse which is disrupting the cloak," Oonak announced. "The radiation is emanating from the star up ahead."

"Don't all stars emit radiation?"

"We've just been hit by another pulse. This is not an ordinary star, Zahn. It's a pulsar. A slow-phase pulsar, but still powerful. Such high-intensity energy pulses coming every few seconds is overloading the cloaking cells, causing some energy to leak back out into space, which means our cloak is severely compromised. We need to find cover from these pulses as soon as possible."

The jagrul was still projecting a small green marker onto Navika's transparent wall. Zahn noticed that it indicated the crescent shape of a moon.

"A moon? The jagrul says our destination is a moon."

"Yes, the moon of Hataaza Darad," Oonak said. "However we must seek cover before—Wait."

Something on Zahn's left caught his eye. It was a jagged black shape, so dark that light itself seemed to fall into it. In moments, it blocked their entire view of the port side of the ship, and Zahn had trouble discerning its true size. Occasionally, it would disappear completely for a moment, only to reappear in the same spot, and he guessed that the pulsar was disrupting its cloak just as it was disrupting Navika's.

He didn't have much time to think about this, because only a few seconds later three dark vortexes appeared in front of them.

"Zahn, under your seat is a mindcap. It will read your thoughts. Put it on and use it to direct Navika's fire while I maneuver the ship."

Zahn fumbled around and put on the cap which was made of a thin cloth covered in a mesh of thin, bright fibers. It fit him surprisingly well.

Outside, more vortexes were forming around the ship.

"Okay, but how do I aim?" Zahn said.

Oonak sent the ship diving down, perpendicular to the star to avoid impacting the vortexes ahead. Even though he couldn't actually feel the ship turn sharply, the sight still made Zahn feel space-sick for a moment.

"Just see the beam going where you want it to go. The battle grid will help guide you, and the cap will interpret your thoughts. I need you to help fight them off until we can find cover."

"What do I do?" Asha said.

"I'm sorry, but I only have one extra mindcap. In this situation, you are a better asset to the mission if you leverage your healing abilities. Did the Amithyans teach you how to reinforce someone's energy field?"

"Yes."

"Then keep your focus on Zahn. He has never done this before. He'll need it."

Outside, another loathsome shadow appeared ahead of them, and five more vortexes were forming around the ship. Once Zahn had put on the mindcap, a red grid appeared all around him, and wherever he looked, a corresponding red square flickered. He imagined Navika's twin plasma cannons firing at the closest shadow, and almost like magic, two painfully bright bolts of white plasma converged from either side of the ship and impacted onto the shield of one of the shadowed ships. He marveled at how quickly his thoughts became reality.

Zahn thought he could see the outline of the ship, a haunting shape that froze his thinking for a moment.

"Keep firing, Zahn! We're almost in the moon's shadow."

As Oonak maneuvered, Zahn felt disoriented as the stars streaked across his vision, yet the red grid remained oriented on their foes, making it somewhat easier to keep his aim. He also felt Asha's support.

The mindcap made Zahn's thoughts seem sharper and more solid somehow. He fired on where he guessed the first craft was and then back at the second. Oonak had to maneuver wildly to keep from being pulled into the gravity wells that were multiplying around the ship. Ahead, Zahn saw that they were heading straight toward one.

Oonak accelerated and narrowly missed the edge of the vortex, and the two shadows pulled far ahead of them.

"Are they retreating?" Zahn said.

"Unknown. Stay focused."

Once they were a certain distance away, both ships held position ahead of them, and Zahn took that opportunity to fire on them both. As he did, plasma bolts impacted onto their hulls.

But it was too easy. Why weren't they moving?

Zahn continued firing, theoretically doing more damage to their ships. Exactly how much, he was unsure because they were so completely dark. For a spilt second between pulsar pulses, they disappeared once more, and Zahn caught a glimpse of what they were in front of.

They weren't creating a blockade, they were in front of an enormous vortex that was forming right behind them.

Both of them fired piercingly green beams into the vortex, causing it to grow at an alarming pace.

The circular disc of the moon was now clearly visible ahead as four more massive shadows approached them from behind.

"Oonak, do you see that? That's the largest vortex I've seen them make yet."

"And four more are approaching behind us," Asha said.

"What do we do?"

"Improvise." Oonak abruptly sent the ship racing upwards. Zahn realized that there was no 'up' in space, but relative to the cabin, he perceived their course as heading upward.

"Brace yourselves. We're going to make a hyper-local timespace jump."

"What does that mean?" Asha said.

Before he could answer, the space around the ship became stretched and unreal, as if a child had painted the scene in watercolor and left it out in the rain.

The interior of the ship roared, and Zahn watched as the moon below slowly faded away. They weren't flying away. It was simply dematerializing.

"Oonak, what's happening?"

"As we accelerate," Oonak said over the growing roar, "it may appear that everything is dematerializing around us, but in truth, *we* are what is dematerializing."

"Isn't that bad?!" Zahn yelled over the roar.

"No!" Oonak yelled. "Don't worry. As we phase out of spacetime, we phase into timespace."

Although they couldn't feel it, Asha and Zahn guessed that the ship was accelerating to fantastic speeds. Unfortunately, it didn't seem fast enough. Four of the Vakragha ships were growing closer.

Zahn looked back at Oonak and noticed that his eyes were once again closed. He was smiling, and although no one could see it, bright flecks of light raced within Navika's nucleus at a frenzied pace.

As if they were a bad dream fading away, the four ships and everything around them faded to darkness as a narrow vortex formed in front of the ship. As it formed, Zahn felt as though the vortex was somehow inside of his own mind, as well.

In a flash, Zahn caught a glimpse of a blinding corridor of pure light. An instant later, there was another flash as they reentered the Ocean of Space, and the roar of the ship gradually returned to a hum.

Below them was the night side of a large, barren moon.

"Whew, that was close." Zahn looked around. "We're still in the nebula?"

"Yes," Oonak said. "We have jumped to the dark side of one of the nearby moons. The prison moon that we seek is on the other side of this planetary system. Thankfully though, here we are shielded from the pulsar's radiation so our cloaking cells will work properly."

Asha and Zahn breathed a collective sigh of relief.

"So that was the timespace drive in action? Kind of takes the idea of a shortcut to a whole new level. Why didn't you do that sooner?" Asha said.

"The timespace drive needs time to calibrate. Once ready, the ship needs to reach a certain relative velocity to dematerialize."

Zahn looked down to the dark surface of the moon.

"I'm just glad we got out of that alive. Those ships weren't just dark. They completely absorbed all light that touched them. Do all Vakragha ships look like that?"

"Navika and I have only come into contact with a few, but all of them followed that pattern, yes."

"So what do we do? If we can't fly to our destination from here because the Vakragha ships will suck us into oblivion, how are we going to get to where my mother is?"

"What about the gate system?" Asha said. "Is it possible that there's a gate down on the moon that we could use?"

"Not just possible, it's provable," Oonak said. "Navika has already detected a gate on the surface below, and no life signs are present. We are about to begin our descent."

As Zahn removed the mindcap and slowly folded it up, Asha sensed his anxiety and looked over to him.

"Don't worry, Zahn. If she's survived out here this long, it means that she has been holding on, and if she's been holding on, it means she still has the will to live." Asha paused for a moment. "No matter how good of a healer I could ever become, I could never give someone that. It's a choice only they can make."

Zahn looked over and considered her words. He thought about how things could be different after he returned home. *Would she ever consider living on Avani? Was it worth asking?*

Below, the moon became larger.

The surface of the moon was barren and rusty with a peppering of small, eroded mountains. Once they were near the ground, Oonak surveyed the area that the gate's gravity signature was emanating from, finding a small cave leading into the side of one of the mountains. They followed it down a few hundred meters, blasted through part of a collapsed tunnel, and followed it into a large, dark cavern.

Upon illuminating the space, they found that the gate was covered in debris and dust. It looked as though it hadn't been touched in millennia.

When Oonak set the ship down beside the gate and told Zahn and Asha to put spacesuits on, Zahn was confused.

"Aren't we going to fly in?"

"No. We have no way of knowing the full reality of the situation on the other side. For all we know, it leads to a narrow passage, in which case Navika would have no way to maneuver without attracting the attention of every creature within 100 klicks of the gate. Even worse, that gate may lead to the daytime side of the moon, exposing us to the pulsar and causing our cloaking cells to become useless. If that were to happen, we would have to face the Hataazans directly."

"Who?" Zahn asked.

"On the other side of that gate is Hataaza Darad, a world completely controlled by the Vakragha Dominion. The Hataazans are their tortured slaves, massive and vicious. Some even claim that the Vakragha created them. We must be vigilant. I have placed each of your resonators in your suits' holsters. They do not fit perfectly, but they are adequate for now."

"Thanks." Asha patted her holster. "Much better than pockets, that's for sure."

"We'll be fine," Zahn said.

After doing a quick check to confirm that they could hear each other through their suits' comms, they headed outside where their suits quickly confirmed that the air was far from breathable. The place was so dusty that Zahn wouldn't want to breathe the air even if he could. Every time they moved, they kicked up a small cloud of reddish dust which stuck to their boots.

"Oon, I just realized something, " Zahn said as he stared at the gate's lifeless controls.

"What is it, Zahn?"

"Well, how are we going to get this gate to work? After all, you said that these gates are tuned for their inhabitants, and none of us were born on this moon. We don't even know what kind of life might have lived here."

"None of us are tuned to activate this gate. I've already tried each of our patterns, so I've instructed Navika to broadcast every DNA pattern in his memory to it. He has been transmitting codes to the gate since we landed, so I'm sure—"

As Asha examined it, the console flared to life, and the flash startled her for a moment.

"There!" Asha said. "That wasn't so hard, was it?"

"But Oon," Zahn said, "why didn't you do that when you crashed on Avani? Why ask for my help?"

"Have you so quickly forgotten? The gate would not respond to me, no matter what I tried."

"So what DNA worked just now?" Zahn said.

Oonak looked up, as though he were trying to remember something, but by now Zahn knew that was the face he made when Navika was telling him something through his mental link. While he watched Oonak, he heard a ringing in his right ear, but since he was wearing a space suit he couldn't do much about it.

"Taarakani DNA?" Oonak said. "That cannot be true…"

Asha walked up to them, carrying the jagrul in a colorless, airtight sphere. "Why? Where is Taarakani?"

"The Taarakani are a race of people who live on the world of Taarakalis. It appears someone has taken this moon from that system, roughly 16,000 light-years from this nebula."

"But why steal an entire moon?" Zahn said.

"Because that is how the Vakragha Dominion grows its power. They have worked this way for millennia, corrupting the natural order of the galaxy."

Asha's eyes widened. "They stole an entire world from its cradle? That's insane…"

"Now you see why it is crucial that they be stopped, at all costs. Does everyone have their cloaking fields integrated?"

One by one, they tested the cloaking devices that Yantrik had given them. Asha had integrated them into their suits' systems so that Zahn only needed to make three quiet clicking noises with his teeth and the cloaking field would be activated or deactivated.

Luckily, there was only one other moon indicated on the gate's console, which made deducing their destination much simpler. Oonak chose the appropriate symbol on the console, the vortex opened up, and they walked through, one by one, directly into the unknown.

Walking through a gate was similar to flying through one, except that Zahn felt rather nauseous afterwards. Yet his discomfort was soon forgotten once he saw what was on the other side.

To everyone's surprise, the gate on the other end wasn't being guarded at all. The cavern was dark, and their suits detected no movement. Even so, they kept their suit lights off and quietly headed over to an opening where light filtered in.

When they reached the opening, they realized that they had just emerged from the inside of a mountain. The surface of the moon was utterly tortured and dry, and rusty rock formations towered high above them. In the brown hazy sky, Zahn could see the tiny disk of the pulsar, and in the distance he saw that the mountain they had just emerged from was part of a severely eroded mountain range that continued down to the horizon.

Zahn turned around and was alarmed to see Asha and Oonak completely clearly for a fraction of a second.

"Oonak! Our cloaking fields are flickering. I think they may be damaged."

Oonak looked up at the sky in disappointment.

"No, Zahn. The pulsar is the cause. I'm sorry. As I predicted, we will not be safe in the daylight. As long as it is daytime, the pulsar will be raining radiation down upon us every few seconds. This also may explain why the landscape is so tortured."

"So what do we do?" Zahn said.

"We find your mother as fast as we can and try not to die. Follow me!" Asha ran ahead with the jagrul under her arm.

They followed her, and soon they were running along a narrow path that was carved into the side of the mountain. The gravity was weaker here, so they made longer leaps as they ran. Above them, the sky grew orange, and around them huge boulders and crumbled rock filled the landscape.

The jagrul continued to project a beam of light toward Darshana's energy signature but in infrared light so they could be as covert as possible. Since their suits' visors could easily see this light, the system worked well.

After a few minutes, they came to a fork in the rocky path, followed the jagrul's waypoint up and to the right, and came to a spiral ramp that led up, into a tunnel. Out of the corner of Zahn's eye, he thought he saw a large figure lumbering around at the bottom of the mountain, but when he looked back, he saw nothing. For a moment, he wondered how much this day was affecting his sanity.

At the end of a short tunnel, they found a long, rusty cavern which stretched down hundreds of meters. Zahn noticed that the jagrul was indicating toward the far end of the room. He was thankful for the light filtering down from above, but he didn't like what he saw.

Along the wall, embedded into the rock itself, were hundreds of bodies.

# CHAPTER 29

## ESCAPING HATAAZA DARAD

Frantically, Zahn ran up to the wall and searched for his mother. There were people of all colors, all shapes, and all sizes. They appeared to be from all over the galaxy, but most of them looked dead or near death. Why bring them all here?

Zahn ran, despite the fact that he knew he should be quiet. He ran past hundreds of people. *Where was she?* He kept running. *She had to be here. She had to.*

The mad dash seemed never-ending, until something made him stop in his tracks.

It wasn't his mother.

Kneeling on the ground in front of one of the bodies was a massive figure, clothed in cold, grey armor. When it turned around, his first instinct was to run as fast as he could, but he controlled himself. Zahn knew that there was no way that the Hataazan could see him now that he was inside the cavern and shielded from the pulsar's radiation. At least, that's what Oonak had said.

Now that it had turned around and was standing tall, Zahn realized it was nearly twice his height. Its face was grotesque with tiny pupils and huge, curling lips which revealed blood-stained teeth. It growled and moved toward him.

Zahn wondered if he should doubt the reliability of the cloaking field for a moment and slowly stepped aside to see if the beast would react. It didn't. Instead, it growled past him and kept heading down the cavern, and Zahn breathed a sigh of great relief. He didn't want to face one of those in combat, even with his resonator.

Curious, he walked over to where it had been and examined the floor. The creature had been standing in front of what appeared to be an old man. The man was completely naked, embedded solidly into the rusty wall. Beside him, protruding from the wall, was a narrow tube with a few drops of red liquid inside of it. Zahn noticed that there were some red drops on the ground as well.

Terrified at what his mother must have been going through during her years of captivity, he continued his frantic search, and just behind him he caught a glimpse of Asha and Oonak. They were straining to keep up with him.

He ran again. He could sense her near now and ran faster than he ever had before. Soon, he felt as though he had seen a thousand faces, and outside of the cavern, he heard the howl of a sinister wind. He was nearly out of breath now.

And then, at the end of the cavern, he saw her.

He ran over and examined her body. Over her mouth was an air mask connected to a small tube that led into the wall. She was quite frail, and her light brown hair was very short.

Here was his mother at last. Here was Darshana.

He felt her pulse. She was alive, but only barely. Oonak rushed over with his scanner, and Asha was right behind him.

"She is stable, but extremely weak," Oonak said. "Asha, do you have the air mask ready?"

Asha carefully removed the air mask that was over Darshana's mouth and placed their air mask over her mouth instead. As she did this, Oonak held his resonator close to the rocky wall where it met her arm, the resonator making a high pitched hum as he squeezed the trigger.

After a few seconds, some rock broke away, and he continued doing this systematically around her entire body. But Zahn felt overwhelmed. After so many years, finally seeing his mother again filled him with a storm of different emotions, but he knew that she wasn't truly rescued until they got her out alive.

Along the other side of her body, he used his resonator to help Oonak loosen the rock around her flesh. As they did this, Asha injected a green liquid into her arm and uttered strange words that Zahn had never heard before. At first, Zahn felt alarmed, but Asha explained that the council had taught her what to do at this moment. He didn't question her again, and instead of panicking, Zahn asked his guides for help.

When the last of the stone was loosed from her body, she tumbled forward out of the rocky alcove. Zahn was in front of her when she fell and caught her in his arms. She felt as limp as a dead fish, and he struggled to hold back tears.

"It's all right, Mom. I've got you now. I've got you now."

Zahn made sure the air mask was fastened around her mouth securely and carried her toward the exit.

Far below them, they felt the ground shake violently.

"We need to leave here as soon as possible," Oonak said over the comm.

Outside, they noticed that it was dusk, and smoke was oozing from the top of the mountain. They weren't on a mountain at all. For the first time, Zahn realized the full gravity of the situation: they had been inside of an active volcano.

In a mad dash, they raced back down the path. As they ran, Zahn noticed that the pulsar was dipping below the horizon, and this gave him some hope. At least it wouldn't disrupt their cloak anymore. Finally, they'd be able to walk around outside without being seen.

When they reached the gate cavern again, Zahn made a quick glance around the corner and noticed two important details had changed. The cavern was now faintly illuminated by crystals along the ceiling, and three of the massive beasts, the same type that he'd had seen earlier, were now standing around the gate.

"Zahn!" Oonak yelled. "You're visible. Move!" Oonak pulled him out of the way of the opening.

"What?" Zahn said. "I thought the pulsar set below the horizon. It's night now. We should be okay, right?"

"It's not that, Zahn," Asha said. "I think cloaking both you and your mother is putting a strain on your cloaking chip."

"Well, I haven't come this far to be stopped now. Don't worry. I'll be more careful."

"No. Take mine," Oonak said. "You need it more than I."

"No, Oonak. I'm not letting you sacrifice your safety for mine. I'll be fine. We just need to cause a diversion."

The ground shook violently again, and their suits indicated that a wave of hot air was passing over them.

"There's no time to argue, Zahn. The volcano is unstable, a fact that we can use to our advantage."

Oonak pulled his cloaking chip out of its slot on his wrist, took Zahn's hand, and rammed it into the empty slot on his right hand. Now that Zahn had one cloaking chip plugged into each glove of his suit, his cloaking field stabilized, but Oonak was now completely unprotected. Behind him, Zahn saw a wave of lava pouring down the path toward them.

"Take your mother, and be safe," Oonak said and ran inside.

From inside the cavern, Zahn heard a trio of deathly roars that sent a chill up his spine. A few seconds later, Oonak darted out of the cavern and ran down the path. Two of the horrible beasts followed him.

"NO! Oonak!"

But there was no response over the comm. Zahn started to run after him, but Asha grabbed his arm.

"Zahn, he's giving us an opportunity," Asha said. "Let's use it while it lasts."

Cautiously, Asha looked around the corner to see the status of the third beast. He was attentive, looking around in all directions.

The lava behind them drew nearer.

"Okay," Asha said. "I know you're carrying Darshana, but I need you to watch my back as we go in. We can't take too long either. That lava is headed this way. Can you hold her and shoot at the same time?"

"Yeah, I think so."

"Don't *think*. Can you or can't you?"

"I can."

"Good. Now even though that beast isn't going to be able to see us, once we fire it's going to have a good idea of where we are, so we'll have to keep moving. If it has explosives, we'll have to move even faster, so I want to get as close to the gate as possible before we fire. Got it?"

"Got it."

Like perfect spies, Asha and Zahn stayed close to the wall, following the perimeter of the room in total silence. Once they were a few meters away from the gate platform, they waited until the Hataazan turned its back on them, if only for a moment.

Once he did, Asha fired her resonator at the back of its head. Twice. Yet the beast was even stronger than she anticipated and the creature's skin barely even melted. Instead, it turned around and roared, its eyes flashing wild colors at them. It couldn't see them, but it fired haphazardly toward their direction. Stalactites fell all around them, and outside Zahn noticed a wave of lava flowing past the cavern entrance, trapping them.

In the chaos, Zahn vaporized a falling stalactite in midair, and jumped away just in time to avoid the resulting debris. He took a breath and carried his still unconscious mother over to a larger stalagmite for cover. Across from him, Asha was using a stalagmite as cover, as well. Through all of this, she still managed to keep the jagrul safe within its spherical shield as she held it under her arm. To Zahn's surprise, it seemed strangely calm.

In the distance, they could hear the beast talking as it approached them.

"Both of you are cowards and fools!" the beast said. "But your death shall be glorious."

"Okay, new plan," Asha said quietly over the comm. "Put your mother beside that stalagmite for a moment and when our friend gets over here, we both fire directly into its eyes. Got it?"

"I'm still surprised that thing can talk, but that sounds good. Which eye?"

"You think you're that good of a shot? Doesn't matter. Left eye. I'll take right."

The ground rumbled once more. Their suits warned them that the air would soon be too hot for anyone directly exposed to the outside, and Zahn thought of his mother.

Just behind him, he heard another roar. His heart was beating fast now. This was it. This was the moment of truth.

"Now?" he whispered.

"Now."

Together, they stood up and fired. In seconds, the beast's eyes smoldered, and it covered them as it wailed in pain.

"Unseen demons, you shall die!" the beast roared, firing toward them in random directions.

When Zahn saw the beast pause to rub his eyes again, he picked up Darshana and sprinted toward the gate.

While he did this, Asha remained where she was and fired at the beast's feet. If the beast couldn't walk, it couldn't be too much trouble. After dodging a few of its clumsy shots, Asha managed to slice open one of the beast's feet.

"For glory!" the beast shouted as it charged toward her.

But it stumbled and crashed to the ground. Slowly, it stood back up, and Asha fired at its eyes again. Now it was blind, and Zahn almost had pity on it.

The beast felt its way along the walls. After a few moments, it finally found the exit to the cavern and stumbled out.

"Great job, Asha!" Zahn said. "There's only one problem. Oonak isn't responding. I've been trying to contact him and— wait, what does this small light on the comm mean?"

"He must have contacted us during the firefight. It's a recorded message. Touch the light."

Zahn did, and Oonak's voice filled their helmets.

"Zahn," Oonak began, "this may not be easy for you, but you must leave without me. I've just placed several small explosives into their thermal regulation systems. This should destabilize the volcano even more, prolonging the eruption and diverting their attention. What is imperative is that you use Navika's timespace drive to leave this system before the Vakragha realize what has happened. You were wearing the mindcap when we made the timespace jump which means you now intuitively know how to jump, as well. Time runs short. You must go. Neither of you should worry. I will find a way out. Even if I have to—"

But he was cut off. The rest was static.

"What? Is that it?"

The vortex was now open, and the ground shook violently.

"Come on, Zahn! You heard him, and this place is about to get a whole lot warmer."

Lava oozed into the room. Zahn looked back toward the cavern entrance one last time but saw no one, and together they walked through the gate.

When they exited on the other side, Zahn didn't have time to feel sorry about what had happened. He carried his mother inside the ship, closed the door, and once again the inner node of the ship filled with pure, cool air. As he did this, he couldn't avoid tracking some of the reddish dust inside.

"Come on," Asha said. "Let's take her into the command bay. I'll work on reviving her while you get us out of here."

The moment he sat down, the dome above the chair lowered slightly. Was the ship already reading his thoughts? Zahn felt awkward sitting in the command chair, but he knew that was what Oonak wanted.

"Navika, Oonak has—"

"Sacrificed himself for our safety," Navika said. "I overheard the comm transmissions, and he gave me direct orders to leave while the Hataazans are still distracted by the eruption. He also ordered me to consider you as the acting captain."

To their surprise, they heard new explosions around them. Zahn looked up and saw that one of the beasts had come through the gate, and then another.

"They're coming through!" Asha said.

"Get us out of here, Navika!"

With impressive speed, Navika raced out of the cavern. Zahn looked back and noticed that a few of the beasts were following them, but soon they were through the cave and back out into the sky. As they raced above the atmosphere, the cloudy sky of the stolen moon soon became the Ocean of Space once more.

Then, just as he breathed a sigh of relief, he heard a hideous voice from within his own mind.

**"Why do you steal what I have rightfully taken?"**

The voice was guttural and revolting. It was so clear that Zahn looked around him in shock, but no one was there.

**"You may think that you have escaped us, but there is no place we will not find you. My servants will be avenged. We consume all. We control all. We are the Vakragha."**

Zahn wondered what Oonak would do. He knew that no good could come from listening to the enemy. Perhaps Asha would know how to stop this voice.

**"If you tell your friend that we are speaking to you directly, she will be the first to die."**

Zahn's eyes widened. His heart was beating fast now.

**"Yes, we can hear your thoughts, and we will find you in the darkness. We *cultivate* the darkness."**

He braced himself for more of the vile voice, but none came.

"What do you think happened to Oonak?" Asha said.

Zahn almost jumped from her words.

"What? Oonak? He ordered Navika and us to leave. What was I supposed to do?"

Asha was quiet.

She released the jagrul from its spherical shield and continued to work with Darshana, who was still unconscious.

After a few minutes, Zahn noticed that Navika was leaving the nebula at a strange trajectory.

"Navika, what are you doing?"

*"To remain safe, we must remain within the moon's shadow. Otherwise, the pulsar's radiation will disrupt the cloaking field."*

"Oh. Thanks, Navika."

*"Of course."*

"Are you okay, Zahn?" Asha said.

"I'm good. No worries, Asha. We'll be out of here in no time."

*"Captain, I'm detecting six Vakragha cruisers approaching us."*

"How is that possible?" Zahn said.

"How is what possible?" Asha said.

"I'm talking to Navika."

"I didn't hear him say anything."

*"Zahn,"* he heard Navika say. *"I am communicating with you directly through the mindcap. No one else can hear me except you. Relaying information is much faster this way. For instance, I can highlight objects behind you, such as the cruisers that are fast approaching. To respond, simply speak within your own mind."*

Images of the view behind the ship somehow appeared beside his field of vision, and within the star field he saw six shadowed shapes, thinly outlined in green, fast approaching.

"Zahn?" Asha called.

"Sorry, Asha. Navika was talking to me."

"Navika," Zahn said through the mindcap, "isn't this a little intrusive? And how can they know where we are? I thought you said we were safe as long as there was something between us and that pulsar."

*"I'd hypothesize that the potent pulsar energy that we were exposed to before may have leaked into the cloaking cells. So it's possible that the field is unstable, causing the cloak to fail periodically. I recommend we use the timespace drive."*

"Right… Wait, how do we do that?"

*"You know how."*

"Sort of. So I just imagine a vortex in front of the ship?"

*"Either tell me the destination or hold the picture of your destination in mind, yes. You may begin visualizing the vortex now, but we cannot jump until we reach sufficient velocity."*

Behind him, Zahn could hear the timespace drive begin to roar again.

"Wait, how do I reach that velocity, though?"

*"Oonak made you captain and you don't know?"*

"Well, I'm pretty sure that—"

*"Incredible. He must really believe in your abilities. All right, here's your crash course in mindcap piloting: energy flows where attention goes. Visualize your desires and the ship will move."*

Zahn imagined the stars moving past, yet nothing happened.

*"Good. We are now moving at 5% impulse. But you'll need to do better than that Zahn."*

"What are you talking about? It doesn't look like we're moving at all."

*"The stars you can see around us are dozens or hundreds of light-years distant—too far to see relative motion. However, just beyond the edge of your vision, you should see a spiral shape within a circle. When the edges of the spiral touch the circle, we have reached adequate velocity to make a jump."*

Zahn looked forward and realized that, somehow, he could see the indicator just beyond his vision. He wasn't sure why he didn't notice it before, but he guessed it was because he'd never looked for anything outside of his field of vision before. It was quite bizarre, as if he now had an eye on the side of his head.

*"Please hurry. We've been discussing this for nearly one second already, and the Vakragha cruisers are now within firing distance."*

Only one second? That's right. Navika had told him that conversations went faster with the mindcap.

He imagined the spiral shape expanding more and more within the small circle and felt the feeling of acceleration as he did so, even though Navika nullified all changes of inertia in the cabin. Somehow, he felt acceleration as a concept now.

*"Good work. Vortex in ten seconds. Wait—incoming fire!"*

Behind him, Zahn didn't like what he saw. Six dark, menacing shapes fired toward them, and as they fired, a small point on one of the distant moons glowed a bright orange.

# CHAPTER 30

## AS PHANTOMS OF LIGHT

As Navika counted down, Zahn held the image of a vortex in his mind and recalled the music they'd heard on Aarava to help him relax. Asha looked back toward him, her eyes wide with fear. "4..." He focused on the Aaravan music and what it felt like the first time they'd used the timespace drive. "3..." Complete calm and focus, just like Oonak had taught him. "2..." It'll be like going underwater for one second. It's easy.

"1..."

The roar reached a fever pitch, and behind them dozens of green plasma bolts raced toward them.

*"Engage!"* Navika said.

Zahn imagined a vortex appearing in front of the ship, and just a fraction of a second later, one appeared. It looked like a sphere of swirling stars, and when they dove in, a vision of perfect light filled his mind.

There was a brief flash, and they were back in the Ocean of Space once more. Zahn looked around, but could only see stars and the faint glow of the galactic core in the distance.

"Excellent work, Zahn," Navika said.

"Yeah, good job getting us out of there!" Asha said.

"One moment," Navika said. "I am detecting traces of Vakragha radiation. It's possible—Wait. That's odd. The radiation traces have vanished. I am now detecting only natural galactic background radiation. Perhaps I am in error. I will begin running diagnostics on my sensors now."

"Don't worry, Navika. Everyone makes mistakes sometimes, and you've been through a lot. We all have."

Asha looked around at the stars now surrounding them. "So, where are we?"

In the excitement of the moment, Zahn had completely forgotten to imagine his destination. He had no idea where they were, so he discreetly asked Navika. Within a few seconds, Navika displayed a hologram of the galaxy to his left. This was the first time Zahn was able to study a complete hologram of the galaxy, and he was surprised to see that one of the galactic arms was partially covered by a murky shape.

"What's that darker area?" Zahn said.

*I am once again speaking to you via the mindcap. The darker area is the current known extent of the Vakragha Dominion. We are 1,027 light-years from the Nirananda Nebula which borders a part of this shadowy region.*

"Hmm. So why did we go so far even though I forgot to picture a destination? I didn't even tell you one."

*I made a judgement and went for minimum safe distance.*

"One thousand light-years is minimum safe distance?"

*With the Vakragha Dominion, yes.*

Then again, a thousand light-years was a mere hop relative to the size of the galaxy. Navika was right. It was enough space that Zahn wasn't going to be watching for every little sensor reading.

"We're in the middle of nowhere, aren't we?" Asha said.

"More or less," Zahn said. "But we're safe. Well, at least once we fix the cloaking cells. Navika told me that the pulsar radiation may have slowly contaminated them. How's my mom doing?"

Zahn stepped up from the command chair and walked down to them. Asha had placed his mother on the long bench. She had even found a pillow and blanket for her.

"I can't wake her up, Zahn. I think she may be comatose."

"Didn't you learn anything on Amithya about comas?"

"She'd been there for years, Zahn. These things can take time. I've stabilized her, but I'm not sure what else I can do for her right now."

Zahn knelt down, held his mother's hand, and looked down to her face. He thought of Amithya, and closed his eyes.

*Please help her,* he thought. *You said you would be with us, helping us in hidden ways. Were you telling the truth?*

Zahn kept his eyes closed for some time as he meditated on this thought.

When he opened them again, he saw strange orbs of light in the cabin, moving over them. For a moment, they were both completely speechless. The orbs seemed divine and otherworldly.

"What are they?" Zahn said. "They're like phantoms of light."

The orbs cast strange lights all around them.

"Do you feel that?" Asha said.

"No. What is it?"

"It's like a presence. A warmth. I think I'm supposed to try healing your mother again."

"Then keep going."

Asha placed both of her hands on Darshana's heart and pushed once. To her surprise, Darshana coughed, took a deep breath, and for a brief instant, she blinked.

"Did you see that? She blinked!"

"Yes. But that doesn't mean she's recovered yet."

Asha kept working as the floating lights indicated other spots that needed attention. At times, Zahn could have sworn that light itself was coming out of Asha's fingertips, and they worked like this for over an hour, Darshana occasionally opening her eyes for a few moments only to close them once more. Even after all of the wonders they'd seen, seeing his mother's dark green eyes again was the best sight he'd seen in years.

Finally, after three hours of intense work and a few short breaks to eat some of the food they'd found earlier, Darshana opened her eyes.

And she kept them open.

At first, Darshana had no idea what had happened. She coughed violently and took a deep breath. Then her eyes locked with Zahn's.

"What happened to you?" she said slowly.

"It's me, Mom. I'm here. We saved you. You're safe now."

Zahn tried to stay strong and not to cry.

"Where?"

"It doesn't matter. You're safe. You're safe."

Darshana's eyes closed again.

"So tired…"

"Here. Have her drink this. It will accelerate her healing."

Asha had brought over a small vial that contained a familiar golden liquid.

"Is that amrita? You saved some?"

"I thought it would come in handy, so I didn't drink it all. Here, Darshana. Drink it slowly."

Asha pressed the translucent vial to Darshana's lips, and she sat up a bit and sipped it. When she finished the last drop, Zahn could easily see the difference. Color was returning to her face, and the light behind her eyes was brighter. Darshana closed her eyes and fell asleep once more. But this was a truer sleep, a deeper sleep.

"Thank you so much, Asha," Zahn whispered. "I don't know how I'll ever repay you."

"What are friends for?" Asha smiled.

Patiently, Asha and Zahn waited. While Zahn stayed by her side and used the ship to track her pulse and temperature, Asha went to work on diagnosing the problem with the cloaking cells. As Navika had hypothesized, the pulsar's radiation had leaked into some of the cells, and Asha set to work on retuning them and resetting the field.

During this time, Zahn hardly left his mother's side. By the time Asha finished her work on the cloaking field, she noticed that Zahn had fallen asleep beside his mother as she slept on the long bench.

Asha walked over and watched Zahn in his slumber. He moved his head slightly every few seconds, as if he were in the midst of a dream, and mumbled something she didn't understand. After a few seconds he mumbled again, and Asha walked closer to try and understand what he was saying.

"Oon says, we're going to make it," he mumbled.

Asha knelt down and whispered into his ear.

"Yes," she said. "Oonak has faith in us."

The thought that Zahn was talking to Oonak in his dream was oddly comforting to Asha, but she frowned at the thought of Zahn waking up and remembering what had happened. She missed Oonak very much, but there was nothing she or anyone else could do about it now.

"But Dad," Zahn mumbled. "She is still alive."

Asha wondered where Zahn could be now. His eyes were darting back and forth behind his closed eyelids.

"Why did you let her go?" Zahn whispered. "Didn't you love her? Didn't you?"

A wave of sadness swept over Asha. When she thought of Zahn struggling even in his dreams, she felt pity. She wasn't proud of the feeling, but hearing his dreams had changed her somehow. She felt she now knew Zahn in a way she hadn't known anyone in a long time.

"Zahn," Asha whispered into his ear. "You're dreaming."

Zahn inhaled slightly but remained asleep.

"But you don't have to dream about that," she continued. "You can dream about whatever you want. Dream about seeing her well again."

Zahn's breathing slowed.

"I wasn't sure before, Zahn, but now I can feel it. With the help of the amrita and the phantoms of light, your mother will recover. I can feel it. Dream of her now. Dream of your home. Dream of walking with her along the silvery sands just like you told me about. Can you see it?"

Zahn mumbled something, but she couldn't understand it. She performed a blessing on both of them that the Amithyans had taught her and sat down beside him as she waited patiently for one of them to awaken.

Then, Darshana did something remarkable: she sat up.

# CHAPTER 31

## THE DISEASE & THE CURE

Zahn woke up right before it happened. He was sitting on the floor admiring the stars, when she abruptly sat up. Holding the blanket to cover herself, she looked around the cabin. At first, he thought he might be imagining it, until she spoke.

"Where am I?" she said. Her voice was soft and weak.

Zahn sat up and gently took his mother's hand.

"You're on a ship. You're safe. How do you feel?"

Darshana closed her eyes for a moment and took another deep breath. "I'm cold. Zahn, what happened to you?"

"What do you mean, Mom? I'm fine." Zahn turned to Asha. "Do you have any extra clothes my mom could borrow?"

"Of course." Asha dug through one of the compartments under the seat.

"What happened to you Zahn? You're so big. I was asleep. There was no time... no sense of time..."

"I know, Mom. You've been gone for a while, but everything's okay now. Asha is getting you something to wear."

"Who are you?" Darshana said weakly as Asha helped her put on an Aaravan robe.

"This is Asha," Zahn said. "She helped us. She's a friend."

"A friend. That's good." Darshana smiled slightly and closed her eyes once more.

Zahn wondered how much blood she might have lost that day before they arrived. The image of the Hataazan and the bloody tube flashed back into his mind, but he pushed it aside.

"I dreamt of you and your father. I dreamt for so long that I began to think that the dreams might be real," she said. "How did you find me?"

"Well, it's a long story, but the council helped, and—"

The jagrul, which was eating some seeds near one of the rear corners of the cabin, suddenly whistled toward Zahn.

"—the jagrul helped a lot, too. But, we never could have found you if you hadn't given me this."

Zahn took the lens out of his pocket and showed it to her.

Darshana smiled. "My old lens. Remember when I gave that to you? We were at the observatory. We were talking about what it means to see."

"Yes, I remember! I remember everything. I just can't believe I'm finally sitting here with you... Mom, everyone thought you were dead. You've been gone for so long, but because of this lens, and a lot of help, I was able to find you."

"Lens," Darshana repeated. Her voice was stronger now.

"Yep." Zahn smiled.

"Zahn, that's why they took me. The lens."

"*This* lens? I don't understand."

"No, not that lens..." Darshana's eyes widened. "Zahn! We did it. We invented a device that could *see* the gravitational connections between worlds, between anything. No longer did we have to wait and observe their motion to calculate it. We could finally see the spacetime curvature itself. We called it the Gravity Lens."

"That's astounding. But I work at the Ashraya Observatory, and I've never heard of that. Was it an observatory project?"

"You work there now?"

"Yes. I'm an observer."

"I'm so proud of you, Zahn. Do you enjoy it there?—No. Must focus. The lens. I was the lead scientist on a small team. It was extremely secret. Zahn, that's why I was taken. Because of the horror that I saw through the lens."

Zahn and Asha were spellbound.

"What did you see?"

"I surveyed all of the planets in our solar system to test it, and I found something that was simply impossible. Zahn, do you remember Rodhas? Do you recall it ever showing any traces of life or possessing any unusual qualities?"

"Well, I was never assigned to survey that planet, but no. I've never read any reports that suggest life. Besides, Rodhas is the farthest planet from our star. It's freezing."

"Yet when you look at it through the Gravity Lens, it violates everything we know about astrophysics. Zahn, it's hollow inside."

"What?"

"It's hollow inside, yet it contains more mass than a gas giant. So I asked myself: how could this occur through natural means?"

"Well, I suppose if two planets formed in the same dust belt... No, that wouldn't work—"

"It's not possible, Zahn. I ran every simulation I could think of, and it's not possible for a planet to naturally form that way. So I had to face the truth. What's going on inside Rodhas is not a natural phenomenon. And then it got even stranger."

"What's stranger than that?" Asha said.

"When I first detected the anomaly, I stayed in the lab all night. I kept the planet under close observation, and during the night I clearly observed that the mass was increasing gradually, hour by hour. It was a slight change, but it was increasing at a predictable rate. I calculated that it would only take about twelve years to reach a mass that would destabilize our entire solar system. And then... well, I can only remember bits and pieces after that—"

Darshana stopped in mid-sentence and studied Zahn's face.

"But Zahn, you're all grown up. It must have been years." The light behind her eyes was brighter now. "How long have I been gone? Zahn, you must tell me. What about Avani? **Zahn, is Avani all right?**"

"When I left, Avani was fine. But that was... well I traded my photodisc so I don't know how long ago that was. I'm sure I could ask Navika how long I've been gone, but honestly, I don't care. We still have time to act. I can feel it."

Zahn glanced back toward the command chair.

"Navika, are you familiar with anything that may be capable of doing what my mother saw through the Gravity Lens?"

There was silence for a moment while Navika considered this.

"According to my Confederation records, there are only two races in the galaxy that are capable of creating such potent gravity anomalies: the Taarakani, who have been missing for aeons, and the Vakragha."

Zahn thought back to how Oonak had sacrificed himself to allow them to escape with his mother safely. No one had ever done something so selfless for him before.

"In fact," Navika continued, "what your mother describes sounds remarkably like the legend in which the Sanguine Suns grew wormholes within planets to conceal them. According to the legend, once a wormhole was unleashed from the core of a transformed planet, the rest of the planets in the system were soon swallowed up, carrying them off into Sanguine Space."

"Wait. Are you saying the Vakragha are growing an artificial wormhole on the edge of the Kuvela system? Near my home?!"

"Indeed," Navika said. "Your mother's findings strongly suggest this."

"The wormholes in the legend are real? Do we have proof?"

"Don't you remember the stolen Taarakani moon in the nebula?" Asha said. "How do you think it got there?"

Zahn was speechless. The thought of his mother being returned was once an untouchable dream. Now that he had saved her, he felt as if nothing could ever be wrong again, until this. The thought that his entire planet might be on the brink of total disaster froze his thinking for a moment.

"And the wormhole is going to kill everyone on Avani?" Zahn finally said.

"Uncertain," Navika said. "Before we reached Avani, Oonak and I came upon a group of people who claimed to have escaped from an enslaved world, though our encounter with them was brief. Therefore, it is possible that the planets are swallowed up and the inhabitants are merely enslaved instead of annihilated. Although, that sounds like a fate even worse than death."

"So if the legend is true, that means Avani could get swallowed up into the Vakragha Dominion like the prison world we just rescued my mother from?"

"The available evidence supports this hypothesis."

Zahn ran up to the command chair and sat down.

"We have to get back to Avani now. We have to warn them. They may only have days left."

"Wait!" Asha ran up to him. "What Navika said strongly supports the existence of the Tulari. You're forgetting the rest of the legend, Zahn. How did the Innocents save themselves?"

Zahn tried hard to think back to when Oonak had first told him the legend, back before they'd even landed on Aarava. But he drew a blank.

"The Innocents found the Tulari, Zahn!" she said. "They found it in a cave deep underground and used it to seal up the wormhole forever. Don't you see? What's happening to your world echoes the legend, and the Tulari is the only effective weapon against them."

"Asha, that's great. I'm glad it might turn out to exist, but how could we even hope to find it? It has been over twelve years since my mother discovered the anomaly. We are out of time!"

A look of dread crossed Darshana's face.

"It exists," Asha said. "Trust me. My father has gathered too much information from too many sources for it to be a fabrication. It exists, and it can bend space around it unlike anything you could ever imagine."

"Over twelve years. Over twelve years…"

"Mom, don't worry. Just let me figure this out."

"Zahn, the anomaly could be on the brink of destroying everything we know."

"Mom, please be quiet for a just a second. I need some silence to think about this. Asha is technically an extraterrestrial, as was the owner of this ship. Ask her about living on a moon base. Ask her anything. Just please give me a few minutes to think. We can solve this."

A silence fell upon the cabin, and Zahn listened to the quiet hum of the ship and contemplated the situation. Darshana looked over to Asha, seemingly studying her.

"You're not from Avani?" Darshana said.

"Ah, no. I thought you knew."

"I assumed from the tone of your skin that you might be from one of the southern continents, but now... Do you mind if I ask about where you live?"

"It's just a small outpost that services travelling starships. My father and I repair them and sell supplies, primarily."

"Extraordinary."

Zahn stood up.

"Okay, it's settled," he said. "We're heading back to Avani, finding this Gravity Lens device, and using it to find the Tulari. After all, if the legend is true, the Tulari is our only hope of saving Avani, anyway."

"Whoa, Zahn! One step at a time here," Asha said. "There's no guarantee that the Gravity Lens will help us find it. After all, my father has been searching for the Tulari for most of his life. Do you honestly think—"

"Do you have a better idea, Asha? First Oonak was attacked in orbit above Avani by a ship that seemed even more advanced than Navika, and now this. Asha, the Vakragha are practically at my planet's doorstep, and every passing minute is a minute that they're closer to consuming my planet whole, and who knows how many others."

"All I was going to say was, we should go find my father."

Slowly, Darshana turned around and looked at them. Her gaze was strangely calming.

"Zahn, from what I'm hearing, I don't think we need the Gravity Lens at all. If what Asha says is true about the Tulari bending space, then it has a unique energetic fingerprint."

"Of course." Asha brightened. "If the Tulari can erase artificial wormholes, then it must have a truly incredible gravity signature. It probably leaves trace radiation, as well."

"But Asha," Zahn said, "the galaxy is huge. There's no way we can scan billions of stars to find it. We need information, some clue that will point us in the right direction."

For a moment, his gaze drifted over to the countless number of stars around them.

"You know, you two make a good team." Darshana smiled.

"Only part of a team…" Zahn looked down to the partially transparent floor.

Asha walked over to him and put her hand on his shoulder.

"Don't worry, Zahn. We'll see Oonak again. I can feel it."

Zahn tried to imagine what Oonak would do in this situation, but his mind went blank. As Asha walked back down to where Darshana was and gave her some water, Zahn was surprised to hear Navika chime in on the situation.

"Sadness in a captain affects the entire crew. Is there anything I can do to help?" Navika said.

"Nothing. Unless you can bring Oonak back or simulate a model of the entire galaxy…"

Then, Zahn's eyes flashed with excitement.

"Wait a second. Navika, based on everything we know about the Tulari, can you create a working model of such an object? And if so, could you extrapolate possible gravitational profiles based on that model, and then scan for any matches?"

"Yes, but extrapolation will limit my accuracy."

"It's our best shot. Do it."

As Navika worked, Zahn looked out onto the stars ahead, and then over to his mother. She was resting again, and Asha was sitting beside her.

Once again, Navika's crisp voice filled the cabin.

"I've constructed as accurate of a model as possible based on all of the available data. But I'm sorry to report that nothing within range or in memory matches that gravitational profile. I'd recommend executing a search pattern, instead."

"Are you sure you accounted for everything, including from the time before you crashed on Avani?"

"I prefer to call it a hard landing, but yes, I did. There is nothing that matches any relevant object of that description."

Zahn punched the padded armrest in frustration. "And I thought we were so close."

He closed his eyes and tried to imagine the Ashraya beach.

"Navika," Darshana said quietly, "did you scan for trace radiation, as well?"

"Only gravitational matches were requested," Navika said. "Zahn, would you like me to?"

"Yes, Navika. Please."

After a few moments, Navika spoke again.

"Again, there are no objects in range of the ship which even remotely match possible radiation signatures of the device you describe. I'm sorry that I couldn't be of more—Wait."

Navika was silent for some time. He had never voluntarily stopped in the middle of speaking before, and they hung onto the edge of his words as if their lives depended on it.

"How… curious," Navika finally said.

"What? What is it, Navika?" Zahn said.

"Your boots."

"What's wrong with his boots?" Asha said.

"The traces of reddish dust on each of your boots contains a highly unusual radiation signature that could have been generated by such a device."

"Dust. Where did you both go?" Darshana said.

Zahn and Asha looked at each other and spoke as one.

"The stolen moon!"

"Do you know what this means?"

"What?"

"Think about it, Asha. Where was that moon stolen from? Oonak said it was stolen from orbit around the Taarakalis system, remember?"

"Yes."

"So, if that stolen moon was bathed in such intense Tulari energy, then the Tulari was either created in the Taarakalis system or it spent plenty of time there, correct?"

"Right…"

"Then it makes perfect sense!"

"What do you mean, Zahn?"

"Navika," Zahn said, "can you restate which two races are capable of creating and controlling artificial wormholes?"

"Certainly. As I said, according to my records there are only two races in the galaxy that are known to be capable of creating such potent gravity anomalies: the Taarakani, who have been missing for aeons, and the Vakragha."

"Asha," Zahn continued, "from what we now know, I think the Taarakani *must* have made the Tulari. What if one civilization created the disease, and the other created the cure? Think about it. The Tulari would be the natural counter to the Vakragha wormhole technology. How else do you explain this correlation?"

"I don't know." A smile crept across Asha's face. "Why don't we go find out?"

"My thoughts exactly."

"I told you," Darshana said. "Great team."

Zahn looked toward the vast array of stars ahead. "Navika, prepare for a timespace jump."

Behind him, he could already hear the now familiar roar of the timespace drive.

*"Destination?"*

"Taarakalis."

# CHAPTER 32

## A DESOLATE WORLD

As the sound of the timespace drive grew louder, Zahn pushed Navika to accelerate faster and faster. "4..." Navika counted down. "3..." And once again, Zahn held the image of a vortex in his mind. "2..."

"1..."

Zahn's focus was resolute. "Now."

He imagined a vortex in front of the ship, and a fraction of a second later, he dove into the vortex and entered the luminous realm once more.

For a moment, he thought he saw space, but once again he saw the luminous corridors spread out before him, followed by darkness once more. Each time this would happen, he heard a rushing noise behind him.

After this happened a few times, he realized that, instead of using an existing corridor as the gates had, the timespace drive actually created a corridor for the ship.

Just as he was getting used to the rhythm, there was a final flash, and they were back in the Ocean of Space once more.

More importantly, they were now high above a ruined world. Below, the surface of the planet appeared desolate and tortured. It reminded Zahn of the stolen moon back in the Nirananda Nebula. Eroded mountain ranges marked the landscape like scabs, and dark patches along the surface hinted at once thriving oceans, now sucked dry.

"Whoa. What happened here?"

Asha couldn't take her eyes off of the tortured landscape.

"I don't know, but I'd like to find out. Navika, any life signs?"

"The surface is almost completely unpopulated. There are only several bipedal life signs on this side of the planet, all in the vicinity of an angular structure. It appears to be a pyramid."

Zahn looked over to Asha who raised her eyebrows at him in a mixture of excitement and surprise.

"Well, that doesn't leave us much choice, does it?" Zahn said. "Take us down to the structure, and be stealthy about it."

Gradually, Navika led them down through thin, wispy clouds. The closer they grew to the surface, the more ruined it looked, as if it had been tortured for uncounted millennia until the galaxy itself had forgotten the reason.

Crowded mountain ranges competed for space along the edge of one of the continents. Between two ridges was a narrow valley, and Zahn could now discern what appeared to be an abandoned city to the south. Dozens of crumbling towers were arranged in circles with small paths between them. At least they appeared small to him. It was difficult to tell from this altitude.

After a few long minutes, they descended into the narrow valley between the two eroded ridges. Ahead, Zahn could see a four-sided stone pyramid built out of dark red rock, and beside it were two towering colossuses. Surrounding the pyramid was a high stone wall, and Zahn directed Navika to land as near to the pyramid as possible.

When they touched down on the dusty surface, Navika confirmed that the atmosphere was bone-dry but breathable, and the gravity was oddly similar to Avani's gravity.

Once outside, Zahn surveyed the scene. From the light, he guessed that it was late afternoon. Ahead, a ramp led up to a large stone door, and all around he noticed some of the survivors of whatever catastrophe had befallen Taarakalis: thick patches of odd, bushy plants that were scattered around the pyramid.

"Asha, what do you think of these?" Zahn said.

Asha walked over and noticed that the top of each bush had a small cone shape which was pointed directly at the sun as it peeked out from behind one of the high walls. She also noticed some tiny thorns, but they looked so small as to be harmless.

"It's unlike any plant *I've* ever seen, that's for sure."

When Asha went to take a small sample, the center cone turned to her and blew a burst of air into her face, as if it were sneezing. She tried again, barely grabbing a sample of the plant in one swift motion before it sneezed at her for a second time.

Meanwhile, Zahn approached the front of the pyramid and quickly concluded that this door was not meant to encourage visitors. A triangular-shaped opening was sealed by a stone door which resembled a wall more than it resembled a door, and all three of them searched around the door for a panel or anything that might allow them to open it. There was nothing.

Feeling out of options, Zahn tried knocking.

The stone was rough on his knuckles, and he realized that the stone might be too thick to even register a knock.

"Navika," Zahn spoke into his wristband, "can you slice this door open? Make an opening big enough for us to pass through."

"Affirmative. Please clear away from the door."

They moved aside as Navika rose a few meters above the ground, and for the first time, they saw what it looked like to be on the dangerous end of one of his plasma bolts. Navika rotated slightly to aim a triangular face toward the door and shot two white-hot bolts of plasma from the bottom two points.

Both of the bolts moved toward the center of the door at first, but were then distorted around the door in a huge arc, eventually impacting on the ground on the far side of the pyramid, melting some of the dirt into a muddy kind of glass.

"What was that? Try again, Navika."

Once again, Navika aimed for the center of the door, and once again his plasma bolt was distorted around the pyramid, impacting onto a patch of ground, melting it in the process.

"Well, I think it's safe to say that whatever we do find inside is well-guarded. Any ideas?"

"What about the flutes we were given on Aarava? Perhaps if we played them together," Asha said.

"This is a pretty huge door. But it's worth a try."

Soon they were all experimenting with the three flutes that the Aaravans had given them. Since Oonak had left his on the ship, even Darshana had one to experiment with, and after much trial and error they found a frequency that made the door rumble. But even when they all played together, the door did not move at all.

After what felt like a half hour, Zahn threw his flute down in frustration. "We've come thousands of light-years—"

"Tens of thousands, actually—" Asha added.

"A long way! And now, we can't even get inside."

Zahn kicked a bush near the door, and it aimed its cone at him and blew air into his face so hard that he nearly fell over.

"Hey!" Zahn reflexively kicked it back.

This time, it blew back at him so hard that he did fall over. Yet when he hit the ground, he was smiling.

He had an idea.

Carefully, he lodged his Aaravan flute into the small opening in the center of the cone. Using his resonator, he melted the opening and was pleased to see that the plant was now firmly attached to the flute. He knelt down, put his fingers over the correct holes, and pointed the flute directly at the door.

He called Asha and Darshana over who had, in vain, been trying to vaporize parts of the door with their resonators.

"Kick the plant, Asha," he said when she was closer.

"What? I don't take my anger out on plants, Zahn, especially alien plants that sneeze in my face."

"Zahn." Darshana walked up. "What are you doing?"

"It's going to be fine, Mom."

Zahn turned back to Asha. "Just kick it."

"Haha, I don't think so. I'm a student of healing, not of kicking defenseless life forms."

"Please, Asha. Just trust me."

Reluctantly, Asha kicked the side of the bush, and a loud whistle emanated from the flute. It was so loud it made Asha's ears ring, and behind them the door moved slightly.

"Yes! Once more, with feeling this time!"

"I can't believe it…" Asha was stunned.

This time Asha kicked the plant as hard as she could, and the plant blew the flute louder than she'd ever heard any instrument play before. Zahn plugged one of his ears with his free hand, and Darshana and Asha covered both of their ears as they watched the door.

To their amazement, it rolled slightly to the right.

"One more time!" Zahn said, still kneeling beside the plant to hold the flute in position.

Once again she kicked the plant, almost uprooting it this time. The wail of the flute echoed across the valley, and slowly, the door rolled open more. Now it was open just enough for a person to get through. They had done it.

But at a price.

Beside the bush, Zahn noticed some blood had dripped onto the ground, and then he saw what had happened to his arm. The bush must have grazed him during the last kick, because he was now bleeding from a series of small cuts along his forearm.

"Asha, help."

Asha and Darshana rushed over and looked at the wound as blood bubbled up.

"I'll be right back," Asha said. "I think I know where Oonak kept the healing gel."

"Asha, what about your healing abilities? Can't you try that?"

"Oh, right. I just, I've never had to stop blood with them before. But you're right. I'll try it."

Asha placed her hands over his arm and closed her eyes. Zahn thought he heard her whisper something, and then her hands glowed slightly. He felt a warm sensation travel up his arm and into his chest.

"Do you feel any better?" Asha said.

"Yes. How does it look?"

Asha took her hands off of his arm, and he could see that the bleeding had completely stopped. Only a few red marks remained, and bits of dried blood brushed off easily.

"Asha, that's astounding," Darshana said. "Where did you learn that?"

"She learned from the Masters." Zahn smiled warmly at her. "Great job, Asha. Sorry about the blood on your hands."

"Don't worry about it." Asha took out a small handkerchief and wiped her hands with it. "Are you still up to going inside?"

"More than ever."

Zahn flexed his arm and walked up to the pyramid entrance. He noticed that it felt surprisingly good, almost better than before he was hurt.

Beyond the door was a narrow hall, and at the other end of the hall he could barely see a large room lit in an eerie glow. He stepped back outside and noticed that a dry breeze was now blowing through the barren valley.

"Does everyone have their cloaking chips? I think we're going to need them."

"Got mine," Asha said, pulling one out of her pocket.

Zahn felt the two in his pocket and thought of Oonak. He wondered what Oonak would think if he knew that they had found the Tulari.

After explaining how the cloaking chip worked to his mother, all three of them activated their chips, stored them safely in their pockets, and walked into the massive pyramid.

Hesitantly, they headed down the narrow hall, and Zahn noticed that even though the walls were dark, they reflected the distant light like polished glass. He wondered what this place looked like when the lights were on.

Soon, they were at the far edge of the hall, looking into a large inner room, and Zahn noticed several details at once.

Huddled around the base of a tall pedestal, three enormous guardians sat with their heads down. Zahn guessed that they were over three meters tall, and they appeared to be sleeping. Or were they in a trance? They each had long black hair that was pulled back and were clothed in thick, red armor, though he could see no weapons.

Zahn's arched his neck to see what, if anything, was set atop the pedestal, and what he saw left him breathless.

Floating in midair above the pedestal was a truly remarkable object. It resembled a giant, glowing pearl, and Zahn recalled how Asha had referred to the Tulari as the Pearl of Great Price, although he didn't actually think it would resemble a pearl as much as this object did. It was much larger than a pearl, but otherwise the resemblance was uncanny.

As it floated just above the pedestal, it radiated a soft white light which stirred within its core like a slowly twisting storm, and the shadows it cast on the guardians below wavered every few seconds. Zahn felt mesmerized, and when he looked over to Asha, she seemed intoxicated with excitement.

# CHAPTER 33

## THE TULARI SANCTUM

Zahn stepped into the inner room.

The moment his foot touched the floor, the entire room filled with light, and the three guardians opened their eyes. With impressive speed, they took a gasp of air, stood up, and pointed their palms forward, toward the darkness.

"Who has entered the Tulari Sanctum?" one of them said. Its voice was deep and reverberated off of the polished walls.

"Identify yourself," another said.

Zahn spoke to the guardian nearest to him, which was the one who had spoken first.

"I am Zahn from Avani, a world many thousands of light-years from here. I have come here because my world is under attack by the Vakragha. Only the Tulari can stop them from consuming my planet whole."

"Why can we not see you, uninvited one?" This one sounded female. She turned toward Zahn, and he saw her angular, yet feminine, face.

"Yes! Be you ugly, intruder?"

"No, my friends and I only wish to remain safe until we can discern your motivations. As I said, my world is in great danger, and I have come a great distance on a Confederation ship. Will you allow us to use the Tulari to save my world? We will return it here when Avani is safe. Please, it is our only hope."

"Mortal!" the first one yelled. "If only you could begin to know how many have come with such a story, yet all were unworthy. It is too powerful for even three mortal beings to wield. Go back to your home and salvage as much as you can before the dark scourge destroys all that you love. That is all you can do. Waste no more time, leave now!"

"No! Being mortal doesn't make us any less worthy. Doesn't a civilization have the right to protect its planet?"

"We have given you our answer."

The guardian folded his arms.

"So you can do nothing to help us?"

"We cannot give the Pearl of Great Price to mortal beings."

Zahn breathed heavily. He couldn't believe that these towering guardians, which had appeared to be wise and mighty before they spoke, had revealed themselves to be so unwilling to help them.

"Well, we aren't leaving until you help us. Billions of people are going to be enslaved by the Vakragha if we do nothing, and I am *not* going to give up now, especially not after coming this far. You're going to have to find a way to help us, or—"

Zahn paused for dramatic effect.

"—or we *will* fight you."

One of the guardians laughed.

"Mortal, there are three of us. Do you realize your folly?"

Zahn stepped back into the hall.

"I'm going to distract them," he whispered. "When I do, use your resonator to nudge the Tulari off of the pedestal, Asha. And Mom, I want you to throw this at the guardian nearest to Asha once she grabs the Tulari. Can you do that?"

Zahn handed her a small ball filled with an orange liquid.

"What are you saying, Mortals?" one guardian said.

"What is this?" Darshana said as she examined the small ball of liquid.

"It's a special acid that Asha's father gave us. It's supposed to slow them down. Everyone ready?"

"Okay."

"Got it."

Zahn stepped back into the light and smiled, even though the guardians still couldn't see him.

"Yes, there are indeed three of you," he said. "And there are three of us, which means you're still at a disadvantage."

In an instant, Zahn darted forward and shot the nearest guardian in the eyes. Asha simultaneously shot the one behind that guardian in the face, and both growled in surprise, covering their faces for a moment.

The third guardian held out his left palm and shot a bolt of light toward where Zahn had been standing a moment before. Zahn rolled forward and dodged the bolt just before it impacted on the wall, causing huge pieces of stone to fly everywhere and litter the floor. Asha used that opportunity to fire a repulsing burst at the Tulari atop the pedestal, but it only moved slightly.

Zahn noticed that Asha's cloaking field flickered for a moment. One of the guardians she'd shot in the eye noticed, too, and lunged toward her.

Asha fired at the Tulari again and finally managed to knock it loose. As it fell, Zahn called out to her.

"Asha, watch out! Your cloak is faltering!"

But she didn't have time. One guardian grabbed her by the neck and pushed her up against the pedestal, choking her.

Still cloaked, Darshana ran up and threw the small ball of liquid at the guardian choking Asha. Her aim was true, and it exploded into a hissing, bubbling liquid which covered the guardian's eyes and mouth. The guardian released Asha and clawed at his face. Nearby, the other guardian noticed that Darshana's cloaking field had flickered and fired a red bolt of light from his palm toward her. It impacted onto her side, and she collapsed onto the ground.

Meanwhile, on the other side of the pedestal the third guardian caught the falling Tulari before Zahn was able to catch it. When he caught it, the guardian made eye contact with him, and Zahn realized that his cloak must be failing, as well. The guardian shot a red bolt toward Zahn, but he just managed to dodge it and rolled behind a large chunk of stone that had been blown loose from the wall. He fired back, but his resonator didn't seem to affect the guardian at all.

He looked at his hand. He was invisible for the moment, so he quietly crawled behind a different piece of rubble. As he sat there, Yantrik's words came roaring back to him.

*"Let me know how they work,"* Yantrik had said.

Zahn would definitely have a few things to tell Yantrik when he saw him again.

If he saw him again.

"Mortal!" one guardian called out. "We have your friends."

He knew that they were trying to trick him into revealing his location, so he remained as quiet as possible. In the distance, he heard one of the guardians cough.

"You shouldn't have come, off-worlder. You are wasting your friends' lives."

Behind him, he heard someone familiar whisper his name.

"Asha?" Zahn whispered a bit too loudly. "Asha, are you okay? How'd you escape?"

She crawled over to him.

"Your mom helped me. But... she was hit, Zahn."

A feeling of shock soon transformed itself into guilt.

"I shouldn't have brought her. I shouldn't have brought her. We should have left her in the ship where she'd be safe."

"Then she would be stuck back on the ship, and we might have been killed already," Asha whispered. "Zahn, we needed her help. She knew the risk."

Zahn closed his eyes, and for the first time since they'd rescued her, he prayed. Within his mind, he called out to his guides for help.

In the distance, he heard one of the guardians approaching.

"I don't think our resonators work against them, Asha."

"I know."

Zahn reached out for Asha's hand and she took it.

"Don't you see?" the guardian bellowed. "Now you must hide from us. You are all cowards, and you must pay the penalty for cowardice."

At any moment, a blood-red bolt of light was going to flood his vision. He heard the footsteps of the guardian draw nearer.

This was it.

He was going to die here.

As a last effort, he took the lens out of his pocket and tried to wedge it into the sonic barrel of his resonator. It was a tough fit, but it was his last idea.

Behind him, he could see the wall growing redder as the guardian approached. He would have only one chance.

"Leave now or perish!" one howled.

"I'm going to stand up," Zahn whispered to Asha.

"What? They'll kill you."

"They're going to kill both of us. I've got a plan. When they're distracted, run back to the ship and start firing into the pyramid's open door."

"Zahn—"

"No time to argue."

He threw a small piece of rubble across the room, and when it hit the far wall, the nearest guardian shattered it with another bolt. Slowly, Zahn rose up from behind the large stone he'd been hiding behind, and he was pointing the resonator directly at the nearest guardian.

At seeing this, the guardian grinned arrogantly.

"I am immune to your weapon, mortal. It will not save you."

"Then shoot me, you beast!" Zahn screamed.

The guardian's eyes flashed like fire, and he blasted Zahn with a blood-red bolt of light. The bolt careened toward him, impacting onto his resonator.

But when it hit his resonator, something unprecedented happened. The bolt of light bounced off of the tip of the gun and headed straight back toward the guardian who shot it.

The guardian barely jumped out of the way in time, and the bolt impacted onto the stone wall behind him, blowing more huge chunks of rock from the wall. Asha covered her face as thousands of small bits of rock flew through the air.

The guardian stood up and dusted himself off.

He looked furious.

"We told you! Mortals are not worthy to wield the Pearl!"

His yell echoed down the halls, and then the sound of the yell was dwarfed by the sound of another explosion, this time originating from outside of the pyramid's walls.

Natural light flooded the inner room, and a gust of wind blew in from the outside. Zahn and Asha looked out from the edge of the boulder and saw a short, radiant figure enter the room through a hall that had been dark before. Appearing to be clothed in light itself, the figure was so bright that they couldn't discern its facial features at all. Zahn noticed that even the guardians shielded their eyes.

The figure spoke in a strong, resonating voice.

"And what about *im*mortals? Are they worthy?" it said.

All three of the guardians held up their hands to block the radiance that was blinding them.

"You are going to give these wanderers what they need."

Zahn wondered who it was that would speak with such authority to these mighty guardians.

"What authority do you have here, Radiant One?" the first guardian said.

As the guardian was finishing his words, the figure held out a hand and lowered it. As his hand lowered, the first guardian became smaller and smaller, and as he became smaller, the pitch of his voice grew higher and higher. When the figure had stopped, the guardian was less than a half meter tall. When it realized this, it screamed in a high pitch and ran off down one of the halls.

As the figure approached the other two guardians, they knelt down immediately.

"Please diminish your brightness, Radiant One. Who are you?" one guardian said.

"I am the child-like laughter under a starry sky."

"Please, Radiant One. Speak plainly."

"I am ageless, and my name is of little importance. That is all you need know."

The figure's radiance diminished slightly, but Zahn still couldn't discern any features. It was still extremely bright.

"Thank you for diminishing your radiance, Unnamed One. We recognize your power, but please tell us. How could these lower beings be worthy of such an unspeakable power as great as the Pearl?"

"Don't you see? Their hearts are selfless in their desire to save those that they love. But not only this. Their selfless actions serve far more than even their own worlds. Indeed, they have allowed themselves to be Instruments of Light that, in time, will serve an innumerable number of beings. Because of this, they wield a rare kind of power. Therefore, you will give them the Pearl. Now."

Reluctantly, the first guardian handed it to the radiant figure, and the figure turned toward Zahn and approached them.

Zahn looked at his hand. The cloak was holding steady, so how could it see them? The figure's brightness was almost overwhelming now.

Asha and Zahn stood up. Even at just a few meters away, Zahn couldn't see his face. The brightness was impenetrable.

"Wield it well," the figure said as he handed it to Asha, who was closest. "And always remember, never allow your enemy to tell you who you are."

"Zahn, the Tulari. I'm holding it. It's real." Asha's eyes welled up. "I wish my father could be here to see this."

"Radiant One, may I ask who you are?" Zahn said.

"I reveal hidden strength in times of darkness."

"But why have you helped us? Did you hear my prayer?"

"What have you learned, Zahn? Have you seized the moments? Have you looked through new lenses and gained new insights? Have you expanded your understanding? Your opportunities have not manifested by chance. We have been guiding you and showing you the way whenever you had eyes to see, ears to hear, and the heart to feel."

"Thank you, Radiant One. I am extremely grateful for your protection. But how do you know this? Who is 'we'? Can you tell me who you are?"

"You must seize this time. Right now, you, your mother, and your friends are the only ones who stand between the Vakragha and the enslavement of your home. Remember, all you need do is to deliver the Tulari into the wormhole itself. Your mother will recover momentarily. Seize this time and go. If you do not act now, Avani will fall."

The figure walked over to Darshana, sprayed a strange pink mist onto her collapsed body, and disappeared back down the hall where he had come in.

For a moment, Zahn watched the dust float around the room as it drifted through a beam of sunlight. Across from them, the guardians dusted themselves off, glanced at Zahn and Asha in disgust, and walked down the hall that the shrunken guardian had run down.

Darshana slowly sat up and looked around, and Zahn walked over and helped her get to her feet.

"I'm sorry I wasn't able to be of more help, guys," Zahn said. "If it weren't for that Radiant Figure, we'd all be burnt to a crisp by now, wouldn't we?"

"Zahn," Darshana said. "If it wasn't for you and Asha, the Radiant Figure wouldn't have had anyone to save when he arrived. Your resonator idea gave us the precious extra minutes we needed."

"Thanks." Zahn smiled. Somehow, she was everything he remembered her to be.

"Who was that, anyway?" Asha said. "I've never seen anything like that."

"Whoever he was, he has a phenomenal understanding of biology," Darshana said, stretching her neck. "That must have been the most powerful healing agent I've ever seen, because I can almost walk normally again. When that red bolt of light hit me, I was completely paralyzed. When I hit the floor, all I could move were my eyes. I almost thought—"

Darshana nearly tripped over a piece of rubble, but Asha caught her.

"—that it was the end."

"Far from it, Mom. Far from it."

# CHAPTER 34

## RENDEZVOUS AT RODHAS

Stepping over the chunks of rubble that now littered the floor, Zahn, Asha, and Darshana walked over to where the sunlight was pouring in to see where the strange figure had emerged from, but they only saw that a similar door had been rolled open at the end of another narrow hall. Zahn ran to the end of the hall but couldn't find any sign of the figure or a ship.

They retraced their steps and followed the first hall back to the partially opened door and emerged back out into the open air. It was nearly dusk now.

Zahn looked over to Asha who was holding the faintly glowing Tulari.

"How heavy is it?" he said.

"Not as heavy as you might think. It's a little warm, too. Touch it."

It did feel warm to the touch, as if it were alive.

After removing his flute from the sneezing bush, Zahn led them down to the ship. Soon, they were racing high above the jagged peaks of Taarakalis, and the dark blue of the sky transformed itself into the Ocean of Space once more.

This time, he told Navika to prepare for a timespace jump to the outer edge of the Kuvela system, but not to Rodhas itself. Instead, he chose the most distant moon of Rodhas. He wanted to retain the element of surprise for as long as possible before they acted, just in case the Vakragha had a way of disrupting Navika's cloak and revealing their position. He couldn't make a mistake now. Too much was depending on him.

"One moment," Navika said. "I am detecting debris in high orbit above the planet that was not present when we arrived."

Zahn thought of the guttural disembodied voice that had spoken to him as they were leaving Hataaza Darad.

"Any idea of its source?"

*"Difficult to ascertain. The debris is primarily a fine metallic dust. However, I can say that it poses no immediate threat to us."*

"Good. Then let's get out of here. We have a planet to save."

The timespace drive roared to life, and this time the roar seemed louder than it had ever been before.

Once again he saw the luminous realm. There was a flash, and then he saw space once more. A flash and then space. A flash and then space. Again and again. It happened so many times that Zahn lost count. It must have happened dozens of times now. Was something wrong? Why not just make one big jump?

A moment later, there was a final flash, and they reemerged into the Ocean of Space, a dark moon looming just below.

*"We have travelled over 30,000 light-years, the longest jump of the entire journey."*

"Whoa. That's almost a third of the diameter of the galaxy, but what about those flashes? It seemed like we were briefly entering space, and then reentering timespace again. Why were we doing that, Navika?"

*"As I suspect Asha could tell you, a jump is defined as a superset of one or more hops. These hops are necessary because of the drive's limited energy reservoir. However, since this energy is returned to the reservoir by the timespace field at the end of every hop, the time between hops is negligible. So, as I said, the sum total of the most recent sequence of hops is over 30,000 light-years, nearly one-third of the diameter of the galaxy. Welcome home."*

"We're not quite home yet, and I'm not sure I understood all of that, but thanks. Can you confirm our position?"

*"We are on the night side of the eighth moon of Rodhas, on the edge of the Kuvela system."*

"Good. Proceed under cloak."

Hesitantly, Zahn maneuvered the ship to the edge of the moon and passively scanned Rodhas. Its cratered surface was a darker shade of grey-green than he had remembered it being from photos. But then again, photos can be deceiving, and he had Navika display a magnified view of the planet while they formulated a plan.

To their horror, angular pieces of the planet's crust pulled back for a moment, revealing shallow shafts that led into a vast hollow expanse. Within it, Zahn caught a glimpse of a dark, menacing shape that was soon blocked by a small swarm of fighters as they emerged from many points on the planet at once. He had unintentionally fulfilled his dream of seeing Rodhas, but he had never expected this.

"Be careful what you wish for," Zahn said quietly.

"What?" Asha said.

"Nothing."

The swarm of small, angular fighters which had emerged from the planet flew around in formation for a few seconds before flying off toward the dark side of the planet. Zahn wondered what they were up to, but was distracted when he realized that both of his ears were ringing. Why did that keep happening?

Zahn looked over to Asha and his mother while he rubbed his right ear. They both seemed anxious.

"So this is the disease..." Darshana's eyes studied the infested world. "And we have the cure?"

"Yes, and I know what you're thinking. I know that we're just one ship facing an entire armada of Vakragha, but we also don't know how much time there is before this wormhole is unleashed. We have to use the Tulari now."

"From Avani," Darshana said. "I could detect the wormhole's mass, but I never thought it would look so menacing up close. I wonder if they're using negative energy to maintain the wormhole's stability..."

"So, what are we supposed to do, Zahn?" Asha said. "There's only one mindcap, remember?"

"Don't worry. We have the Tulari. We can do this."

"I just wish I could be of more help. I'm a pretty good pilot, you know."

"How could I forget that? You saved us from the marauders, and then you brought my mother back to health, something I don't think I'll ever be able to fully repay. You've already been crucial to our success, Asha. Don't feel bad if you can't do as much now. We never would have even gotten here without you."

Zahn closed his eyes for a moment.

"Anyway, I just asked Navika, but he says he can't exactly split up into two ships. So we'll just have to work with what we have."

In the back of Zahn's mind, he heard a quiet ping sound.

"There's got to be something," Asha said.

The ping sound came again, and he wondered if this was Navika's way of quietly getting his attention.

"What?"

*"We are being hailed by a vessel that is requesting an encrypted channel. However, I do not recognize the ship's identity. Would you like me to grant the request?"*

Zahn furrowed his eyebrows. Somehow, he felt a familiar presence, but he had no idea who this could be.

"Any chance that opening a channel will make us easier to be detected by the Vakragha?"

*"Doubtful, as this is a narrowband transmission originating from behind the seventh moon of Rodhas. The Vakragha would need to have a ship directly between us and the source to intercept it, and there are no ships detected in that area."*

"Understood. Establish the encrypted channel and put it on surround so that everyone can hear."

Moments later, the sound of static briefly filled the room and then resolved itself into a gruff yet warm voice.

"Are you reading me? Is this the captain of Navika?"

"Yantrik?" A look of disbelief crept across Zahn's face.

"Zahn! Is that Zahn I hear?"

"Yes! Is that really you, Yantrik?" Zahn was stunned to silence for a moment. "How did you know we would be here?"

"Let's just say I got a bright idea. Strange fellow, too. Kept talking about purity of the heart and lenses or something."

"Dad! You're okay! How did you find us?"

"Is that my little Asha? Hi! I'm doing just fine. Your old dad knows how to fight off a few marauders by now. Anyway, during the attack I shut down the power for the entire outpost and threw out some junk to make it look like I was evacuating. They blew that to bits as I'm sure you can guess. Then I waited in silence until they eventually left. I don't think it was me they were after, anyway."

"Dad, it's wonderful to hear your voice. You'll never believe what we've been through. And Dad, we found the Tulari!"

"I know! That strange fellow who brought me here mentioned that you would be 'wielding the pearl', and that I would be needed, as well. By the way, why don't I hear Oonak?"

Asha and Zahn fell silent for a moment.

"He sacrificed himself so we could rescue my mother from captivity," Zahn said. "And he told us to leave without him."

"Oh, I'm sorry to hear that. He seemed an honorable man."

Zahn reminded himself to focus on the task at hand. For all he knew, the Vakragha would detect them at any moment.

"Yantrik, I'd like to confirm your location. Navika is detecting from your narrowband signal that you're on the far side of the seventh moon."

"Navika is correct. I'm not too far from your position, but far enough that when we attack, it should divide their fire. And I brought a surprise for Asha."

Beside the command chair, Navika displayed a hologram of a maroon, crescent-shaped fighter ship.

"You brought my ship!" Asha said.

"That's right," Yantrik replied. "You can thank your strange friend for that. He asked if he might bring me and your ship to where we would be needed most. He said it was vital that we come. When I said yes, there was a flash unlike any I'd ever seen, and I found myself here."

"Who was this person with such power?"

"Well, he showed up at the outpost a good while after the attack. Could barely even make out his face, he was so bright. I asked him how he got to be that way, but he only chuckled. Like I said before, strange guy."

Zahn and Asha looked at each other. "The radiant figure!"

"What? You've seen him around? Any idea who he is?"

"No," Zahn said. "But he's already helped us once. Whenever he shows up, he seems like an angel."

"Yeah, I can see why. I wish I knew his trick on how to get us here so fast. Anyway, Asha's ship is heading to your position now. Don't worry, I calibrated the cloaking cells carefully. Tell Asha to let me know when she's ready, and then we can finally see what this Tulari can do. I've spent too many years searching for it to miss it in action now."

Out of the corner of his eye, the mindcap showed Zahn that Asha's ship was requesting to dock, and he accepted the request. After a few seconds, he heard a hissing sound behind him, and Navika told him that they were now docked. To his surprise, Navika also informed him that her ship had sent detailed radiation readings which he had just used to further improve the cloaking field at close range.

"Thanks, Yantrik! That helps."

"Exactly. Every little bit helps."

On her way out, Asha grabbed her bag and the sphere containing the jagrul bird, which was now sleeping beside the long bench. She reassured Zahn that she would be of much greater help now that she had her ship, but Zahn stopped her.

"Wait," Zahn said. "Mom, go with her. You'll be safer with Asha than with me and the Tulari, and I'm sure you could be of help to her."

"Are you sure, Zahn?" Darshana said.

"Trust me, Mom. It's better this way."

"Be safe, Zahn." There was a sadness behind her eyes.

"Mom, we're about to launch a covert attack on an alien base hidden within a hollow planet. I don't think anyone is going to be safe for this."

"Then be lucky."

Zahn embraced his mother tightly.

"I can do that."

Once they were in the central node, Asha helped Darshana put on an extra flight suit that she had kept on her ship for emergencies like this.

"Darshana, have you ever fired a plasma cannon before?"

"No, but I could learn."

"Can't think of a better time than now. You'll take the auxiliary cannon."

In a strange silence, Zahn watched as the door slowly closed, leaving him alone for the first time in what felt like days.

After a short conversation with Navika, Zahn decided that the best way to deploy the Tulari would be to place it in the central node of the ship, and then open the door to blow all of the air out, taking the Tulari along with it.

When he asked, Navika assured him that his core nucleus would be fine. The cables that connected Navika's nucleus to the ship were extremely strong, and Zahn got the idea to wedge the Tulari between a few of the cables above the door. It was secure enough to prevent it from falling out and rolling around, but was easy enough to push it out of the cable mesh if he tried.

When he sat back down in the command chair, Asha was hailing him.

"We're all set here," she said. "Darshana already seems comfortable with the weapon interface. Between all of us, we're going to make these Vakragha wish they'd never been born, or hatched, or whatever they do. Do we know how they reproduce?"

"Navika, do we know that?" Zahn said.

*"The reproductive cycle of the Vakragha is currently unknown to the Confederation."*

"Guess not. Okay everyone, report in."

"Asha reporting in through a secure narrowband channel."

"Darshana, standing by on same channel."

"Yantrik, standing by."

"Good. Okay, here's the plan. We're going to wait for a shaft in the planet to open again. Asha, when it does, I want you and your father to make a low pass and take out as many surface cannons as you can. While you have the Vakragha distracted, I'll get into position. When I give the signal, I want everyone to retreat, since using the Tulari could very likely destroy the planet along with the wormhole. They don't even know we have it, so we have surprise on our side. Does everyone understand?"

Everyone did, and when a part of the planet's crust slid back again a few minutes later, they descended upon the Vakragha like invisible ghosts descending upon unaware prey.

Yantrik and Asha dove under the planet's atmosphere, fast and low, taking out dozens of cannons as Zahn set in a course to enter the planet through a large opening nearby. Once he finally got a glimpse of the core through the opening, an alarm sounded throughout the ship.

*"Zahn, we are being exposed to intense radiation emanating from the core of the planet. It's a modulating wave of energy, and exposure will likely overload the cloaking cells, revealing our location. Wait— I'm detecting a swarm of fighters heading toward our position. This radiation must also prevent the swarm from staying cloaked, as well."*

As Navika finished relating this, Zahn saw a swarm of the small angular fighters in the distance open fire on him.

Dozens of narrow, green bolts of plasma flew toward the ship, and Zahn evaded as many of the bolts as possible and returned fire. He felt a rumble as a few bolts impacted onto the ship. On an impulse, he raced toward the planet's northern hemisphere, his cloak recovering in moments.

Meanwhile, Asha and Yantrik were dealing with their own challenges. Whenever they passed over an opening, the surface cannons saw them, demanding immediate evasion. In the process, Asha's ship sustained a direct hit, and her shield strength was instantly cut in half. However, they had already destroyed a good number of cannons, and Darshana's aim was better than she had anticipated. She had destroyed almost as many as Asha had.

In the midst of their evasion, Zahn contacted them.

"Navika is detecting intense negative energy emanating from the wormhole inside the planet which disrupts the cloaking field," he said. "We aren't safe above the shafts. I was attacked by a swarm, but I was able to find cover. Wait... I'm detecting a massive vessel emerging from one of the shafts. It appears to be a Vakragha flagship. I'm going to try and find another opening on the other side of the planet. Be vigilant."

Zahn knew he was racing against time. He flew Navika over the northern tip of the planet and beyond, to the other side of the world. In the far distance, he was relieved to see another gap in the crust opening up, and no ships were in sight.

And then, he heard the vile voice once more.

**"I will devour your heart, Avanian."**

Once again, the voice was horrible and revolting. Like a vile whisper inside of his own mind, it was so clear that Zahn glanced around the cabin, but no one was there.

"No," Zahn said aloud. "I have a surprise for you."

**"Not even the Tulari can help you. Your journey has been in vain. Your failure is inevitable."**

"What? How do you know we have the Tulari?"

**"The Amithyans told us. They have a hidden base on Taarakalis. They have deceived you."**

"Liar! The Amithyans helped us save my mother. They are from a Transcendent World. They would never deceive us, and you will not succeed in enslaving Avani!"

**"I am Razakh, Autarch of Hataaza Darad, and I will take what I may. The Amithyans led you to the Nirananda pulsar because they sought your death."**

For a moment, Zahn wondered what it would mean if that were true. Is it possible the Amithyans had lied to them? No. It wasn't logical. But if this Vakragha was the overseer of Hataaza Darad, that would explain his determination.

Had he overseen this wormhole as it grew? That was too much of a coincidence to be pure chance.

**"Your inner conflict is ironic, Avanian, since we are no different than you in the end. You, too, are a devourer of life. Yet you refuse to see this truth."**

"I am not a devourer of life or an enslaver of it, and I don't believe your lies! The Amithyans were generous and kind. They would never deceive us. Their identity *is* Truth!"

**"You delude yourself just as every other childish species does. You devour life, just as we do. We have witnessed this. We devour on a grander scale, but we are both violators of Free Will. Under our control, your race will learn this and other terrible truths of the galaxy."**

"No! We must eat to survive, and we do not enslave our crops. We cultivate them, and without them we would die."

**"How do you know that we have not cultivated your world, as well? Your world is ripe for harvest now, Avanian, and the harvest is inescapable."**

As Razakh finished saying this, Zahn noticed that the shaft he'd seen open up earlier was going to close before he would reach it, and no other openings were visible.

"Zahn," Asha said, "my ship has sustained another direct hit."

Zahn forced himself to push the Vakragha's words out of his mind for the moment.

"Are you both okay?"

"Yes, but I have to fall back. We'll do what we can from a greater distance."

"Just be careful, Asha. I can't lose her again."

"I won't let that happen, Zahn."

Asha's ship pulled up and headed back toward the eighth moon. On their way, they noticed that the flagship was no longer anywhere to be seen, so in the middle of her retreat she briefly moved the ship in front of one of the shafts before dashing away again. She knew it was risky, but she also knew that the information could prove crucial.

It did. Inside, she saw that the wormhole was now filling about half of the volume of the hollow sphere. From the readings, Asha was amazed to learn that the entire planet had been reduced to a mere shell, and she could see a superstructure on the inside surface of the sphere that was keeping it intact. All along the superstructure was a network of cones that had small points like needles protruding from them.

On the far end of the hollow sphere, she saw a glimpse of a massive black vessel that light itself seemed to fall into. She knew at once that it was the flagship Zahn had mentioned earlier, and it was heading to an opening on the other side of the planet.

Asha learned all of this once her ship was safely behind the moon. All of that information had been gathered in the split second she had dashed in front of the large opening.

"Zahn! The flagship is about to exit on the far side of the planet. Are you there?"

"Yes, but I don't see it. I'm waiting for this shaft to open. I'm detecting a vessel right behind it, but it's the only opening I've found on this side of the planet. I'm going to wait out of view of the shaft and keep my cloak intact as long as possible. Wait. It's opening now."

"We've got to go back to that opening," Darshana said. "We've got to take the flagship by surprise. Zahn needs us."

"When did you become a tactical officer?" Asha said.

"This will give Zahn a chance to launch the Tulari into the wormhole. Trust me."

"And how are we supposed to hit the flagship? There's a wormhole between us and it. Even if we could fire off a volley and escape before getting hit again—"

"Tell Yantrik to break off his attack," Darshana interrupted. "He needs to get into position above that opening. Asha, remember the superstructure over the inner sphere that's holding the planet together? He should be able to reflect his fire off of that inner sphere."

"I'll be there in under a minute," Yantrik said over the comm.

"What?" Asha was stunned. "How did you hear us?"

"Darshana left the comm on, and I'm glad she did. That's a pretty smart idea. In fact, I'm going to try it. I'm going to fire a volley at the superstructure at different angles. One of these shots has got to hit 'em."

"Be sure to take into account the wormhole's gravity," Darshana said.

"Already have."

As Yantrik's ship raced by the opening, he fired about a dozen shots into the massive hollow sphere. Just as Darshana had predicted, most of them bounced off of the inner surface of the sphere and a few headed toward the flagship which was halfway out of the planet now. Only a few would have a chance at impact.

But, to Yantrik's relief, one of the shots made contact.

"Great job, Yantrik!" Darshana said.

Back on the other side of the planet, Zahn was already in position, indirect of the shaft so that his cloak stayed intact. Navika detected a faint flash of an impact beyond the shaft, and Zahn knew that it was his opportunity to open fire.

In moments, he got into firing range and launched two white-hot bolts of plasma toward the flagship, impacting on what Zahn guessed was the command pod of the ship, though the shape was so dark that he couldn't be sure.

The ship returned fire toward his general direction, so he dashed back into an area above the planet that he knew was safe. Yet, as more sections of the crust opened up, Zahn had to focus more on where he was flying than where he was aiming.

Dozens of small fighters poured out of the shafts now, raining green plasma down upon him. A moment later, a section of the crust slid open under him, and he knew that his position had been revealed. With all of his focus, he evaded the oncoming wave of fire, pushing the ship's impulse drive to its limits until, to his relief, the shaft under him closed a few seconds later.

But it wasn't enough.

One of the green bolts of plasma impacted onto the ship, causing an alarm Zahn had never heard to sound throughout the cabin. The sound gave him a sinking feeling in his stomach.

*"Somehow, that last bolt passed right through our shields."*

Now that Zahn had acclimated to the mindcap, they could have entire conversations in mere seconds now.

*"The impulse drive has sustained a direct hit. I'm sorry. You must manually disable it."*

"What? Why?"

*"The impulse drive is not responding to my attempts to restart it and is entering a cascade failure. Perhaps the combination of you pushing the impulse drive to its limits and the wormhole's exotic radiation signature created—"*

"Stop theorizing! What do I have to do?"

*"You must manually disable it within the next forty-two seconds, otherwise the impulse drive will implode from the inside, critically fracturing the hull and depressurizing the ship. I have created a lighted path along the wall to guide you."*

"What about evading the flagship?"

*"Without the impulse drive, evasion is impossible. Go!"*

Zahn got up and ran to the central node of the ship which was now filled with a thin white smoke. He coughed and felt lightheaded. Through the smoke, he could barely discern a series of glowing dots leading to one of the three rooms he hadn't entered before. He stumbled over to it, and the door slid back.

Instantly, he was hit with a wave of hot air, and his eyes were nearly overwhelmed by what he saw inside. Strange cylinders and clusters of spheres connected by thousands of narrow tubes covered the floor and walls. On the far end of the triangular room, where it came to a point, was a large cone which contained a rapidly spinning pool of energy. Three cables were connected to the back of it which led down into the floor.

"Remove the green cables," Navika said. "Twelve seconds."

Zahn grabbed all three of the cables with both hands.

They wouldn't budge. He pulled again.

"Eight seconds."

He heard a hissing sound coming from the cone, and a white vapor filled the room.

He pulled has hard as he could. "5…" Then, he realized that there was a locking mechanism that he had to rotate slightly before they would detach. "3…" He unlocked them as fast as his hands could move.

"Come on! I have not come this far to fail now!"

"1." He pulled all three with both hands and closed his eyes.

To his relief, they came loose, causing him to tumble backward. As he tumbled, he smacked his head on the hard crystal floor, and a wave of nausea came over him. The room spun around him, and his vision became blurry.

"Zahn, the flagship is nearly in range. Zahn, are you all right?"

For a moment, Zahn thought he saw the radiant figure.

Was this how it ended? Was this how he was going to die? Surely, he had drifted above another shaft and was completely exposed by now. Without an impulse drive, there was no way he could get into position and shoot the Tulari into the wormhole now. His plan had failed.

*He* had failed.

Somehow, he thought he could smell the Ashraya beach within the cabin, but he knew this was impossible.

He blinked his eyes and was stunned by what he saw. Above him, he thought he saw the radiant figure shining through the smoke, reaching down to him.

A hand pulled him up to his feet.

His vision became clear, yet no one else was there. Had he imagined it? Zahn wasn't sure what was real anymore.

A new strength came to him. He knew what he had to do, and as he walked back to the command bay, a vile voice filled his mind once more.

"Do you see the truth yet, Avanian? Have you accepted your parasitic nature? Acceptance is your only choice. Without your impulse drive, you are powerless in space. Your friends are surrounded on all sides. If you allow me to collect you and your weapon, I will let your mother live."

Zahn ignored the voice and sat down in the command chair.

*"There you are! I was beginning to get concerned. You have successfully prevented the cascade failure, and we continue to cruise at near maximum impulse speed. However, the Vakragha flagship is heading toward us, and we will arrive above another open shaft in less than a minute, completely exposing us once again."*

"Understood."

Zahn contacted Yantrik and Asha.

"My impulse drive is out," Zahn said. "And I can't maneuver. I only have one option left. I want you to know that I love you all. Each of you has changed my life, and for that I am forever grateful. Now you must all clear away from the planet as quickly as possible. I'm going to destroy this base, one way or another. Mom, I love you. Tell Dad I love him, too. Can you do that?"

"Zahn! Just wait a minute. What's your status?" Asha said.

Zahn didn't respond. He was high above the planet now, still speeding away from the evasive maneuvers he'd done earlier. Far below him, a section of the crust opened up. In moments, another swarm of small fighters flew out of the planet and headed straight for him.

"Zahn! What are you doing?" Darshana said.

"Mending the balance."

As he said this, he closed his eyes and imagined a vortex in front of the ship. Behind him, he could hear volleys of plasma bolts impact onto the ship's hull.

*"If I've inferred your plan correctly, it is truly temerarious. But also brave. If we die here, I want you to know that it's been an honor to know you, Zahn. Perhaps this will work, after all. Or perhaps it will fail spectacularly. In either case, I want you to know that I think Oonak would be proud."*

"Thank you, Navika. I couldn't have done it without you."

Horrendous images of mutilated figures covered in blood suddenly flooded Zahn's mind. He saw Avani's oceans turn to black pools of death and the silvery sands burnt to ash. He struggled to push the images away, and the vile voice returned.

**"This is your fate if you resist. Martyrdom will not help your world. Surrender and your mother will live. You are not a man of action, Zahn. You are only an observer after all."**

"Not anymore."

Zahn inhaled deeply and intently held the image of a vortex in his mind. One appeared, and they plunged in.

# CHAPTER 35

## FLOATING IN ETERNITY

Time stopped.

Zahn perceived the wormhole folding up underneath him, and then all was radiant nothingness. Space and time no longer had any meaning.

Ahead of him, he thought he saw a small child.

After a few moments, Zahn came to his senses and realized that the small child he had seen was actually him. His entire life was passing before his eyes. Visions of moments flashed before him: exploring the Ashraya archipelago trails when he was small, the day his mother had disappeared, the first time he'd walked up Zikhara alone, and the first day he went to work at the observatory. Finally, the replay reached the moment when he'd met Oonak for the first time, and it reminded him of how much he missed him. Oonak had sacrificed himself to save his mother, and that would never be forgotten.

Soon, he saw their arrival at Rodhas and the battle. He saw it from a higher perspective, and then he saw the white flash: the moment he'd made a timespace jump directly into the wormhole.

Now that he'd seen this life review, he felt lighter, as if a weight had been lifted off of him. Had he died? Was this what death was like? When the light of the white flash dissolved around him, he realized that he recognized this place. He'd seen the briefest glimpses of it whenever he'd used the gates or the timespace drive.

He looked around and realized he was floating, completely alone, in the midst of a brilliant radiance. All around him were countless luminous corridors arranged like webs, and in the distance he heard the sound of soft flutes and birds.

For the first time, he was seeing all of this without being in a starship. He was floating in the midst of timespace itself, and no sign of Navika could be found.

*I'm dead. I'm dead, aren't I? What about Asha? For that matter, what about Mom and Yantrik? This isn't how it's supposed to end.*

In the distance, a white orb of light was approaching him. It spoke to him with the clearest voice he had ever heard.

"Greetings, Zahn."

For a moment, he was silent.

"Am I dead?" Zahn finally said.

"You are... intact. You may now relay your desired coordinates within spacetime. However, be aware that there are serious risks and consequences for inserting oneself before one's own time."

"So, I'm alive? I survived the jump into the wormhole?"

"Technically, you no longer exist in the physical universe at any point after the jump. However, because your vessel contained a piece of my fractal nature, I did everything in my power to coordinate the nexus event so that I could eliminate the anomaly while retaining the integrity of the instrument and its keeper."

"Wait a minute. Did you just say that you sealed up the wormhole *and* saved my life?"

"It is my purpose."

Zahn laughed a laugh of joy and relief. He had done it. They had done it. Together.

"So you're the Tulari? But how? How did you save us? And have you always been able to talk?"

"I am indeed the consciousness of the Tulari, and the precise orchestrations of the event are far beyond your understanding, I assure you. Suffice to say that I displaced you from that area of spacetime before you or your vessel could be damaged... and yet a part of me is still there, in that last instant, assuring that the wormhole collapsed, is collapsing, will collapse, in on itself."

The Tulari paused.

"I apologize. That may sound confusing to you. Verb tenses are difficult in timespace being that time is far from linear here."

Zahn looked around and tried to understand this place, but it was simply too much to take in. All around him, points of light flashed through luminous corridors. But there was so much more. Shapes he couldn't describe turned in on themselves, and sacred geometry slowly spun around him. He tried to examine the Tulari, but it was too radiant.

"We are floating in Eternity, you know."

"Whoa."

The orb of the Tulari pulsed.

"As I said before, you may now relay to me your desired coordinates in spacetime, though be mindful of my earlier warning. You are not the first to call upon my powers, and there are limits to how I may assist you."

"Why?"

"I preserve the integrity of the warp and the weft that makes up the fabric of this Universe. I prevent all manner of paradoxes and incongruities, and I maintain the balance between the two realms. It is my eternal function."

"Spacetime and timespace. I must be one of the few that have visited both, aren't I?"

"All come here, all depart from here, and a part of all is here."

"What does that mean?"

"For some, this is a place of reflection before a new cycle."

Zahn tried to remain focused. If he really was outside of time now, he could find out what happened to Oonak. He might even be able to save him.

"Did I understand you correctly before? There's no way I can travel into the past?"

"As I stated, there are serious risks and consequences for inserting oneself before one's own time."

"What if I just want to observe my past? I don't want to change it."

The Tulari was silent for a moment.

"That is permissible. If you remain completely hidden and inert, the danger is minimal."

"Can you tell me what happened to Oon?"

"Who is Oon?"

"He's my friend. He sacrificed himself for us back on Hataaza Darad. If it wasn't for him, we never would have escaped with my mother alive."

"If you allow me to read your memories of this event, it would increase the probability of me locating him."

"Sure."

The Tulari came closer, and Zahn could see that it was quite similar to the object that they had retrieved from Taarakalis, except that instead of being solid, this orb was made of pure light. The light moved closer and closer, until it touched his forehead, and for that instant Zahn felt firsthand the Tulari's great power.

"I see," it said. "Such bravery. I shall find him."

The Tulari bolted away with incredible speed, and Zahn was left alone in the vastness.

He looked around and thought he saw a familiar pyramid shape in the distance below him and tried to move. But once he tried, he realized that it was nearly impossible. He could no easier move forward or backward within timespace than he could move forward or backward in time back at home.

He waited for what seemed like hours. There was no way to measure exactly how long. At first, he thought he might be able to judge the passage of time by the changing of the songs, but the songs blended together perfectly, and he couldn't tell when one ended and when one began.

Finally, he saw the white orb in the distance, and in an instant, it was right in front of him.

"I have found the entity known as Oonak."

"Good. What happened to him after he left us?"

"He is in the midst of collapsing stone. He is saving you and others. He is motionless."

"*What?* He can't be dead. He's too smart to get trapped or killed. Look again."

"He is dissolving stone. He is meeting a great beast. He is sneaking away."

"Yes! Where did he go?"

"I cannot say."

"What do you mean you can't say? Why not?"

"I cannot show you anything that has happened after the moment that you entered timespace. It is my duty not to infringe upon the timeline."

"But he's my friend! I need to know where he'll be."

"Does it surprise you when I say that this is not the first time I've heard someone say those words? Please, do not be downcast. Remember, you may still see firsthand the events that I have described to you, and not all have that chance."

"Then let's do it. Show me what happened to Oonak after we separated. I know you can't show me anything after the point we entered timespace, but show me as much as you can."

"Granted."

# CHAPTER 36

## A SLEEPING DRAGON

The entire scene played out in a series of five short glimpses seen from a distance, as though he were watching it from above through a spotless window.

In the first glimpse, he saw Oonak run down the path etched into the side of the volcano as two of the beastly Hataazans chased after him. As fast as he could, Oonak followed the path past huge boulders and crumbling rock, but the beasts slowly caught up to him. Zahn watched as Oonak darted into a large opening that led into the ridge.

In the next glimpse, he saw Oonak in a large cavern, throwing two explosives into a massive, hissing machine which had a mess of cables and pipes protruding from it. The cavern branched off into several narrow tunnels leading back up and out of the volcano. Oonak followed one of the tunnels, which became unstable. As the ceiling collapsed, everything went dark.

In the third glimpse, he saw Oonak rub his head, activate his suit's lights, and begin searching the tunnels for a way out. As he searched, Zahn saw him eat some kavasa berries, and after many hours Oonak discovered a huge creature that was also trapped in the cavern mazes. When Zahn saw the creature, he was stunned. Oonak was standing beside an enormous winged lizard with silver, scintillating scales. It was a star dragon, and this one didn't appear to be a hologram at all. Oonak melted the collar around the dragon's neck with his resonator, and when it fell, its scales glowed faintly.

In the fourth glimpse, Oonak and the dragon were fighting dozens of beasts within the caverns. The star dragon blew a stream of blue fire onto them, catching most of them ablaze. As the dragon did this, Oonak took care of any beasts that got too close. The ones that got set on fire ran around in mad circles, eventually running away in terror.

In the fifth glimpse, he saw Oonak step into a large pocket over the dragon's belly where there appeared to be plenty of air. Behind them was the same gate that Zahn and Asha had used to get back to the stolen moon, and a few seconds later the dragon stepped into the vortex. After that, the vision faded.

"That is all you are permitted to see," the Tulari said.

"Why?"

"As I have already explained, I cannot show you anything that has happened after the moment that you arrived here. The current slice of spacetime you have just seen is all preceding the instant that the nexus event occurred."

"By nexus event, you mean how you took me here to timespace, don't you?"

"Yes."

"I didn't even get a chance to see where he jumped to."

"Zahn, this cycle is now complete. I must now return you to spacetime at the exact moment at which you left."

"What? But we could both be destroyed! With the wormhole gone, who knows what will happen in the aftermath."

"Timing is paramount with regard to free will. Space, on the other hand, can be bent."

"So we can reappear in another location as long as it's the same instant we left? Can we jump anywhere in the Universe?"

There was a long pause.

"Not precisely. For our purposes, my range is limited to the Aravinda Galaxy. If you create a clear enough picture of your destination in your mind, then I could send you anywhere within your galaxy. Knowing what you now know about the events leading up to the nexus event, I advise you to choose your home, or nearby. Remember, your impulse drive is still offline."

"Right. By the way, did I hear you correctly? Did you call our galaxy the Aravinda Galaxy? Who calls it that?"

"The Eternal Ones."

"Out of all names, why did they choose that one?"

"Aravinda is a name signifying expansion and growth. I see that on your world there is a kind of flower that you call a lotus. This flower begins under layers of mud, yet overcomes this obstacle to reach the sun. This is the meaning of Aravinda."

"What a beautiful metaphor…" Once again Zahn tried to study the surface of the shimmering orb, but its radiance was overwhelming. "The Taarakani didn't create you, did they? They were just protecting you. You're much older than their civilization, aren't you?"

"Remember, once we reenter spacetime I can no longer see time rolled out like a carpet beneath your feet. I will be where you left me, on your vessel. But in my dormant state, you will be on your own."

"Wait, so if this ever happens again, can I use you again?"

"Of course, but the Vakragha seldom employ the same strategy twice. What is your choice, Zahn?"

Two possibilities clashed in Zahn's mind. On one hand, going back to Avani would get him and Navika home safely, but what about everyone else? He recalled Asha and his mother retreating to behind the eighth moon.

He sighed.

As much as he didn't want them to worry about him, the Tulari was right; going directly home was the safest choice.

"Let's go home, Tulari. It's time for a reunion."

# CHAPTER 37

## AS GLASS SHATTERING

What Darshana, Yantrik, and Asha saw was a truly spectacular sight. The moment after Zahn jumped into the wormhole, there was a flash unlike any the Kuvela system had seen in aeons. So bright it was, that the windows on Asha's and Yantrik's ships polarized to full opacity within a fraction of a second to avoid harming their eyes.

Just as their windows were regaining transparency a few seconds later, they beheld the planet begin to crumble under its own weight. Dozens of sections of the crust slid open as countless numbers of fighters fled.

But they were not fast enough. Deep within the planet, there was an explosion. Massive cracks formed on the planet's surface, and as glass shattering into a billion pieces, the planet split into hundreds of jagged fragments which were consumed by the dying wormhole within. One by one the escaping ships were sucked into the churning maelstrom, now all that was left of the tortured world.

As Yantrik and Asha raced away to safety, even its moons were pulled in. From a safe distance, they saw that even the flagship couldn't escape this fate and was struggling to keep from being consumed. Yantrik detected a small pod leave the flagship as it was being pulled in, but once the flagship had finally lost this war of opposing forces, the pod vanished along with it. Just to be sure, Asha scanned the debris field but found no life signs.

Yet all of it was bittersweet.

Zahn was gone.

# CHAPTER 38

# THE HATCHLINGS

In a bizarre flash of nothingness, Zahn found himself sitting in the command chair on Navika once again. Yet something had changed, something so fundamental that Zahn took it for granted. It took him a few moments, and then it hit him: the walls were opaque.

He'd grown so accustomed to being able to easily see the surroundings around Navika that seeing the pearl-colored walls made it seem like an entirely different ship to him.

"Navika, where are we?"

*"Zahn, are you all right? We were separated. One moment. I will scan the area."*

"Yes, I think so." Zahn felt his pulse and his forehead. Aside from some bruises he'd gotten during the battle, he seemed fine.

In a flash, the walls became transparent once more. Wide trees towered all around them, and the sun filtered through a canopy of blue leaves above them. Beside the trees were short, sapphire shrubs and a familiar gravel path, and Zahn smiled from ear to ear.

He was home.

"We're home, Navika... and we rescued my mother. Can you believe it? Everything is going to change now."

*"Yes, and there is a breezy morning out there waiting for you. For now, go and enjoy your world. Don't worry about me. I can stay cloaked for as long as you need."*

"Wait a minute... Wait a minute. You're being kind to me. You always seemed suspicious of me before, but now it almost sounds like you respect me. Did I pass a test or something?"

*"You just saved your world from total enslavement, Avanian. Deduce for yourself."*

"Yeah, but I had a lot of help, too. Can you send a message to Asha and everyone else back at Rodhas? Or whatever remains of it, at least."

"*Yes. Speak now.*"

"Guys! I'm alive. I can't explain now, but I'm alive, and I'm on Avani. Navika's impulse drive is knocked out, but I still made it home. If there are any problems, let me know. Otherwise, I'll explain everything when you guys get here. Come soon!"

Zahn stood up and took a deep breath. He was about to set foot on Ashraya again for the first time in what felt like weeks. Exactly how long, he wasn't sure.

"Okay, Navika. Stay here. I'll be back in a bit."

For the first time, Zahn heard Navika laugh.

"What's so funny?"

"*Zahn, how could I not remain here?*"

"Oh, right. Without your impulse drive, you can't move. Of course. Well, you know what I mean. Stay hidden, stay safe. All that jazz."

Zahn walked back into the central node room and saw that the Tulari was just where he'd left it, tangled in some of the cabling that led up to the ceiling. When he opened the door to the outside, he was hit with the fresh aroma of Ashraya's forests. It was a scent he had missed very much.

Slowly, Zahn set foot on his home planet once again. He did it slowly so that he could savor it, for he knew it was a moment that would never come again. He walked over to the nearby trail and followed it up and around to his front door. When he knocked, his father opened the door and embraced him.

His boy had come home.

Later that day, Zahn found himself walking barefoot on silvery sand once more, and this time his father was walking with him. To his left, Zahn could see the beautiful Ashraya Bay, and beyond that he saw faint outlines of islands in the haze along the horizon. To his right, he could see a forest path leading around a canopy of large blue leaves.

As he walked, he noticed the blue canopy spread apart as if some invisible hand was passing through the leaves. And then, Yantrik, Asha, and his mother emerged from the bluish shade of the forest.

When his mother saw Zahn and his father walking along the beach, she ran out to them, embraced Zahn tightly, and kissed his father with a kiss unequaled by any other kiss Zahn had ever seen. They kissed again and embraced each other tightly. Twelve years had felt like a lifetime.

Soon there were tears on all of their faces, even Vivek's.

Darshana hugged her son once more, ruffling his hair just as she did when he was young.

"How did you get here after the explosion? We saw you disappear, and then the whole world shattered."

"It's okay, Mom. The Tulari did it. It saved us."

"But you are the one who searched through the light-years, Zahn, and you found me. You and your friends rescued me from that unimaginable prison. You freed me from a place where I felt so alone, where I'd lost myself."

Zahn held both of his mother's hands and looked into her eyes. "But you were never truly alone, Mom, and you never will be. Our souls are connected. That's one of the things I've learned. We each live in each others' hearts. You, Dad, and now Asha, Yantrik, and Oon, live in the deepest place of mine."

Asha ran up and embraced Zahn tightly. Even her face seemed to glow, and he got lost in the feeling of being near her.

"And who is this, Zahn? Friends of yours?" Vivek asked, looking over to Yantrik who was still wearing his graphite jumpsuit covered in zippered pockets.

"Ah, I'm afraid I'm not so great at emotional introductions. The name's Yantrik," he said, offering his hand to Vivek.

"Pleased to meet you."

Zahn and Asha ignored them for a moment as they gazed into each other's eyes. Zahn had a question, but was now the right time to ask it?

"Dad," Zahn said, pulling his gaze away for a moment, "these are some of the best people in the galaxy, no question about it. This is Asha and Yantrik. They live on an outpost all the way over by—well it's really far away. Without them, I'd probably be orbiting Rodhas in a billion pieces right now."

"Well, you know me," Yantrik said. "I'd die before I'd miss the Tulari in action."

"You should have seen it, Yantrik! It's much more than we expected. You might not believe me, but it's alive."

"It's alive?"

"It's alive, and it is very wise." Zahn paused. "Yantrik, I think it might be as old as the galaxy itself."

"Incredible…" As he said it, the word itself seemed to become infused into the air around them.

"Zahn," Vivek said. "I want to apologize for how I acted when you left. I was letting fear control my reaction to the situation. If I'd had more faith, I would have wished you godspeed. I want you to know that."

"It's okay, Dad. I know it wasn't easy losing Mom, and I certainly didn't bring her back without a lot of help, seen and unseen. In the end, I was given a great gift, an epiphany I had while I was in timespace… I realized the truth."

"What truth?" Darshana said.

"That there is a truth beyond the sky that touches us all: we are not alone in this galaxy. We are protected and guided more than we could ever realize. This truth is even greater than the first truth that I went looking for, which was whether you were alive."

Everyone considered this in silence, and Zahn drew himself back to the therapeutic feeling of the sand beneath his feet. The crisp scent of the ocean made him smile.

"Do you think we have any chance of seeing Oonak again?" Asha said. "I still can't believe what he did for us… Do you think he escaped the eruption alive? He's not really gone, is he?"

"No." Zahn smiled. "If I know him, he's just getting started."

As they walked, Zahn waved Asha to walk with him closer to the ocean. Now, the moon was nearly full as it hung above them in the darkening blue sky.

"Asha, there's a question I've been meaning to ask you since even before we landed on the stolen moon, but I guess I never found the right time to ask it before now."

"What is it Zahn?"

"Asha, I've felt that there was something special about you ever since you first revealed your face in that dark hall."

Asha smiled.

"When the planet shattered, I woke up in timespace, and I thought I was dead. Do you know who I thought of first?"

Asha's eyes fell softly on him. "Who?"

"I thought of you, Asha. In all of my life I've never met anyone like you. When I thought that I was dead, I felt so much regret that I would never grow to know you more." Zahn looked deep into her warm brown eyes. "The Vakragha will return. I can feel that, and I want you to be with me when they do. So I ask you, will you and your father consider moving here to Avani? My folks and I will help you get anything you need."

Asha's eyes peered into him deeply. There was a hint of something buried within them. What was it?

"I know; it's a big question, but what does your heart say?"

The hint of a smile was on her lips, and she considered this in silence as all five of them walked down the silvery beach, letting the warm breeze soothe their hearts after their long journey. And beneath that same sand, tiny rockturtles began to hatch. Soon, they would make their way across the beach to their new home, beneath the seas.

Yet far beyond all of this, within the shattered remains of Rodhas, an unnatural light pierced the darkness. Tiny at first, it grew into an ominous green glimmer within the debris field. This glimmer attracted bits of dust and rock around it.

And just as abruptly as it had appeared, the light vanished.

# AD CONFLUENTEM FLUMINUM ASTRALIUM

"YOU WERE QUITE RIGHT. These stories are forever intertwined. It is incredible to see how far Zahn came in such a short time. Did he ever suspect that he was being prepared for something even greater?"

*"I never asked him. If you like, I suppose we could ask his guides."*

"It just seems Zahn suspected he had guides even before he was told. It certainly explains his faith in joining Oonak. Somehow, he instinctively knew that he was never alone, didn't he?"

*"His guides helped prepare him for possible futures. While he always had choice, they always saw the probabilities."*

"That also explains his actions later, doesn't it? How he was able to do what he did. By the way, what happened to Oonak?"

*"So many questions! Come back tomorrow. I will answer them all."*

"Can you tell us about the second Transcendent Stone, as well?"

*"There is much to learn and much to share. Come prepared tomorrow, and I will tell you the mystery of the Island on the Edge of Forever."*

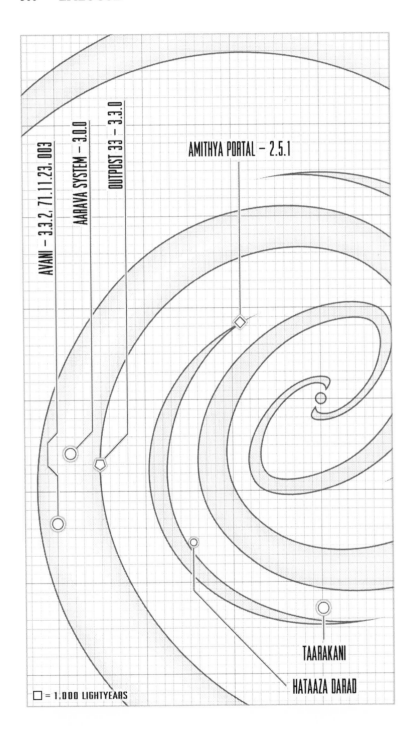

AVANI — 3.3.2. 71.11.23. 003

AARAVA SYSTEM — 3.0.0

OUTPOST 33 — 3.3.0

AMITHYA PORTAL — 2.5.1

TAARAKANI

HATAAZA DARAD

☐ = 1,000 LIGHTYEARS

# AFTERWORD

Congratulations for completing *The Truth Beyond the Sky*, the first book in the Epic of Aravinda series.

Did you enjoy this story? Let your voice be heard! These days, readers, not publishers, are the gatekeepers.

By leaving a review, **you harness your power** to decide which authors thrive, and I would be forever grateful if you would take a minute to write an honest review on:

- Amazon
- Goodreads
- Your blog/website
- Or wherever you bought this book!

As an independent author, I depend on the support of readers like you. The story you've just enjoyed is truly the tip of the iceberg in the growing Epic of Aravinda series. The 2nd book in the series, *The Island on the Edge of Forever*, is the next step in your journey.

In fact, I've gone ahead and included a sample of the first chapter of that book after this note for your reading pleasure.

Remember, only with your help will these kinds of stories continue to reach the people they are meant to reach, and perhaps change the world in some small way in the process.

Share & Enjoy!

*with a galaxy of gratitude,*
*Andrew M. Crusoe*

p.s. Check out http://myth.li/ to find more stories like this one and learn how to get free books!

FREE PREVIEW

# THE ISLAND ON THE EDGE OF FOREVER

## SAMPLE OF CHAPTER 1

ASHA FELT A CHILL SWEEP THROUGH HER BODY.
She was a young girl, sitting amidst a glimmering landscape
of technology. All around her were flickering lights and rows of
equipment scattered across the large, swooping workspaces that
filled the room. And above her was a large glass dome that
revealed a once clear sky, now thick with ominous clouds.

Asha winced. Her father hadn't mentioned a storm. She
looked back down to the small metallic sphere on her lap and
twisted part of it. Dozens of points on its surface flared to life as
it left her hands and floated up into the air.

She watched the sphere fly around in careful circles. "Do you
think I have time to fix one more, Dad?"

Her father walked over and put his hand on her shoulder. In
the reflection of one of the machines, Asha noticed that most of
the pockets on his graphite jumpsuit were strangely empty.
Times really had changed.

"Absolutely, Asha," he said. "We're not due at the docks until
evening, so we still have time to eat, pack, and settle into our
quarters. Don't you remember?"

"Right." Asha leapt up and walked over to a large bin filled
with dozens more of the metallic spheres.

"Heh, just look at all of this." Yantrik said, wandering over to
another table covered in a bizarre assortment of wires, half-built
contraptions, and tiny metallic parts. "It's too bad there wasn't
more room for the entire inventory."

"But Dad, didn't you say we wouldn't need this old stuff?" Asha walked back over and sat down at the workspace, running a blue beam of light over the sphere. "I thought you said we'd be able to bring everything we truly need."

"Don't worry, Asha. We are. I guess your old dad has trouble letting go sometimes."

Asha watched her father pick up three small dice with twelve sides each and roll them onto the table. The dice clattered onto the metal surface, all coming up as single dots, the lowest score.

Yantrik laughed. "I guess it's a good thing I gave these up! Still can't roll to save my life. How's that pod coming along?"

Asha turned back to the sphere she was holding, made a final twist, and snapped it back together again. "There you are," she said. "All fixed. You're all healed."

Yantrik walked back over to his daughter, brushing some of his long black hair behind his ears. "Just fixed, Asha. People we heal. Machines we fix, okay?"

They watched as the sphere rose into the air and began scanning the room with a sharp, magenta beam.

Asha turned to him and studied his face. "Do you ever think I could heal someday? I know there aren't many healers left, but what if I found someone, you know, to teach me?"

Yantrik sat down onto a chair next to her, his dark brown eyes full of compassion.

"You can be whatever you desire, Ashakirta, as long as you find the right teacher."

"Thanks…" She trailed off in thought. "Except, what if I'm not good at it? What if I have no talent?"

Yantrik put his hand on her shoulder. "Asha, none of us start out with great skill. Time will bring that. It's the intention that matters. Remember that."

Asha embraced her father tightly.

Thunder rumbled above them, and Yantrik scanned the darkening sky above the dome.

"Something's wrong. Climate Control forecasted clear skies."

Just before Asha could reply, the comm around her father's wrist whistled. He glanced down to it and darted over to one of the windows that overlooked the city.

"Impossible," he whispered. "There's no way they could have gotten here this fast. Even with…"

Asha jumped up from her seat and ran over to the window. But before she could reach it, her father turned around and picked her up.

"What is it, Dad? Why don't you want me to see?"

Yantrik was reading something on the comm around his wrist, but he tilted it away from her view.

"I'm sorry, little one," he said. "We have to leave. Now."

A flicker of despair flashed behind his eyes. Still holding Asha with one arm, he grabbed a thin, crimson case with his other hand.

With his knuckles, he pressed some of the glowing buttons on the panel beside the door and ran out, daughter in one hand, case in the other.

Asha held on tightly as her father ran down a twisting stone ramp that led to the lower levels of the tower. Soon, the light of day had left the tunnel, and only the red overhead lights remained, like tiny always-watching eyes along the ceiling. Asha shut her eyes and buried her face into her father's shoulder. Even though she was mature for a seven-year-old, all of this felt like a nightmare she couldn't wake up from.

She heard a hissing sound and a clunk. The air felt cooler now. A part of her wanted to know where she was, but another part wanted to stay in her father's safe embrace. She didn't want to think about what was coming. They had talked about it for months now, and some of her friends even seemed excited to settle on a new planet. But the full ramifications of the plan were still unthinkable to her.

She felt herself accelerate and was tempted to open her eyes again, but decided against it. After a few moments, the wind kicked up and blew her long brown hair all around her. Her father was running again. She heard the sound of an airlock. Or was it an elevator? She felt a rising sensation in the pit of her stomach, breathing deeply to try and calm herself.

"Look," her father whispered. "We're aboard."

Gradually, Asha opened her eyes and an expansive room flooded her vision. They were moving upward in a transparent elevator, and far below was a huge cargo bay with many levels of platforms above it, all lit from below. In fact, there was no sunlight here at all, and she stared in disbelief at the huge room until they passed into a dark space.

A moment later, the elevator stopped and slid open, revealing a crowded room filled with dozens of uniformed people darting to and fro. At the end of the room on the far right was a wide window with a long console below it. Beyond that was a surreal sight: roiling, crimson clouds.

Yantrik went over to a control panel on the far end and set Asha down on a chair next to him.

"She's not supposed to be here!" one of the officers barked. "Someone get her out of here."

"If she goes, I go." Yantrik pulled out a silver medallion from one of his zippered pockets and flashed it at the man, who deflated slightly at seeing the small disc.

"Yes, sir. Just, don't let her touch anything."

Asha looked over to her left and noticed a row of smaller hexagonal windows spaced along the wall, just above her head.

A female voice echoed throughout the space.

**"Priority alert to all stations: liftoff sequence engaged."**

Asha felt a rumble beneath her feet, and the clouds outside washed by.

She turned to her father, who was engrossed in what he was doing at the controls, along with dozens more officers, all immersed in different tasks.

"Dad, are we really leaving now? Forever?"

Her father remained silent, typing in commands as if his life depended on it. Ahead, Asha could see a few stars, but part of the view was obscured, as if a perfectly black, jagged shape were obstructing her view.

She looked back to her father's screen and watched as the tower they'd been inside and the glittering city around it shrank into the distance. She would never again see the ruddy mountain ranges, sheer cliffs, and pristine streams that she grew up with, and a deep sadness swept over her.

By now, her father had minimized the rear camera feed to a quarter of the screen. Most of the screen was taken up by navigational data and other symbols Asha didn't understand.

Despite the camera feed being smaller, she could still see a few major features of the city. Once again, she tried to find the research tower they'd been in, and quickly spotted it, admiring its elegant dome one last time before a piercing green beam of light shot down from the sky, slicing the tower in half. In what seemed like slow motion, one side crumbled apart, exposing dozens of rooms. Words left her as she beheld thick green beams of death crisscrossing her beloved city, setting entire districts aflame in mere seconds.

Asha wept.

Her father pulled himself away from the controls and took her hand. "I'm sorry, Asha. I'm sorry this had to happen." She saw that her father was filled with despair, too.

"But why?" she managed to say through the sobs. "Why are they doing this? Don't they realize what they're doing? How can they be so heartless?"

Tears streamed down her face, and her father wiped some away with his sleeve. Ahead, she noticed they were approaching a colossal ring structure, hanging in space.

"Asha, they don't *have* hearts."

Another announcement rang around them.

**"Please be advised: gate jump imminent."**

"They don't have *hearts*?" Asha watched as the void in space grew larger. The paths of light that were etched into the ring now glowed, appearing like a halo in the sky, and the starlight at the center of the ring twirled in a mad spin.

"Exactly, and that is why we will survive."

And before another thought could enter her mind, the swirling maelstrom engulfed them, and all became darkness.

...

This concludes the free sample. Here's the book synopsis to give you an even clearer idea of the adventure ahead:

When Asha accepts a mission to recover a sacred stone capable of raising the dead, she doesn't expect her ship to be attacked high above an unknown world. Asha and her commander, Mira, are dragged into the planet's wild ocean, and Asha barely manages to escape a vast underwater complex.

Once she reaches the surface, she discovers a mysterious island that comes to life with dancing villagers and roaring bonfires every night, only to vanish without a trace each morning, leaving her feeling alone and confused.

Yet there are greater struggles ahead for Asha. Having followed them, the Vakragha are desperate to find the stone first, bent on using it to revive their greatest mastermind. And when Asha finds Mira on the verge of death, the full burden of the mission falls on her shoulders. Time is running out, and Asha must rely on her courage, intuition, and healing skills to have any hope of survival. But she soon discovers that the Vakragha aren't the only ones searching desperately for the sacred stone....

A tropical Sci-Fi adventure inspired by the Big Island of Hawaii, THE ISLAND ON THE EDGE OF FOREVER is the 2nd book of the Epic of Aravinda.

Get the book in ebook or paperback here:
http://amazon.com/author/crusoe/

# HOW TO GET FREE BOOKS

ONE OF MY favorite parts about being an author is that I get to connect with you, my faithful readers.

To do that, I created the **Aravinda Mailinglist**, the most reliable way I've found to keep the lines of communication open. Every week or two, I send out a brief update on what's new, including new releases, cover reveals, and book giveaways!

And by signing up, you'll instantly receive your free Sci-Fi Starter Pack. So what are you waiting for?

Sign up here: http://myth.li/newsletter/

*see you starside,*
*Andrew M. Crusoe*

Made in the USA
Middletown, DE
29 January 2019

4